WHISPERING WALLS

Choman Hardi is the author of critically-acclaimed books in the fields of poetry, academia, and translation. *Whispering Walls* is her debut novel. She is an educator, poet, and scholar whose work is informed by an intersectional approach to inequality, renowned for her pioneering work on issues of gender and education. Since 2010, poems from her first English collection, *Life for Us* (Bloodaxe, 2004) have been studied by secondary school students as part of their English GCSE curriculum in the UK. Her second collection, *Considering the Women* (Bloodaxe, 2015), was given a recommendation by the Poetry Book Society and shortlisted for the prestigious Forward Prize for Best Collection. It was also translated into French in 2020. A selection of her poems was published in Italian in 2017. Funded by the Leverhulme Trust, her post-doctoral research, *Gendered Experiences of Genocide: Anfal Survivors in Kurdistan-Iraq* (Routledge, 2011) was named a UK Core Title by the Yankee Book Peddler. Her translation of Sherko Bekas' *Butterfly Valley* (ARC Publishing) won a PEN Translates Award.

For more information, you can visit her website:
www.chomanhardi.info

ACKNOWLEDGEMENTS

I am grateful to the Arts Council England for a writing grant in 2004/2005 which made the first draft of this novel possible and to the UK Research and Innovation, who through their support to the Gender, Justice, and Security Hub, gave me the opportunity to redraft and complete this novel.

Special thanks to Romesh Gunesekera who mentored me through the first draft and to Shaun Levin for helping me restructure, rewrite, and edit. I am grateful to Joel Hamilton, Dr. Jennie Williams, and Dr. Lucy Williams who read the manuscript and provided invaluable feedback and encouragement. Many thanks to my editor, Goran Baba Ali who trusted in me and responded to my inquiries with sensitivity and wisdom, to Holly Mason who did the copyediting, and to Ronit Lentin who proofread this book.

WHISPERING WALLS

Choman Hardi

For dear Nicky,
With lots of love,

[signature]

Afsana Press
London

First published in 2023
by Afsana Press Ltd, London
www.afsanapress.uk

Whispering Walls is a work of fiction. Although it contains real, historical
events and mentions of real personalities, all characters, places, events,
organisations and institutions in this novel are either products of the
author's imagination or are used fictitiously.

Typeset by Afsana Press Ltd
Printed and bound in Great Britain by Clays Ltd, Elcograf S.p.A.

A CIP catalogue record for this book
is available from the British Library

ISBN: 978-1-7399824-5-4

For my mother

FIVE WEEKS BEFORE THE WAR

CHAPTER ONE

Lana

After ten hours of interpreting in the Immigration House and a bumpy journey on the Bakerloo line, she got off at North Wembley. It was a dimly lit station where few passengers got on or off. The platform was drowned in orange light and the hazy air made everything look depressing. She pointlessly stared at the red brick wall as the doors opened and walked into the cold evening with one sluggish step. His name echoed in her head like a rhythmic heartbeat, a steady drumming: Amer! Amer! Amer! She walked up the stairs, turned left out of the station, and entered the little supermarket to pick up bananas, bread, and walnuts. The petite Mrs. Khan and her tall, grey-haired husband had saved her from starvation on many nights.

'How are you *pyari*? You look tired.'

'It's just work,' Lana said.

'No time for cooking again?'

'No,' Lana shook her head, 'I'm still waiting for you to teach me how to cook Bhindi Bhaji!'

'Easy,' said Mrs. Khan, 'I bring recipe for you, but you must promise to cook! Make time for family.'

'I promise to try,' Lana said while crossing her fingers and smiling at Mrs. Khan.

Sometimes, to counter her disappointment in herself, she

invited her friends over and put on a banquet, frying walnuts and raisins to top a large plate of traditional pilau, baking layers of aubergine, onion, meat, and tomato in a glass pot, and boiling the chicken with dried limes to the point of disintegration. She chopped cucumber and garlic into the yoghurt sauce and decorated the table with olives, pickles, and wine. Yet however much she tried, she couldn't recreate that sense of warmth, food, and family that reminded her of her childhood.

There were two homes in London which made Lana feel as safe and peaceful as she had all those years ago. One of them was her brother Hiwa's house and the other was her friend's flat. Nazah's basic flat in the big council estate near Latimer Road station was a haven for her. From the bottom floor she could smell the homely food, Kurdish music played in the background, colourful kilims decorated the floor, and a transparent pot of tea was always brewing on a candle. Nazah represented all the good things about her culture: generosity, hospitality, and kindness.

Occasionally, Lana was invited to read poetry in a European city and met Kurds who kept the warmth and connectedness going, starting families, building community centres, creating networks, and eating and sleeping in each other's houses. How the stateless recreated their homeland everywhere made her tearful, or maybe it was nostalgia. The past was far from perfect, she knew, but at times she longed for it. Her homeland broke her heart continually. She despaired of the endless conflict when people destroyed each other through gossip, backstabbing, and betrayal. Every time a woman got killed for 'honour' or committed suicide to escape oppression and violence, she grieved. When she thought of the deadlocks of religion and law that favoured

4

men, she was furious. Each time, when she was hurt, she decided to keep her distance and not expose herself again. But however much she distanced herself, she kept getting closer. She could not escape her homeland's grip.

Lana walked full of her own thoughts. She didn't respond to the beggar who wanted some spare change, didn't help the old man who was lost, didn't feel for the child who was crying and being dragged along by her mother. She crossed the road without looking both ways and turned right onto Byron Road. It was the most appropriate place to live for a poet. Where else in London could she smile every time she saw the name of the road? But this evening she just put her head down to protect her face from the drizzle and walked towards number 1, Byron Court. She opened the door of her ground floor flat, hanged her keys and coat on the rack, and stopped to inspect what she saw.

Is there a crack in the wall? she wondered.

Her fingers reached out to feel it but to her relief, there was nothing. She lay down on the untidy sofa, closing her eyes. Under her closed lids colours exploded into cloud shapes, changing from red to burgundy to purple to blue. A bright dot was crossing the field of her vision and she followed it. She opened her eyes for a split second and the light bulb became an overpowering dot of light which kept shifting. She remembered lying down in the garden and squinting at the sun which burst into so many shapes and colours within her eyelids. It was like rippling lava that gradually dimmed until it completely dispersed. Suddenly an image of Amer flashed through her mind. Her thoughts started racing again and she got up and turned the TV on to silence them. She lay back down while listening to the guests

5

debate the justification for the war. Lana knew the arguments on both sides but couldn't help listening. She'd become addicted to them, going from clarity to confusion about it all. She found herself against the war when talking to the war supporters and defending it when talking to the anti-war campaigners.

She suspected that things were less complicated for certain others, those who have their own nation state, who aren't living under a dictatorship or in a violent patriarchy, who are not poor or dispossessed. She didn't want to be a stateless woman anymore, didn't want to fight. Many of the battles in her life had been forced on her, she didn't choose them. She turned the TV up and went to the kitchen to heat up the left-over rice and stew from yesterday, but her mobile rang and she ran back to the sitting room to answer it. The screen showed images of the Kurdish mass exodus in the aftermath of the last gulf war.

I must call them, she thought.

'Hello,' she said, before having time to check who was calling.

'*Ewaret bash*, good evening!' Twana said, and she closed her eyes in disappointment.

She walked back into the kitchen and stirred the rice while holding the phone between her ear and shoulder. Twana asked her whether she knew about the meeting on February 17.

'Yes, I received your email.'

'We're expecting you,' he said. 'I know you're busy, but this is a difficult time, you must come.'

'I'll try,' she said while putting the lid back on the rice.

'Don't try, just come,' he said firmly. 'I'll be there earlier, come before the others if you can.'

Lana felt breathless for a second, wanted to tell him to get lost.

'I'll see,' she said instead, firmly controlling her anger and not sure if she was going to go at all. 'Let's see what happens.'

Will he call me? she wondered as she put the phone down, Will he make me wait forever?

CHAPTER TWO

Hiwa

'I'll start tomorrow,' he said to his wife and little daughter as he stood in the chaos. 'I promise!'

Hiwa had intended to keep his study neat but over the years more and more things found their way into his room. The shelves were crammed with books he hadn't looked at for years: programming, poetry, novels, and history books in Kurdish, Arabic, English, and even Persian, a language he'd wanted to learn but never quite managed. In the corners and under the shelves, cardboard boxes were filled with letters, photos, tapes, bank statements, and receipts. Even the sofa-bed by the window was cluttered, only when Lana stayed the night was it cleared in her honour. The more important books, the ones he glanced at from time to time, Amin Zeki Beg's *A Short History of Kurdistan*, Nawshirwan Mustafa's *Going Around in Circles*, Sherko Bekas's *Butterfly Valley*, were in piles around his desk. Getting up from the desk you'd have to negotiate your way around them to get to the door. Some of the piles twisted around, creating untidy staircases that looked flimsy.

'This will be your room soon,' Sozi told Shilana as she carried her on the hip. 'It will be tidy and pretty!'

'Pitty,' Shilana said.

'Yes, pitty!' she confirmed, 'Do you think *daya* can find her

8

way out of baba's maze?'

Hiwa smiled watching Shilana clap her hands in excitement as her mother carried her through the stacks of books in slow motion, pulling faces, and pretending to be lost. He knew that Sozi thought of his stuff as waste he should have disposed of years ago.

'We made it!' Sozi said as she reached the door. 'Let's hope *baba* will make it too.'

He'd bought the flat on Gayton Road in 1994, after two years of living in Kilburn and sharing space with strangers. The first floor flat was large and lively. The sun, when there was any, streamed through the kitchen in the morning and through the sitting room in the afternoon. The two rooms were separated by a low wall, allowing him to cook for his family while watching his country on TV. The news was regularly interrupted by Shilana's outbursts, demands, giggles, chatter. She'd popped into their lives after twenty-one hours of hard labour in August 2001. At first, he tried to help his wife through labour by holding her hand and encouraging her to breathe, but soon he realised that it was no use.

'Don't touch me please!' Sozi had pleaded in a broken voice. 'I'm in too much pain.'

Neither the reading nor the prenatal classes had prepared Hiwa for this. The blood vessels in Sozi's face were ruptured and she was covered in red dots by the end of it. Eventually, when the tiny baby was raised in the air for them to see, he burst into tears. They were tears of relief and joy, a realisation that his life will forever change.

A girl, he'd thought, I'm the father of a girl.

Still haunted by his failure to protect another girl who came under his guardianship a lifetime ago, he feared failing his daughter and not protecting her from the looming disadvantages. He was also afraid of his own shortcomings as a man, his long-held views about what a girl can or cannot do. Determined to give Shilana time, to prepare her for the world, and to tell her things that he wished somebody had told him, he spent Mondays and Wednesdays looking after her, taking her to playgrounds, reading her stories, playing with dolls, cars, and Lego, and painting with her. Yet despite his love for her, he avoided sorting the study for eighteen months. Sozi was not disheartened by his excuses. She nagged him lovingly, between hugs, kisses, and reassurances. She was persistent but patient, leaving enough time between one reminder and the next.

That night after putting Shilana to bed, Sozi wrapped her arms around his neck and whispered, 'I love you.'

'I love you more,' he whispered back.

'It's not possible,' she said.

'Come to bed and I'll show you.'

He pulled her hair backwards so that her forehead was raised to his lips, and his hands started undressing her. She was his lost homeland, beautiful, yielding, and constantly drawing him close. Later when he fell asleep while resting his head on her arm, he felt light and giddy. It was as if all the butterflies of stress had left his body —he'd felt their fluttering wings going down his legs— and all that was left was contentment.

Hiwa dreamt about trying to clear the study and unloading boxes that were full of stone, but they remained heavy and couldn't be moved. The books and letters he tried to sort were blank. While flicking through dozens of blank pages he panicked and thought that someone had stolen his past, someone was trying to wipe out his existence. The more he tried to tidy up, the more unruly and crowded everything became. The space in the room kept shrinking until he lost control of the flooding papers and flying books.

His heart was racing when he woke up at six the next morning. He felt a chill in his back and realised that his wife had cosily wrapped the duvet around herself, exposing him to the cold. His neck and shoulders were hurting from the effort of trying to catch and move things in his dream. Noticing Sozi's calm face and peaceful breathing, Hiwa wondered how she managed to look so innocent when she'd deprived him of warmth on a cold night. He gently pulled the duvet towards himself, making her turn towards Shilana's cot, and settled down again hoping for better dreams.

There's no rush, he thought, I'll start in a few hours.

Soon he was calmed by Sozi's warmth and rhythm and slept until he woke up to the sound of his daughter's talk in the kitchen.

'*Hem! Hem!*' she said. Food! Food! It was one of her favourite words.

She shortened words, made noise, giggled, and slammed her dimpled hands on the table to show anger or delight. Sometimes, to make her feel at home, he spoke her language and they managed to talk, argue, and disagree with each other without words.

'*Babbab!*' she would say, it sounded like a swear-word.

'To *babbab*,' he would respond with the same passion: You are!

Hearing the comforting voices while lying in bed —the kettle boiling, a plate banging on Shilana's plastic table— Hiwa's face relaxed into a smile. He thought about the gaping bookcase in the sitting room, the shelves expecting to be filled, and shut his eyes again. His wife had prepared everything for him, throwing out her dressing table to make room for his computer desk in the bedroom. Her mahogany dressing table had a swing oval mirror in the centre, with four drawers on each side. Her jewellery pieces, neatly placed in storage trays, were packed into the drawers on the right. The ones on the left included organiser trays for her makeup. To scale down, she'd given away some of her stuff and the rest was placed in the cabinet, all a big sacrifice, he knew.

It was thanks to Sozi that the bills got paid before the red notices arrived and there was always food in the house. Freelance work was the wrong kind of job for Hiwa and the continuous burden of writing invoices and cashing cheques wore him out. Queuing at the bank, the post office, and the Tesco checkouts depressed him. There were times when he forgot to invoice people or by the time he tried to deposit a cheque, it had expired. Then Sozi came, taking over banking and correspondence, improving his life.

Hiwa heard her footsteps in the corridor and knew that she'd still be wearing her red nightdress and carrying Shilana on her hip. The two of them were always talking to each other, Shilana in her '*dada*' and '*baba*'s and Sozi answering back in her hybrid language: 'Of course, *gullekem*, we'll get ready.'

They came onto the bed and tickled him until he turned around.

'Good morning!' he said with a voice full of laughter, and she replied, '*Bvvvv!*'

'We'll leave in a bit and give *baba* space,' Sozi said, 'won't we?'

Shilana laughed, showing her tiny teeth, four at the top and six at the bottom.

He sat up holding his daughter and looking at Sozi's lean waist and round thighs from the back. She called them chicken legs.

'They're perfect,' he would say to her.

She got into her blue jeans and brown jumper before turning to take Shilana from him. Sitting on the edge of the bed, he watched his wife change their daughter briskly, talking to her to distract her from what she didn't enjoy: having her head pushed through the tight collar of a purple jumper. Shilana ran to him, and he swung her from side to side before letting her go. Sozi then picked up the car keys and left.

'See you soon *baba*,' Sozi shook her daughter's hand into a wave.

Hiwa went to the kitchen, soaked in the silence, and rested his back on the wall. Already feeling tired about the day ahead, he made himself a thick coffee and flipped through the TV channels. In dozens of countries across the world people were getting ready for the anti-war protests over the weekend. The European leaders were 'still split about Iraq,' the newsreader announced, and his colleague was going to follow with a report about the consequences of this disagreement. He closed his eyes and imagined bombs falling like rain, imagined the land rolling over and showing its guts to the world, imagined the spray of dirt and blood on his face.

It doesn't have to be like that, he said to himself, it can't be like that this time.

Fine rain was falling, incessant and soundless, reminding him again that he was away from his homeland. Back there, raindrops rapidly hit the ground and flooded gardens and roads. Back there, there were definite seasons, frosty winters, scorching summers, a few months of green, and a few months of gold. The carpets were unrolled and laid out for autumn and winter and packed away for the summer. Despite the heat, he loved summer for its fruits: grapes, figs, cantaloupes, watermelons, and apricots. All the colours, tastes, and smells used to remind him which quarter he lived in.

Every part of the world needs a Vivaldi to document its seasons, he thought.

Grateful that his wife was not there to see him take his time, he walked past the large mirror in the corridor. His large brown eyes, surrounded by long dark lashes, were lively, brightening up his face. His black hair was growing too long, and his beard was four days old. He rubbed his chin and remembered his wife's complaint the night before.

'You're stinging me,' she said while gently stroking his head.

'I love stinging you,' he told her.

He walked away from the mirror whistling Ali Mardan's song, 'I want a kiss right now/ I won't leave it till midnight.'

He opened the door to the study and stood in the door frame. It was Thursday morning, 8:45 am, and the calendar on the wall revealed 13th February 2003. He looked at the bookshelves, the boxes, and the book piles all over the floor. In a distant land, seas, fields, and mountains away, his dead siblings stirred in their graves. His brother Kawa's large blue eyes smiled, and his sister Tara sat up in anticipation. As if she'd been waiting for this moment for years and was holding her breath. Hoping to make her happy, Hiwa stepped forward as Sherko Bekas' words echoed in his head: 'Drop by drop the rain writes flowers/ as tear by tear my eyes compose you.' His favourite Kurdish poet spoke his truth at so many crucial moments in his life. Hiwa picked up the first large box and brought it to the middle of the room before putting it down and opening it. All the things that were waiting to be released prepared to stretch their wings.

'Go on,' Tara whispered, 'free us!'

CHAPTER THREE

Gara

Friday was supposed to be a day of rest for Lana and Hiwa's family in Slemani, but their brother Gara used to say that it was only a resting day for the men. As men met in teahouses and mosques to discuss politics, religion, and sport, women heated the *hamam* for the long weekly wash, hand-washed the sheets, mended and, if there was electricity, ironed clothes, deep cleaned the house, hand-picked stones from rice, and looked after guests. They worked hard to keep life going.

Gara would spend his Friday mornings in the Sha'ab teahouse, one of the city's oldest places where men mingled. The walls were covered by portraits of Kurdish intellectuals, artists, and poets, mostly men. The curling cigarette smoke created a fuzzy atmosphere which made the old black and white pictures look more dated. Despite having assistants, *kak* Omar served his best customers himself. He remembered how they liked their tea: thick with plenty of sugar, thin with no sugar, and everything in between. Whether Gara had planned to see friends or not, the teahouse was the best place to keep in touch with men from different periods of his life and of all walks of life. Some of his old teachers frequented Sha'ab. They would huddle in a corner, wrinkled by age and experience, sipping their sweet tea in between conversations.

Once *mamosta* Faraj came to him and said, 'We take pride in your good work and take some credit for it.'

Another time one of his late brother's teachers was tearful when he told him, 'It's cruel when the young die before the old. I will never forget Kawa!'

Gara felt at home there and reaped the benefits of living in his birthplace, maintaining a network of relationships, and feeling the pulse of the city. Being a regular at the teahouse made him approachable and trusted, important qualities for a journalist. Sometimes stories were brought to his attention here and people approached him with information. But no matter where he was and however much he enjoyed himself, he usually went home to have lunch with his family, his wife, his son, and his aunt.

The car radio declared that the price of plastic sheets continued to rise as people bought them in anticipation of the war. Gara took a deep breath and wondered whether covering doors and windows with plastic sheets could protect people from possible gas attacks. He considered buying plastic sheets and then dismissed the idea. Despite the last piece of news, the radio played Piramerd's song about Slemani in the snow: '*Bayani bw le khaw hastam ka rwanim bafra bariwa/ Slemani alley Belqise taray ziwy poshiwe,*' (At morning I woke to find snow had fallen/ Slemani is like Balqis, wearing a silver veil).

He arrived home and found Aveen preparing lunch in the kitchen while little Kawa was standing by her feet. The *hamam* was humming in the background, the pressure cooker hectically announcing that the meat was cooked, and the windows were steamed up. He could smell the cooked meat, beans, and rice which made him feel hungry. Kawa was fully dressed with his shoes on, pulling his mother towards the door.

'*Baba* is here,' she said joyfully. 'Look!'

The boy turned back and ran to Gara who picked him up.

'How are you bebe *gyan*?' he kissed his son.

He then put one arm around Aveen's waist, but she gently escaped him. She didn't like public displays of affection. She said it was out of respect for Sayran who hadn't been loved like that.

'*Daya* doesn't love me,' he complained to his son.

Kawa giggled and Aveen frowned in response. He then dangled Kawa from side to side.

'Who is my flower?' he asked his son and Kawa replied, 'Min.'

'Who is my soul?' he asked, and Kawa laughed, 'Min.'

'Who is my eye?'

'Min.'

Aveen vigorously washed the empty sugar box, trying to scrape off the hardened sugar from the bottom. She then put the box upside down next to the tea box on a dry towel and stirred the rice before turning the gas down. She took the pressure cooker off the hob and put it in the sink to cool.

'*Bakeh*,' Kawa said to Gara, meaning *bakheke*, the garden.

'Yes, *bakeh*,' he replied, 'but let's say hello to *pura* Sayran first'.

He went to the sitting room where his aunt was sitting on the sofa by the *aladdin* heater and putting the duvet covers back on. Sayran was surrounded by sheets and naked duvets queuing to be clothed. She looked up at the two of them.

'Hello *pura gyan!* We're going to walk in *bakheke*.'

'Welcome back,' Sayran said while waving at them. Her face wrinkled into a smile. 'Bye bye *gullekem*,' she blew Kawa a kiss who blew a kiss back with both hands, 'Bye bye.'

Gara opened the door, and they were in the little entrance where the shoes were lined up and the coats were waiting to be taken out. He opened another door, and the dry cold attacked their hands and faces, making Kawa scream with joy. Both doors closed behind them and the two of them started walking and running on the small patch of grass. The garden hadn't thawed yet. Kawa was jumping up and down and Gara was bent over, his arms stretching around his son in case he fell. Within his limited freedom Kawa ran around giggling, making sure that he trod on all the erect blades of grass until they cracked under his feet. He loved the crunch.

Gara looked up and saw that his aunt's face was turned towards the *aladdin* heater with its circle of blue flames. At times, she was as fragile as a thin sheet of glass before a hammer. He knew that sometimes sorrow was so close that scratching could make it resurface. Even though the miseries of the past had ended, it all seemed flimsy, like the flickering blue flames in the heater. He thought of all the families who were taking refuge in the cold mountains in fear of the coming war and felt a sudden chill in his bones. The rain seeped through layers of clothing. Large drops dripped from the rims of women's dresses, the end of men's trousers, from their arms and armpits. No one could see further than two metres.

Not again, he waved away the thought of another exodus, No one will give birth in the rain. It will be different this time. Twelve years have passed so things will be different.

'Lunch will be ready in a few minutes,' Aveen said as she joined them in the garden.

Kawa stood between his parents, held their hands, and jumped each time they lifted him up. For a few seconds it looked as if he was flying as they cheered him on. The three of them came back inside while Sayran was speaking on the phone, 'Why do you call so often?'

Aveen folded up the two made up duvets before leaving the room. She came back with the empty tea and sugar boxes and disappeared into the back of the house. Gara was always impressed by the way she utilised time. The phone call gave her a few extra minutes before serving lunch and she was going to use the time to refill the boxes from the pots by the staircase. Kawa wanted to follow his mother, but Gara grabbed him, 'It's cold down there,' he said. 'Stay with *baba*, *gullekem*,' and he threw his son into the air. Kawa laughed with every jump and Gara wished that he would always be there to catch his son if he fell.

'It's not as bad as they make it out to be,' Sayran said. 'Everyone is... as usual.'

He squeezed and kissed Kawa.

'Gara's just got home,' Sayran said into the phone, then looked at Gara and offered the handset. 'Lana wants to talk to you.'

Gara put Kawa down and took the phone.

'How are you Lana *gyan*? Don't worry, we will buy enough plastic sheets to protect ourselves from the gas attack.' He laughed as his aunt scolded him for scaring Lana. 'I'm joking, I'm joking. We'll be okay,' he said, trying to calm his sister down. 'But I wasn't joking about the plastic sheets. The radio just announced it.'

Kawa took advantage of his father being busy and went after his mother to the back of the house.

'*Daya*,' he called after his mother, '*Daya*, look! *Jooja*!'

'Just a minute,' his mother said. 'I'm coming.'

He then started jumping up and down and kept shouting, '*Jooja.*'

Sayran picked up a book and aimed at a retreating spider, but she missed.

Kawa continued to call out, '*Jooja, jooja.*'

CHAPTER FOUR

Lana

Lana was grateful that none of the hustle and bustle of Friday night affected North Wembley. The neighbourhood had its own culture, quiet at night, controlled, and understated. Despite the silence, she was unable to sleep until late and even when she did fall asleep, she kept waking up, tossing and turning, and waiting for the day to break. Insomnia wasn't new to Lana but recently it had taken on a different intensity. She would spend most of the night awake but not alert enough to get out of bed. She would lie down, rest on her right side when her left side was numb, and turn over to lie on her stomach when her back ached. The duvet was in the way, the bed sheets wrinkled under her cheek, the pillow was too high or too low. It was a constant fight with the bed in the dark. She was defeated in these late-night wars and woke up with dark circles around her eyes. She opened her eyes around nine on Saturday morning. The curtains were drawn but she could still sense that the sky was covered with thick clouds. She closed her eyes again, too tired, and achy to get up, until Nazah's phone call forced her to leave her bed.

'You're not sleeping, are you?'

'I just can't get up,' Lana said in a husky voice. 'What are you up to?'

'I'm in Hammersmith. Want to join me for a walk in Holland

Park and then lunch at my place?' Nazah said cheerfully.

'Holland Park in this weather?' Lana was more tempted by lunch at Nazah's than a walk in the park.

'You only need an umbrella,' she said defensively, 'and the flowers are lush in the rain.'

'I believe you, but I will skip it this time.'

The plan was to vacuum and dust the flat, do the piled-up dishes, change the sheets, and wash the clothes. Yet for about an hour, all she managed to do was think about all the things that needed to be done while lying down, eyes half closed. She was about to drift back to sleep when she remembered her conversation with her family the previous morning. Before leaving for work she'd searched for the phone card amongst her papers on the table, and dialled the number on the card, the long pin code, followed by her family's phone number.

'*Balle*!' her aunt answered.

'*Pura* Sayran *gyan*,' she shouted, 'how are you?' There was a brief silence before her aunt bombarded her with questions about herself, Hiwa, Shilana, and Sozi. This was always followed by 'Why do you call so often?' Her aunt worried that she would go bankrupt if she called regularly. The fun always started after these inquiries.

'How is your pain *pura gyan?*'

'I'm good *basaqa*. The painkillers you sent are wonderful. I only take them when I really need to, so that they last me longer.'

'Take them whenever you need them,' Lana said. 'I'll send you more, don't worry.'

There was a brief silence and Lana knew what her aunt was thinking. There was no guarantee that she could send anything, anytime soon. No one would be travelling to the country, while a war was looming.

'Is everything okay with you? What are people saying about the war?'

'We are fine,' Sayran said, 'Don't worry about us. It's not as bad as they make it out to be. Everyone is... as usual.'

'What does Gara think?'

'He's just got home,' then she mumbled, 'Lana wants to talk to you.'

'How are you *baqurban*?' Gara asked in a playful voice, 'Don't worry we'll buy enough plastic sheets to protect ourselves from the gas.'

'Oh Gara, please don't say that.'

She could hear *pura* Sayran scolding Gara, forcing him to say he was joking.

'So people are seriously afraid?'

'Some people have fled to the mountains, but it is unnecessary.'

'What makes you so sure?'

'They can't afford to get it wrong with all the opposition and protests.'

Lana was continually baffled by this optimism about the war despite a grim history. Einstein was right, madness is repeating the same thing and expecting a different result. She bit her lower lip but didn't want to argue with her brother on the phone. She heard her nephew Kawa yelling in the background.

'What is it?' Lana asked, 'Why is he shouting?'

'Because he's seen a *jooja*,'

'Is *jooja* an insect?'

'It could be an animal, a bird, an insect, or a ghost.'

'A ghost' left its echo in Lana's mind and made her more anxious.

It was midday before Lana woke up. She made herself a tea and started washing up. When the plates were draining, she sighed in relief and ate some walnuts while sipping her tea. She then stripped the bed, duvet and cushion-covers and put a wash on. She walked around the flat collecting the clothes that were lying around under chairs, by the bed, and in the bathroom, separating the clean clothes from those to be washed. After putting her clean clothes back in the cupboard, she straightened her back and stretched. The washing machine was making a steady noise. She watched the clothes spin in the machine and wondered how women, even those who had full time jobs, managed the constant and repetitive tasks of maintaining a household without losing their minds. She wondered how all her mother's efforts to make a tidy woman out of her had failed. She'd disappointed her mother and her ex-husband and had defied society's expectations of her. Cooking was never a problem for Lana, it was cleaning that she found depressing.

Feeling hungry, Lana searched the fridge and resorted to an old quick recipe, lentil soup. She washed the lentils, mixed them with a handful of rice, and boiled them, adding fried onion and garlic when the ingredients were cooked through. She ate a bowl of warm soup with two slices of brown bread but longed for okra stew flavoured with tomato, onion, and garlic.

Mrs. Khan is right, she thought, I need to make time for life.

After hanging the washing in the bathroom, Lana compulsively flipped through the BBC, the CNN, and the Kurdish satellite channels eager to know if there had been any developments. She then switched the TV off, searched through her CDs, and put Rafiq Chalak on. His clear voice both calmed and saddened her, making her feel the wounds and sorrows that she hadn't personally experienced, but they were a part of her life anyway. It reminded her of hopelessness in the face of uncontrollable events, of maddening loneliness, of the gulf caused by heartbreak, injustice and grief, a gulf that disconnected people from their loved ones and made them feel powerless. How lonely survivors of trauma and grief are, she thought.

The evenings were the most difficult. Every night she got home, put some food together, then sat down and waited. Usually, she was too tired to read or write and all she could manage was listen to music, watch TV, have a bath, or phone home. She knew that this time it was her call, she had to do it, but having left it long enough she was worried that he may not want to hear from her anymore. She sat with the phone in her hand as Rafiq Chalak sang *Arami gyanm*, My soul's peace. She dialled his number and waited as it rang at the other end. When it reached the answerphone, she was unsure whether to leave a message, but before making up her mind she started talking.

'Hi Amer, it's me. I just want to say that I understand if you're still angry with me. I'm sorry about what I said. You're a good man, and you deserve better.' She hung up without saying goodbye. It was obvious, he didn't want to hear from her anymore. Her heart hurt, as if she had been stabbed hard.

She slowly got up and made herself another cup of tea. The wind was curling around her flat. She imagined the place taking off into the sky in a Marquezean manner, imagined looking down at the ground from her window in the sky. She wondered what kind of gap her place would leave on earth, and whether

her perishing would make any difference to the world; maybe to the people who cared about her. Otherwise, she would be a piece of disaster news, a face flashed on the TV screens when 'Last night's gale' would be spoken about.

She walked back to the sofa, grabbed her tea in both hands, and closed her eyes. She knew she shouldn't listen to Rafiq Chalak at such times, but that was precisely why she listened to him; he enhanced her mood. She wondered for a second if she had the right to be angry with Amer.

But how could I be? she asked herself, I was terrible.

The day it went wrong, she was angry with Amer and his laid-back manners. She'd always been apprehensive about his Arabness and how her family and community would react to him. She asked him whether his community would have a similar problem with her ethnicity.

'Nobody will come to the wedding,' he teased her. 'We'll just have to do it alone in an empty hall full of imaginary friends and family.'

She glared at him.

'Come on,' he said. 'Why do you always expect the worst?'

She responded by saying that of course he doesn't find this relationship difficult because he is the hero, he is 'the Arab man who is fucking a Kurdish woman.'

Amer stopped in his place, astonished. 'I can't believe you said that,' he said.

She immediately regretted it but was too stubborn to apologise. She looked at him defiantly, without answering.

'What kind of a feminist are you?' he asked her, 'You think

27

that love is something a man does to a woman?'

Amer shook his head and mumbled something to himself. Then he turned around and said, 'And I'm still "the Arab man" to you!' He stared at her for a second, giving her a chance to speak but she didn't, and with these last words he walked out of her life two weeks ago.

I ruined it, Lana thought as she sipped her tea. It's over.

She had met Amer four months before when she had a reading at the Poetry Cafe in Covent Garden. The narrow four storey building housed the Poetry Society's readings, writing workshops and meetings. The small cafe on the ground floor was separated from the reading space in the basement by a thick curtain. Lana went from interpreting all day straight into the cafe. Wearing blue jeans and a worn pink top, she felt improperly dressed for the occasion. Her scarf was pink, red, and orange, her black coat covered her to her knees, and her brown boots looked old and discoloured. Still, she hadn't forgotten the most important thing: her poems.

She was to read with two well established poets and being the youngest and least well known, she would have to read first. She disliked reading first. The late comers always walked down the stairs in the middle of the first poet's reading. The curtain wasn't a good sound insulator. There were always people talking and laughing upstairs and it took them some time to register the reading and calm down. Yet she knew that she was expected to be grateful for being given the opportunity to read to an audience who had, most likely, come to listen to the other writers. She shyly grabbed a glass of orange juice, and after greeting the organiser and the other writers, sat quietly in a corner. A few familiar faces walked in and Charlotte, who she'd become friends with through poetry, came and sat with her.

'I saw your name on the programme and thought I must come along,' Charlotte said.

'Thank you, that is very kind… you didn't have to.'

'Don't be silly. Believe it or not, I actually enjoy your readings.'

Lana didn't know what to make of English people, they were either too reserved or too friendly, which was confusing for people like her. After six years of living in London, she still wasn't sure who she could or could not hug, and she came across as shy and awkward. She'd also become sensitive to women touching her. Once she shared a room with another woman at a conference and the woman came close to her a couple of times, too close, Lana thought, and this made her feel uncomfortable. She'd developed a similar phobia towards children and could no longer casually talk or play with them like she used to. She remembered how, when she went shopping with her mother as a child, the shopkeepers picked her up and kissed her. Some tickled her and gave her sweets. All these things seemed like a film now, not her own memories which she could sentimentally think about. She was too detached from those days, those people.

Now she was a shy foreign woman who spoke 'very good English' but every now and then mispronouncing a word gave her away. When she talked fast, sometimes she confused the pronunciation of 'saw' and 'sew', 'ankle' and 'uncle', 'ant' and 'aunt', 'Blair' and 'blur', and 'warm' and 'worm'. She could hear herself making these mistakes, but it was usually too late. Other than these occasional mistakes, her friends told her, 'you sound like any other middle-class British woman', which she found rather strange. Despite being the baker's daughter, she'd studied English literature and worked for an international NGO back in her country. She'd become middle class in her own community but was she in the UK? A friend once teased her and said, 'You like to be working class, but you're not.' It wasn't the desire to be working class that made her doubt her middle class status but rather confusion about where she stood in different contexts. She felt working class amongst English people, missing many of their everyday cultural references. Some days, listening to people's conversations around her, she wondered whether they spoke a different language.

'So what are you going to read?' Charlotte said.

'I don't know, some old stuff and some new.'

Charlotte was smiling, 'Something old, something new. That always works.'

She didn't know why Charlotte was kind to her, but she knew that this is how it is in life. People have a soft spot for certain others and sometimes this is not even reciprocated. Some people had always supported Lana regardless of whether she did the same for them. She tried to remember who had her unconditional support. There were members of her family, of course, like Hiwa, Sozi, Gara, Aveen, her aunt, and her friend Nazah, but who else? While thinking about this, a shadow approached them.

He was a handsome man with tanned skin, black hair, and long dark eyelashes.

'The Middle East!' Lana thought and hoped that he wouldn't try to talk to her.

Charlotte clearly knew him, 'Hello darling... how lovely to see you... this is my friend Lana,' then she turned to Lana,

'This is Amer!'

Something moved inside Lana, a little turning of the stomach.

'Nice to meet you,' she said while shaking his hand.

'You too,' he was smiling widely and looking at her intently. 'You look like you come from my part of the world!'

But before she had a chance to reply, the organiser was right in front of her: 'Are you okay to start?'

'Sure!' Lana was relieved. She got to her feet, turned to Charlotte and said, 'I'll see you downstairs then.'

'Yaah, just getting a drink for Amer.'

Lana nodded and left them, smiling at Amer before she turned away.

So he is coming down, she thought, and ruled against changing her choice of poems or the stories that went with them. If he doesn't like them, it is his problem.

The basement was full, and the microphone was working properly for a change. She and the other two writers, both women, sat on the sofa to the right of the microphone. Sue Derby was doing her usual warming up of the audience, making a few jokes, a few announcements about the next readings, and then she turned to look at the writers.

'We're very lucky to have three wonderful poets with us tonight, some of London's most exciting women poets.'

Why add the word 'women' to 'poets'? Lana thought. Surely they can see us.

She sipped her orange juice and checked the audience. They were the usual crowd of poetry goers, simply dressed and polite looking. They listened attentively and she wondered why they got Sue Derby's jokes but not her own. Maybe it was to do with

31

her delivery, or with where she came from, or the kind of poetry she wrote. Nobody expected her to be funny. Sue described her poems as 'important,' and Lana thought: There goes all the possible smiles for me.

Charlotte and Amer were sitting towards the back. Lana could see Charlotte's enthusiastic face, but Amer was part-hidden by the person in front of him. Maybe they were a couple? But before she could make up her mind the audience was clapping for her to start. She got up and adjusted the microphone, it was always too high for her. To her surprise a few people smiled, and this made her relax. Reading poetry made her come out of her shell. Her voice was crisp and clear, and she looked at the audience as she read. She told little stories between her poems, some of which were supposed to be funny. Before reading *The Seventh Wedding Invitation*, she explained how in Kurdish, smart or pretty little girls are told that they would marry seven times. This was supposed to be a bad omen, meaning no man would put up with them, but Lana reclaimed this idea and celebrated being the 'bad woman' who divorces six men because they don't please her.

In the break she went straight to Sue and the other writers, apologising that she couldn't stay for the second half. She was feeling exhausted and needed to prepare for tomorrow. Just as she was wrapping her scarf around her neck, before stepping out of the door, Charlotte tapped her on the shoulder.

'That was great… won't you have a drink with us?'

'I'm sorry, I need to pack for tomorrow. Going to the poetry course, did I mention it?'

'No, you didn't. That should be great fun.'

Amer was standing in the back of the café, looking at the poetry pages on the wall.

He didn't like it, I knew he wouldn't, she thought and gave her friend a hug before leaving.

Rafiq Chalak had stopped singing and the wind made the windows shiver. She stood in the kitchen and listened to the wind. It reminded her of Hussein Arif's short story about a windy night in the mountains when the wolves came to eat the young family who had refused to live with the others in the village. Was she doing the same to herself? Was she choosing the lone life over togetherness so that the wolves could eat her?

It was late now but she wasn't sleepy. She ran a bath and added a few drops of lavender oil to the water to calm herself. The bell rang and she straightened her back in alarm, it was too late for visitors. Maybe it was the wolves, she thought, maybe she was running out of time. She didn't move for a few seconds and then there was a knock.

'It's me!'

She automatically ran to the door, opened it, and there he stood, scruffy and knocked about by the wind.

'It's me,' Amer said again as he opened his arms.

She grabbed his hands, pulled him in, and embraced him in disbelief.

'I was waiting for your call,' he said. 'You took your time.'

CHAPTER FIVE

Hiwa

The rain had stopped, but he felt the dampness in the pages of his books and papers. He was starting to realise that clearing the study would take longer than planned. He'd spent the weekend, including the evenings, among the scraps of paper, photos and tapes that embodied his past but was still creating more mess than order. There were separate piles for the different kinds of paper and the largest pile consisted of rubbish: papers, receipts, Christmas cards he didn't know why he'd kept, and letters from people whose names he didn't recognise anymore.

He had an urge to keep things in case they would become useful one day. He used to have a similar problem with his cupboard which kept getting more crammed. It took Sarah, the woman who later broke his heart, a year before she persuaded him to give up his old shirts and trousers to the charity shop. His mother Ahoo recycled everything. She used the wool from old jumpers to knit new ones, altered shirts and dresses for the younger children, and cut old sheets and left-over fabric into square pieces to make patchwork quilts. He missed sleeping in the heavy quilts, the love that went into making them made them cosier.

Sozi and Shilana were in the bathroom. He listened to his daughter as she played in the lukewarm bath and knew that she was surrounded by her ducks and bubbles.

'Yuck,' Sozi told her. 'You can't eat that, *pisa!*'

He loved children's open minds about things, how they wanted to experience everything, touching and tasting indiscriminately. At times he only realised that a dog barked outside when his daughter said 'wa waw.' She was alert to all the sounds he'd become accustomed to, and he wished she would maintain her freshness.

He stopped shovelling through his papers to look at family photographs harvested from various envelopes and boxes. There was a picture of the women of the family smiling at him. He guessed that Gara had taken the photograph. It was dated 02/07/1992, more than a year after the death of their brother Kawa, and a few weeks before their mother would die. Sitting on the floor, Ahoo had a tray of tea glasses and saucers, a pot of steaming tea, and the sugar box in front of her. She was wearing her traditional clothes: long black dress, black waistcoat, and black slip and *sharwal*. Her thin white scarf couldn't tame her bulky hair, it stood stiffly.

The younger women were huddled around his mother. On her right Lana was smiling, leaning on Ahoo's shoulder, in black pyjamas. Aveen was sitting next to Lana wearing a black night gown. She was all covered up, her hair tied in a ponytail and her legs tucked under her body. She was looking at the camera with a faint smile. On the left *pura* Sayran was waving at the camera, looking pale. Her navy gown looked too big for her. Hiwa couldn't remember whether her rheumatism had already flared up by that time, but her handwriting was shaky at the back of the photograph: 'Hiwa *gyan*, we miss you so much. Come and

35

visit soon. We pray for your health and happiness.'

His mother was the only one who looked happy in the picture, her teeth showing as she smiled. She was the one who would die soon, and he wondered whether the others already knew this at the time. It felt like a landmark picture taken to remember her, sitting cross legged by the steaming *semawer*, and pouring tea for everyone. His mother's sweet tea was perfumed with the right amount of cardamom and cinnamon. He has never since drunk tea that tasted so good. Even when Sozi and Lana used the same recipe it was never the same. He was convinced that people poured a bit of themselves into the things they made. Some people couldn't cook not because they didn't know how to, but because that bit of themselves which they put into their cooking was not right. All his life he had searched for a woman who was not only lovely in herself but also in the things she touched, made, cooked. That was why Sozi had occupied his life so quickly. She could transform a room making slight alterations and cook in a rush, making the most basic ingredients taste good. He imagined the best ingredient came from her daring vision, the sweat of her hand, the spray of her breath.

Hiwa looked for a space to separate this picture from the rest. He stood up and cleared a small corner at the edge of his desk. He put the photograph down, facing upwards, and stood there inspecting it for a second before going back to his piles on the floor.

Shilana was yelling in the other room. She didn't like being dried and clothed. This was her cue that it was bedtime.

'*Baba*,' she called to him crying, 'bababababa.'

He was tempted to respond, to go and rescue her from this

oppression. She often appealed to him at times of crisis, urging him to side with her against her mother, but he stayed out of these conflicts.

He flicked through childhood photographs, some too blurred to make out. A photo of Kawa in shorts with scabby knees stood out from the rest. He was staring into the camera with those clear blue eyes, one hand on the mud brick wall. It was taken before their mother banned him from standing by the wall. After seeing the holes in the wall increase, she started watching her middle son and soon realised what the problem was. Every time she caught him pretending to play by the wall, she'd give chase but couldn't catch him. He'd spend the day hiding until she pretended to have forgotten. Gradually, it seemed as if she'd stopped noticing his clay eating habit, or maybe she gave up fighting him.

Hiwa searched his mind for an image of the road where he lived his youth. Had he known how much he would miss the dusty roads and golden twilights, he would've paid closer attention to the daily details—the bumps on the ground that tripped him up, the stones that lay at rest until a child tumbled them over, the bright light which made the mud brick walls paler, the cracks that crept up on houses, the sweet honeysuckle drooping from the walls.

Every morning he'd wake up after several calls from his mother, sit around the sifra with his siblings and gobble up the warm bread, sour yoghurt, and sweet tea, then leave home, turning left at the bottom of their dirt road, then left again onto the street. The narrow street was always buzzing with its small shops, the small mosque drenched in blue and inscribed with

37

holy words, and the public *hamams* with their domed tops, one for men and another for women and children.

Because of water shortage or rising oil prices some Fridays they couldn't wash at home, and their mother took them to the public *hamam* instead. All the neighbourhood's women and children would be there, sitting on low wooden stools all around the huge hall. Under the taps, which were two metres apart, the water gathered in a small stone basin. Women scooped bowls of water out of the basin to pour on themselves and their children. The public bath was much bigger than the bathroom at home and, sometimes, he managed to escape his mother's grasp and play with the other children in the middle of the steamed-up chamber.

Everything seemed so simple yet mysterious inside the dome. Women were doing all sorts of interesting things, putting henna in their greying hair; shaving their legs, armpits, and private parts; massaging each other; washing each other's backs. And the most fascinating thing was when they lifted their huge breasts to wash the hidden space underneath. Once a woman shouted abuse at him for staring at her and he ran back to his mother, scared that he may get a beating. Had it not been for the *natir*, the huge female attendant, banning him at the age of twelve, his mother would have continued taking him there, insisting that her son was 'just a child who didn't know anything.'

On the narrow street, women were always haggling with the stubborn and experienced shopkeepers over the price of fruit, vegetables, dry food, sweets. Some of them were wearing an *abba* that covered them from top to toe, others walked around in their 'modern' clothing. He remembered the men turning their heads to watch the women as they passed by. A friend of his father once told him that women were the suns and men were the sunflowers. For years he thought this was romantic. Only after loving and listening to women, did he realise that they didn't enjoy being gawked at. He realised that men's hassling was routinely romanticised and normalised. Women came to believe that the way men treated them, looked at them, and harassed them was normal. They learnt to walk on without responding or reacting, they were silent.

The shop owners sat on small stools in their traditional dress and headwear. They saw to their customers in between entertaining their guests—old men who moved about slowly, sat by the heater with their coats on during the winter, and in the summer they sat at the edge of the shop, sweating, and drinking iced water from the thermos. Sometimes the old men teased the children, asked them who their parents were, and told them funny stories about their father or mother when they were kids.

At twilight, when fathers came home, the road was filled with the smell of food, the sizzling oil, fried onion, and the aroma of rice topped with meat and raisins. Little was left from those hundreds of walks that took him from home to the outside world and back. He never thought that one day he would be ripped away from that place, those meals, the togetherness of his family, the ordinariness of life, and the simple daily routines. He thought that life would remain straightforward, that his siblings would grow old around him, and that their house would remain uncontaminated.

Sometimes the smell of honeysuckle, or a spray of dust in the wind, would take him back to those days. He would stop, close his eyes, and briskly relive those moments. He longed for that period before his father's accident, Tara's suicide, Kawa's murder, and his mother's decline from grief. Maybe he longed for his innocence, for the seasonal routines that grounded his experience of home. He regretted not looking at his *daya* all those mornings when she poured him tea and gave him warm bread before he left the house. He couldn't remember their conversations at breakfast, lunch, and dinner. He couldn't remember what he thought and felt at the end of the seasons. And worst of all, no new experience could match the intensity of those days, nothing was as rich in colour, taste, and smell as the memories of that poor road. It was as if, with the loss of that life, his senses were numbed. He couldn't feel the same excitement and enthusiasm about anything anymore. All of Europe with its lush landscape, seas, and mountains couldn't make him feel like he had all those years ago.

Maybe it was because I was young, he thought, or maybe displacement dulls your senses, and nothing matches the vigour and vibrancy of your homeland.

The photographs were colourful windows to another world, crystallised moments in a family history. They sparkled at certain angles, reflecting so much light that the image disappeared. He decided to organise them in chronological order and imagined his daughter looking at them one day, imagined telling her stories about her aunts and uncles. He compared two similar pictures which were taken ten years apart. In the old one Aveen was smiling and holding Kawa's hand. In the other, and striking a similar pose, Aveen was smiling and holding Gara's hand. He wondered how a woman could be in love with two brothers who were so different from each other. He put the two photos aside and considered the only picture he'd brought with him, carrying it in his wallet as he travelled to Iran, and then to Syria, until he finally arrived in the UK. Throughout his journey, he'd taken out Tara's photograph and looked at it. Once a young man who accompanied him for part of the journey teased him about it. Hiwa remained silent, leaving his co-traveller to imagine all sorts of stories about this beautiful woman. Tara must have been fifteen in the picture. She had full lips, green eyes, and long black hair, and he tried to imagine what she would look like if she were still alive today.

His finger traced the edge of the small picture, which was now marked, tiny white lines running through its surface. He got up once more and put the photograph on top of the others at the edge of the desk. He was bent down surveying her face again when he heard his daughter's tiny footsteps rapidly approaching the room. She came in, her hair was loose and wet from the bath, she was wearing her green pyjamas and her eyes looked greener than usual. Shilana stood for a second inspecting the papers and calculating what she should attack first. Hiwa looked at his daughter, as if for the first time, and jumped backwards in shock. He suddenly realised who she looked like. He rushed towards her and picked her up mid-air just before she jumped on his photographs.

'Dear God!' he said while holding her close to his chest. 'Oh, dear God!'

He walked out of the room carrying his daughter like precious cargo. She was resisting him with all her strength, hitting him with her fists, and trying to push him away. But however much she tried, she couldn't escape his grip. He was touched by her struggle, and it made him even more certain, she was as stubborn and beautiful as Tara. This little girl is what she must have looked like all those years ago when he himself was a child—the green eyes, the silky dark hair, the small nose, the round mouth. He'd jumped with this realisation and now he was sweating.

'Shhh,' he said gently while trying to rock his daughter. She smelt of soap and fresh clothes.

'She ran out the minute I turned my back,' Sozi said in the corridor while holding her arms out to take her daughter back.

'It's okay, I'll put her to sleep.'

'I thought you wanted to work on your things.'

'I've done enough for tonight,' he said.

Sozi kissed her agitated daughter good night and let them walk to the bedroom. Shilana gave her an angry look, a look that said, 'You're letting me down.'

Sozi laughed, stopped them at the door, and gave both of them a hug.

He walked around the room rocking Shilana and singing a lullaby to calm her down. 'Wolves of the night! Wolves of the night!' he sang to her, 'Go away so that Shilana can sleep.' He didn't like the second part of the lullaby which told the wolves to go to other people's houses and eat their children instead of this one. He told the wolves to go and eat the sheep, the goat, and the donkey instead. 'Go to the sheep's house, eat the son and the daughter, and save the parents for later.'

They always struggled putting her to bed, as if she was worried about missing something during her sleep. Sometimes Shilana entertained herself playing with her teddy, other times nothing could contain her, she would get bored, she would moan and cry. He worried that the world wouldn't provide enough entertainment and freedom for this girl.

Shilana gradually settled down, sucked her thumb, and rested her cheek on his shoulder. He put her on the bed, gave her her comfort blanket, lay down next to her, and gently tapped her back while still humming.

'I'll tell you a story,' he said in a trembling voice, 'a story about a little girl like you, a girl you would've loved had you met her, and she would've loved you.'

Shilana looked at him while she held the blanket under her nose and continued sucking her thumb. She was listening, she loved stories.

'Thirty-nine years ago, on a cold winter morning in Slemani a baby girl was born,' he told her quietly. 'Her parents named her Tara because she was as lovely as the bridal veil. She had a brother who was two years older than her. He called her Tatty and everyone else started calling her the same.' Shilana lifted her head up and then she was still again.

'Tatty looked up to her brother but he looked up to her even more. He only got the courage to protest and to ask for what he wanted because he knew she'd support him. She didn't like to do what she was told, this little girl; she had a mind of her own.' He smiled remembering his strong-willed sister as he stroked his daughter's head.

'She liked football. She loved playing with the neighbourhood boys and got into fights with them. She always had an answer for everything. Her parents thought that she was born a girl by

43

mistake. They were worried that she'd never fit in.

'It was a small place, you see, a place where women worked hard—cooking, cleaning, and raising their children, where they grew old and sick too soon, where many of them were not cared for, a place where everyone knew everything about everyone else, where people were warm and caring, they always helped each other, but they also tightly controlled each other.'

He paused and realised that he was narrating his sister's life for the first time. After all these years, he was finally giving it a context, there was cause and effect, things happened in a certain order, and they could be explained. In the past he'd seen it in chaotic fragments which were meaningless and unexplainable. Shilana wanted to resist sleep, but it came in waves, heavy waves that she couldn't escape.

'That place was too small for Tatty. She knew that something was wrong in the neighbourhood. She didn't want to become another woman who worked hard to satisfy everyone else. She was too beautiful, talented, rebellious, and she had a dream. She wanted to act on stage. But as she grew up, she realised that she could never fulfil her dream. And when she was receiving one blow after another, she was hoping that her brother would help her. She hoped that he would support her to live the life she wanted.

'Tara lived in Slemani and she died there. She didn't realise her dreams because the world wasn't ready for her, her family wasn't ready for her, no one was, not even her own brother who loved her so much. Everyone was such a disappointment, life itself was. She died, and her place of death was put behind a wall, but she's never forgotten. You know, sometimes people are more powerful when they are dead. Sometimes when life becomes a meaningless prison, death doesn't seem so bad.'

Shilana was now asleep, peacefully breathing dreams. Was she dreaming of the other girl, he wondered. Did she realise who that little girl was? Her innocence made him tearful, his voice shook for a second.

'Sleep my darling. I'll help you realise your dreams. You can be sure I won't abandon you. I won't let the world impose its restrictions on you, I won't let you down.'

Did she understand what he was promising her? Was she assured that things will be different for her? His heart was still beating fast and he was wondering if this was his second chance. He walked out of the bedroom, his head hanging low. He went straight to the sitting room, where his wife was watching TV and rubbing cream onto her feet. She turned around and looked at him as he sat next to her. He held his head in his hands and started crying.

CHAPTER SIX

Lana

Just before 7 pm, Lana arrived at the Kurdish Cultural Centre in South East London. The large events hall was used for parties, seminars, *pirsa*, and weddings. The heating never worked properly and there has been talk of repainting the whitish walls for the past five years. The dark colour of the carpet was chosen to be dirt resistant and during every gathering younger people debated about what it was. It was a crossover between brown and grey. A large Kurdish flag covered the wall behind the stage.

Lana had missed the first meeting a week earlier when, Twana told her, they discussed the possible disastrous consequences of the war. They had outlined an action plan but a few days after the meeting, there was talk of Turkish involvement in the war. This changed the second meeting's agenda. The question that became the focus of the gathering was how to prevent a Turkish invasion.

Like most Kurdish political gatherings, this too was chaotic and full of emotion. A man blamed the Kurdish parties for wasting years fighting each other instead of organising for such a day.

'We're so unprepared,' a woman said. 'We have no clue how to prevent the worst.'

Another man shouted from his seat, 'What about the chemicals? Who is providing us with protection?'

Baram, who chaired the session, looked defeated. He begged people not to interrupt each other. Drakhshan who had been a loved teacher back home, raised her hand and when she was allowed to speak she came to the front and spoke in a calm voice.

'I think this isn't the right time to talk about the past. War is on the way and the best we can do is to prevent the worst. I came here because I thought we would discuss the Turkish threat. I hope we can focus on that today and reach an agreement about what to do.'

A few people at the back clapped as she sat down. The rest just whispered to each other disgruntledly. A committee was selected to take matters forward. Several people volunteered, and some were forced to step in. Lana was asked to take part and realising how desperate everyone felt, she didn't refuse. This meant participating in long meetings to decide on an action plan and to carry it forward. She told herself that this is the last time she would get involved, only because it is urgent.

The committee was divided into smaller sub-committees to facilitate efficiency. Those whose English was good were responsible for drafting a letter to MPs and the Prime Minister, and to the US President. A group of polite and patient men and women were chosen to contact members of the Kurdish community on a daily basis to urge them to act. Another group was responsible for getting permission for a demonstration, organising logistics, and making the banners. The last group was to work on a website and to coordinate with other Kurds in Europe and America.

Lana was in the letter drafting sub-committee which also decided on the slogans for the demonstration. 'No Turkish intervention' was something that everyone agreed about but whether to say Kurdistan, Iraqi Kurdistan, or Iraq led to much debate and conversation. The conservatives were saying that at that moment it was best not to use the word 'Kurdistan' at all, not to provoke Turkey, Syria, Iran, or the international community. They were also saying no Kurdish flags should be displayed in the demonstration. This angered the rest of the committee.

'Our flag has been up for twelve years,' a man fumed, 'and now you're expecting us to lower it so as not to upset our enemies?'

Others were arguing that if they can't say Kurdistan right now, they would never be able to say it in the future.

'Till when?' a young man argued passionately, 'till when will you be timid? When will you dare to say what you want?'

'Such things are not gained by words,' some of the older men argued. 'It's hard work, and we must work for it silently.'

Lana found herself between different groups who wanted to carry forward different agendas; between different personalities who passionately disliked each other and disagreed with each other; between different political groups that needed to be reminded how important it was to stay united at this time. Being a woman, some of the men tried to side-line her. The intensive way men talked and argued exhausted Lana who had to do the same if she was to be heard. Everything kept her in a continuous state of panic. She knew that there was little she could do in the face of all the forces involved but the way everyone acted and talked passionately, the way every single detail had to be debated and agreed upon, made her feel that she was doing something important.

CHAPTER SEVEN

Gara

The whistling kettle on the *aladdin* heater woke Gara from his siesta. He looked round, registering his surroundings. The windows were steamed up and the smell of tea perfumed the air. His wife, son, and aunt cozied themselves around the *aladdin*. The carpeted room was warm, but a gust of cold air rushed in, giving him the shivers. The back corridor and the bathroom were ice cold except on *hamam* days. All the doors were closed to isolate the heated room from the colder parts. But the cold air attacked from under the doors and through the window frames. The sky was clear blue which meant that the wind was strong and piercing. Little Kawa was excited about the new set of colouring pencils his father had bought for him and was scribbling vigorously. Sayran sat on the sofa by the heater, her knees covered by a blanket. Her hands and feet were frozen again, and she'd become 'a burden' on others.

'It's okay,' Aveen told her while touching her forehead, 'You don't have a fever.'

'I just need to rest,' Sayran said.

Gara watched Aveen's slender figure bend in front of him as she poured his tea. Still covered in a fluffy blanket, he sat up and leaned on the sofa. He loved falling asleep while others talked as it reminded him of his childhood when the house was full of people. He looked at his son who was drawing a picture of *daya*, a massive head with short arms and legs. Sayran's face was tensed up as Aveen sat on the back of the sofa and gently massaged her shoulders. He looked out the window and wondered whether it would be another dry winter.

'Rain!' Aveen appealed to the sky. 'Rain for the empty reservoirs.'

He looked at her with amazement. She regularly expressed his thoughts and feelings as if she could read his mind. The sun was going down and the light was dimming so she turned the light on.

'I don't like darkness,' Aveen said. 'It's not romantic at all.'

'Not even when you are with the right person?' Sayran asked her teasingly.

'No!' she replied. 'I like to see things.'

'Wait until you're older,' Sayran told her, 'and you'd want the lights off.'

The three of them laughed and Kawa looked up at them, his mouth agape. He stopped colouring and came and sat next to his mother, showing her his paintings. With every new page Kawa got a kiss from his mother, she kissed his thumb, his index finger, his palm, his wrist, his eyes, and he kept laughing. Suddenly Kawa looked up and stopped laughing.

'*Jooja*,' Kawa said as he pointed forward.

The three of them looked at where he was pointing but found nothing.

'There's no *jooja*, *gullekem*,' Gara said.

Kawa got up and tried to open the door to the back of the house.

50

'Open,' he looked back and begged his mother, 'open, open.'

'There's nothing,' Aveen reiterated.

But Kawa kept trying to open the door. She opened the door and walked into the corridor with him. Gara followed them and looked at the floor and walls, hoping to find an insect.

'See? There's nothing,' Aveen said.

Kawa looked around him. '*Jooja*,' he kept saying.

FOUR WEEKS BEFORE THE WAR

CHAPTER EIGHT

Hiwa

Despite Sozi's protest about the cold, he decided to spend Wednesday morning playing with Shilana in the Harrow Recreation Ground.

'She'll catch a cold,' Sozi said, before leaving for work.

'I'll wrap her up,' he reassured her.

He put her wellies and puddle suit on, covered her in a soft blanket, and gave her the banana and kiwi smoothie that she loved. This was the only way to keep her in the pram without her making a fuss. The minute they arrived, she quickly got out of her pushchair and ran, a newfound joy. Her puffy purple suit made her look shorter than she was.

You're too young to run, he thought. Why are the females in this family in such a rush?

He chased Shilana as she shrieked and laughed, oblivious to the crisp air. He pushed her high on the swing, caught her as she slid down the slide, and helped her climb the climbing wall. Eventually she became tired and grumpy, grabbed a piece of her comfort blanket —cut into four pieces to make it lighter for her to carry— and lay down in her pram. He knew that she needed one more thing to fall asleep and gave her the lukewarm milk bottle which she grabbed with both hands. He circled the park, following the public path alongside the green lawn. He could smell the wet earth, the satisfied blades of grass. The lime trees, chestnuts, and oaks rustled, swaying gently in the wind, their leaves clapping in unison. The open sky was blue. Flocks of birds followed their leaders, going back and forth as if in a military exercise. The tennis court was empty. He observed the neat rectangles on the ground and the net dividing the opposing sides. Everything was calm, like a quiet mind. On the other side of the green patch, a small building with locked doors declared itself to be The Stage. Some afternoons the doors were opened to let the stage come out into the park. Here, musicians and poets communicated with those who were taking the time to listen.

When war and sports divide, the arts unite us, he thought.

He hadn't experienced that sense of community, connection, and revival which the arts provided since Shilana was born. The last event he went to was when his sister read poetry at the Troubadour. Over the course of the evening, the four poets made him feel love, sadness, anger, and pleasure, all at the same time. The poems countered the emotional blunting he felt, the numbing that turned him into a passive receiver of life's twists and turns. Over the years, he'd become less capable of empathising, responding appropriately to tragic events, and feeling strongly. He knew that he should feel outrage and sadness about the horrors in the world. He also knew that he needed to feel strongly in order to act. The arts had given him the opportunity to understand and feel what he should feel. He remembered a major moment of realisation gifted to him by a film.

In her attempt to help him connect to her world, Sarah had watched *Sophie's Choice* with him. As he watched Sophie struggle to make a choice, attempt to hold on to both her children, realise

55

that she cannot, and choose her son over her daughter, Hiwa broke down. For the first time in his life, he felt the pain of the Holocaust and understood the long-term scaring effects of trauma. On a personal level, he understood his mother's pain when she chose him over Tara and sided with him against her. Even after her death she wanted him not to feel guilty and to be safe. She persuaded him to leave the country and start a new life. He understood her guilt and regret, even when he wasn't there to witness it.

Hiwa completed his circle and stopped for a second to inspect the lush ground he was leaving behind. He then left the park and turned onto Hindes Road, observing the three-storey houses, lingering longer on the yellow brick rather than the red brick. He admired the organised hedgerow and skyline, the comfortable and even pavements, the clean roads.

How much work has gone into planning each road, he wondered. How many people have put their heads together to make this happen?

He thought of the ad hoc and impromptu nature of some residential roads built in his homeland after 1992. Sometimes a new road emerged without planning, houses were erected before the infrastructure was in place – paved roads, sewage systems, and electric poles. When the Ba'athist violence was over, forcibly displaced populations dumped in the fringes of the cities moved closer and built themselves practical homes on public land. This created deprived "*shaabi*" neighbourhoods with limited services that were later engulfed by newer, better organised ones as the cities grew.

So much is determined by war, he thought. Survival

overshadows concerns about comfort and aesthetics.

Living in London had educated his eyes, helping him to see better. It had refined his senses and helped him to understand. He painfully noticed what was wrong with the roads, neighbourhoods, and systems, more so than those who never left the country.

'Distance and new experiences bring clarity,' he said to his sleeping daughter. 'You'll realise this when you grow up. I hope you can take a few steps back when things are unclear. I hope you can turn away and turn back again. I hope you'll see what you've been missing.'

CHAPTER NINE

Gara

He couldn't sleep and turned over to face his wife. Her chest was gently rising and falling. Kawa was asleep, breathing heavily through his mouth as his nose was blocked.

'Are you awake?' Gara whispered.

Her body moved.

'What does he see?' he said.

'It may be nothing.'

'We can't see it but that doesn't mean it's nothing.'

'Since when do you believe in the invisible?' she said.

'I've never thought that we experience only beings that exist.'

Aveen didn't respond. She put her hand on Gara's chest and gradually her breathing synchronised with his. 'Let's not worry yet,' she said. 'It's probably nothing.'

Kawa coughed. She turned around and stroked him until he settled down again. Soon, she too was asleep.

They named their son Kawa because they couldn't escape Gara's brother. There was no way around it. He was constantly present, silently lying down between them, listening, watching, and even touching them. Sometimes Gara felt that Kawa was also holding Aveen as she lay in his arms. He felt Kawa's hand on his shoulder, on his back, as he bent over his wife kissing her.

Kawa was always there, neither reproaching, nor angry, just

close and quiet, making sure that he wasn't forgotten. Naming their son after him was also an attempt to escape the guilt they felt, as if they were trying to tell him that he wasn't dropped, that he was still part of their lives, included in their thoughts and prayers. It was a tribute, a mutual recognition of his memory, of their love for him. Did he accept their offering?

Little Kawa carried the name gracefully, totally unburdened by its weight, innocent of its meaning to his parents. He was generally a happy boy, capable of amusing himself with a piece of paper for hours. He could be serious and thoughtful, rather like a philosopher, puzzling over the ways of the world. He had no outbursts of rage, wasn't stubborn. He didn't have his uncle's blue eyes, nor did he have his curly hair, rather large brown eyes and straight brown hair. He had his mother's thick lips, a heavy lower lip that kept his mouth open at times. His little nose was Tara's, the same neatness. From his father he'd inherited his long fingers and toes. Every time Gara mentioned this, people laughed at him. It was as if he was desperately trying to prove that this boy who looked nothing like him was really his son, the fingers and toes proved it.

He watched his son carefully as he grew up, wondering whether he and Aveen were capable of producing a copy of his brother. He wondered if the boy would look, walk, or talk like him, whether he would inherit his uncle's personality. At times he worried that by trying to acknowledge his brother they had been unfair to their son. Would he grow up and find the truth and blame them? Would he complain that they had been selfish, that he shouldn't carry the weight of their guilt, nor their attempts at mending things with a ghost? Were they just trapping themselves in the past? Would this innocent and desperate gesture unleash chaos and misery later on? Would their sins catch up with them? Some days Gara thought he would have to pay the price for it. It had all started on a spring twilight five years earlier, when Gara forgot Kawa for a few moments and kissed his brother's widow on the neck.

The family lived through seven years of grief with Aveen. When her pain was fresh, she thought of Kawa every day, her tears flowed like rain as she sat amongst them. Gara watched her cry for years until she was stuck in a place where her colourful memories were fading, where she was no longer capable of producing tears, and had to work hard to remember Kawa and feel his loss. He observed her struggle when she had to create an atmosphere to mourn for him. She would surround herself with his pyjamas – the ones she kept in a plastic bag to preserve his smell, his silver flute, a pack of the cigarettes that he used to smoke, and an aftershave she'd bought after her return from Iran because the smell reminded her of him. She smelt his clothes, inhaled the cigarettes, and touched his flute, putting her fingers where his fingers had been. But Gara knew how cruel time was—his smell left the pyjamas despite her efforts to hang on to it, and the flute became just a cool metal surface lacking any connection to him.

When friends and relatives tried to console Aveen, when they told her, 'time will heal,' and 'people start their love story at your age,' she cried in response. Once she got angry and shouted, 'Why can't you leave me alone? I had my love story, I married my love, I became pregnant, I lost my husband, and then my baby. What more is there for me to see?' She believed that she'd lived her life too swiftly and there were no more beginnings for her, the only thing she expected next was her own death.

Gara knew that she tried to feel pain in order to feel something, to stay alive, to know that she was still in the world of those physical beings who had wishes, desires, and regrets. For as long as she remembered him, Kawa wasn't dead, not completely, and neither was she. Watching her suffer was easier for Gara than the deadening silence that sometimes came over her, when she looked like a ghost, like an empty shell without a past or a present, when she was unable to feel or respond to anything. The nothingness, the silence, was the most terrifying thing for Gara, as if she was dead but hadn't made it to the other world. He felt her loneliness amongst those who could still feel pain and pleasure. He watched her as she stared at others, as if from a very long way away, not commenting, nor reacting. This is why when her memories were reduced to meaningless and incoherent fragments, she started narrating them to herself.

Aveen recited her memories aloud, reminding herself about his every move. Gara recalled how his aunt and sister worried about these lengthy recitals she descended into when she thought they couldn't hear. They tried to interrupt her trances and bring her back to the present. Once his aunt told Aveen, 'The dead are disloyal. Just remember that they never answer back, they don't even visit you in a dream.' As a young woman Sayran had made the mistake of hanging on to a dead man and she was trying to protect Aveen from it, but it was no use.

61

Gara knew that Aveen was not losing touch with reality. It was only because she was so painfully aware of the present that she tried to escape into this private world. She tried to take a break from the heavy weight of 'now', to lose her sense of time and live those moments again.

That afternoon when she tried to reconstruct Kawa and ignite his memory again, Gara stood by the door and listened.

'Every time you came to our house I watched you, not knowing that you knew.' She said. Gara could tell from her voice that she was smiling. 'I watched you from the upstairs window, from the kitchen window, from the keyhole of Berhem's bedroom door. I was supposed to bring you tea when you came. I knocked on the door and waited until Berhem took the tray from me. If he said, "just come in," I would drop the tray by the door and walk away, embarrassing him. You were so beautiful, and I was worried that you would see straight through me. What a game of hide and seek, do you remember?

'Then it was your turn to watch. That day when I walked out without an umbrella, crying into the rain like mad, I never realised you were standing around, hoping that I would come out. It was one of those days that I felt I would go crazy at home. I only wanted to go for a walk, just to be in the rain and breathe in the cold air, but my mother made a huge scene, as if I was committing a crime. We shouted at each other until we were tired, and I ran out feeling that I was a prisoner, watching my life pass by without having a say in it. I must've walked for an hour in the rain thinking that no one's problems were bigger than mine. How silly I was!

'You followed me all the way and wanted to come and talk

to me, but you worried that talking to me meant betraying your friend. Eventually when we met, how funny it was! Wearing my flipflops, I'd tucked the sides of my long dress into my underwear and was washing the back courtyard, the broom in one hand and the hose in the other. I was singing at the top of my awful voice, "*Kajale Kajale/ jwan u narm u jikale...*"

'The next minute both of you were standing over and watching me. "This is my little sister," Berhem said, trying to embarrass me, and it worked. You looked beautiful in that light blue shirt. I quickly pulled my dress out, stood straight and said, "Welcome." Just like that and I quickly turned away thinking I could end it there. Your voice was playful when you said, "I didn't know you were a singer. That's real talent there." Berhem laughed and I looked at you all confused, not knowing what to say.

'How brief our time was together... how brief, my love,' her voice broke. She kissed the flute where he placed his fingers and the floor he'd walked on, and when her lips were on the cool tiles she started crying aloud.

'Aveen,' Gara said, standing in the door. She looked at his figure in the doorframe, the light behind him shone through his shirt and she got confused.

'Kawa,' she cried and rose, but just before she hugged him, she realised it wasn't Kawa.

'Oh no,' she said, 'no,' her legs were failing.

Gara grabbed her before her knees hit the floor, his knees landing close to hers.

'That's enough,' he told her in a voice close to begging. 'Please stop doing this.'

She couldn't control her tears, her chest was rising and falling.

Gara held her as she cried. He held her and, without thinking, he gently kissed her neck.

For a few days after the kiss, Gara left home before breakfast and came back late, hoping to avoid her. He felt ashamed of kissing a woman who still mourned for the man she loved, for his own brother. He felt guilty towards Kawa who would've never done this to him, if he was the one in the grave, leaving behind a young widow. But most of all he was terrified by what he felt. Suddenly, his depression, his anger, his lack of interest in marrying all made sense, he loved her. And since he couldn't trace the beginning of this love back to a particular moment, he felt that he'd always loved her, maybe even when she was married to Kawa?

The burden of this thought was too great, Gara avoided people's eyes. He taught his classes and stayed away from the teachers' common room. He was less patient with his students, less generous in his marking, and taught at a faster pace. Since Lana's marriage and departure, a year before, he'd been living with Aveen and his aunt. Soon after Lana left, Gara worried that Aveen too may leave. Berhem came back from Sweden and tried, for the second time, to persuade his sister to go with him. Part of him wanted her to leave, she'd mourned for too long, and it was time to move on. But part of him hoped she'd stay.

'Aveen is part of our family,' he told Berhem. 'I understand if she wants to leave but it will be her choice, not ours.'

At the time he didn't know why he wanted her to stay, 'Maybe because I'm used to her,' he thought to himself selfishly. 'Or maybe because she reminds me of Kawa.' Now he was embarrassed by the lie he'd told Berhem, embarrassed by how he'd deceived himself all these years.

This is treason, he thought. It's selfish and greedy.

He remembered the canvases and acrylic paints he bought for her over the years, hoping to help her start painting again, convincing himself that he was being a good and supportive brother-in-law, trying to help his brother's widow. She thanked him but never used the material. Maybe she already knew about his intentions, Gara thought, and she tried to discourage him from trying.

That week when he was desperately trying to avoid Aveen, he briefly saw her twice and was grateful for his aunt's presence. He noticed how Aveen's face was calm, and she seemed unaffected by what had been.

She never noticed the kiss, he consoled himself. She was crying, didn't feel it.

But one night as he turned the key and intended to tip toe to his room, she was waiting for him in the sitting room with a lantern by her side. He was immediately disillusioned. Sayran was asleep in the back room where the two women slept and Aveen had apparently stayed up to talk to him.

'*Slaw*,' he whispered guiltily, expecting her to have a go at him.

'*Slaw*,' she whispered back, standing up in the dark.

His throat was dry, and he waited for her to say something, the silence made him uncomfortable.

'I'm sorry,' he finally said, as she wasn't going to say anything.

'No,' she replied, 'I am.'

'I know,' he wanted to say. 'I understand that you don't love me, I know I'm stupid and selfish.' Instead, he said, 'It's okay!' Then after pausing for a second, he added, 'It's really late now.

Go to sleep and don't worry about anything, I won't bother you again.' He then quickly walked towards his room without looking at her.

He wished she'd pretend not to have noticed, that she would ignore him instead of making it clear that she knew he wanted her, but she didn't want him back. In that one week his emotions had found a focus and his hopes immediately collapsed before they had a chance to be expressed. The following days he avoided being at home as much as he could, trying to show her that it wouldn't happen again. He worried that she may leave, after all these years.

How stupid of me, he told himself. She's been living under the same roof, what more do I want?

One Friday morning, just when he was about to leave, Sayran came to his room.

'What is wrong?' she asked him, looking worried.

'Nothing,' he told her and then quickly corrected himself. 'Nothing you should worry about.'

She looked at him suspiciously, not believing, 'You're not ill, are you?'

'No, I'm not,' he said laughing, wishing that was the problem.

'Any news from Hiwa and Lana?' she asked.

'I don't know anything, I swear,' he reassured his aunt while hugging her.

In the evening when he got home, he went straight to his room. Minutes later, while he was unbuttoning his shirt, about to change into his pyjamas, Aveen was standing at his door.

'You misunderstood me the other night,' she said. 'I meant to say I'm sorry that I've been so selfish, prolonging my misery and making you all suffer.'

She didn't wait for his answer, she turned around and was gone. Gara sat on the edge of his bed, her words echoing in his head.

You're not selfish, he wanted to shout behind her. You're good and loyal.

He wished he could tell her that she wasn't the cause of their suffering, his family's suffering started long before she set foot in it.

Maybe it's this tragic house, he thought while looking around his room. There are too many ghosts in this house, too many ghosts we cannot escape.

CHAPTER TEN

Lana

It was Friday evening, the end to a blissful week of making up, when she arrived at Amer's place. She hung her coat beside his and left her shoes in the corner. Unlike her flat, everything was neat and elegant. The floorboards were dark brown, and a large red carpet covered the middle. The second floor flat had no curtains. There was minimal furniture: one sofa, one coffee table, a single comfortable chair, and a small TV. This was another area where gender norms failed, Lana thought. Amer was a much better housekeeper than she was. He wasn't the kind of man who blamed her for being untidy. If he didn't like the state of something he would deal with it. Seeing him collect cups and wash up made her feel guilty. She would start clearing up alongside him and apologising, making him laugh.

She sat on the sofa watching TV as he went to bring tea. The repetitive news couldn't capture her attention, she was happy. As a child, she'd heard from the neighbourhood women that the bliss of making up was worth the hassle of fighting.

'That first cuddle after a long silence,' *baji* Halaw had said, 'nothing is nicer.'

'A man is never more generous,' *haji* Aysh had confirmed, 'never more eager to please you.'

The women in their traditional clothing spoke about the

'mysteries of manhood.' Those big hipped, busty women, who smelt of their clove necklaces, talked with the wisdom of old age and years of sharing stories. They laughed about how keen men were on sex. They relayed stories about embarrassing moments when their husbands had implored and lied to the guests and to their children to have a quick cuddle with their wives in the shadowy back rooms. They talked about the sturdy, unyielding men who walked around acting and talking confidently as masters of the house, masters of the community, and the country. At times they were reduced to gentle and needy creatures who trembled with love and desire. It was these secret moments that the women talked about at length, because no matter how dominant their husbands were, they were reduced to a wreck if their wives didn't love them.

'You need to fight every now and then,' *baji* Halaw believed, 'so they know your worth.'

But as Lana let herself back into that sticky sweetness, into hours of holding on tightly, she knew that it wasn't just because he was keen, it was because she'd missed him. In a constantly changing world, she found in him a stable person who cared about things, loved generously, and worked hard; she found in him the kindness and generosity of her home culture and the tolerance of her new one. Unlike what the neighbourhood women of her childhood had told her, he wasn't the only one who trembled with love, his body wasn't the only one that bloomed into yearning. She craved his breath, his voice, his skin, the musky smell of his body as it locked into hers.

It was the war that spoiled everything, the war that was

coming over the world like a dark cloud that couldn't be stopped. It threatened her happiness, reminded her how fragile it all was, how it could be destroyed at any moment. She embraced him with all her might in fear that this war might take him from her. She made love to him each time as if it was the last time. And he held on to her and loved her back. When the news predicted disaster, when their shared homeland was under continuous scrutiny, its history examined, its power structure analysed, its unity questioned, they held each other close.

Lana switched the TV off and went to the kitchen. He was radiant in his light green shirt. His flawless brown skin glowed and she was filled with the desire to kiss his eyelids, his lashes, his straight nose, his full lips.

'I'm making you real tea,' he said as he made himself a cup of chamomile tea.

She grabbed her black tea and raised it to him.

'*Supas!*' she said in Kurdish.

'*Al'afoo!*' he answered in Arabic.

They walked back into the sitting room and spread themselves on the sofa.

'Are you coming to the party tomorrow?'

'What party?'

'Charlotte's birthday, the Aquarian,' he said, making a fish face and turning his hands into fins by his cheeks.

'Oh no, I promised to go to my brother's,' Lana said. 'I've already cancelled once.'

'Don't worry, there will be plenty of quirky people.'

'Isn't it bad luck to have the party after your birthday?'

'Doing it early is supposed to be bad, not late,' he said.

'How aquarian will you go?'

'I'll wear something blue. We're strange enough as we are... Anything on?' he nodded towards the TV.

'The same old stuff,' she said, leaning back into the sofa. 'Why didn't you go to the demonstration? I thought you agreed with the crowd?'

'I agree that the war will unleash horrors.'

'They destroyed the Nazis, and that ended it in Germany.'

'Exactly!' Amer said. 'They really destroyed the Nazis and with them they destroyed a large section of German society. That can't happen in Iraq. And the one million strong army that was utilised for—'

'But I keep thinking,' she interrupted him, 'when the war was over, the remaining Nazis became ordinary citizens. Don't you think the same could happen in Iraq?'

'The Nazis had no support,' he said. 'Everyone told them that they were guilty. It was shameful to have been part of the Nazi regime. The Ba'athists are different. They have support and sympathy from the pan-Arab nationalists across the world.'

'And from the Islamists, anti-Americans, and anti-imperialists.'

'And there is a lot of bad blood and rivalries between the different groups.'

'And no good leaders,' Lana said thinking of the Kirkuk oil fields which would be fought over by all.

'No, there aren't,' he said. 'They haven't learnt from the past.'

It's the wall, Lana thought, the wall between us and our past tragedies that obstructs learning, it makes us suffer from amnesia and dooms us to repeating the same mistakes. She took a deep breath.

71

'The Kurds may not want to stay in Iraq,' she said. 'Your lot won't like that!'

'My lot, huh?' he said with raised eyebrows. 'I think it would be a shame to lose the diversity that makes Iraq special.'

'You can't make decisions for us,' she sat up, her nationalism rising.

'I'm not deciding,' he said, 'I'm stating my preference. I like us to be from the same country, don't you?'

'It's like an abusive marriage,' she said. 'A man beats his wife but every time she wants to leave, he says, "You can't leave, I love you."'

'I shall stop talking,' he said, 'I'm on dangerous grounds here.'

There was a moment of silence before she started speaking in a calm voice again, 'I too thought about joining the demo but the thought of joining pro-Ba'athists, Arab nationalists, Islamists, and others who don't give a shit about our destruction puts me off. Such hypocrites!'

'What about rising above?'

'It's easier said than done.'

'One day, when you're ready,' he said, as if he could foresee the future.

She stared forward and wondered how and when she could stop being angry about the blind spots of truth and justice.

'I don't want to be angry,' she said. 'It's exhausting.'

'Let's not be angry then,' he said while getting up. 'Let's go to the Turkish restaurant.'

Lana laughed. A few days before, she'd walked out of a Turkish shop leaving her groceries at the till when the owner asked her where she was from and then told her that he'd never heard of

Kurdistan before.

'Where is it?' the shop owner asked her. 'Can you show it to me on the map?' knowing too well that she couldn't.

'You know where it is,' she responded and walked out, not buying the goods.

She hugged Amer and they rocked together from side to side, as if dancing to some imaginary music.

'If they ask where I come from, you'll have to answer them... don't want to fight.'

'This lot are good guys,' he reassured her. 'They won't freak out if we say Kurdistan.' He then pretended to be ignorant and spoke in a Turkish accent, 'What was it? Turkistan? Gorjestan?' making her laugh.

'It'll be okay,' he said.

They wore their coats, put on their shoes, and locked the door behind them.

The morning after the Poetry Cafe event four months earlier, she took the train to the poetry course in Devon, carrying the October rain in her thick hair. She'd woken up fluent in her three languages. This put her in a good mood because some mornings she couldn't speak any of them properly. She'd wake up speaking broken Kurdish and it would go downhill from there. But as she stripped off her damp coat on the train and arranged her bags on the seat next to her, sentences ran through her head, singing, dancing, and some of them even shouting. She was full of the music of words. She felt that she could write a poem in all the languages she knew, real and imagined, and she was convinced that it would make sense. She took out a piece of paper and a pen and stared out the train window before writing:

> The blue table echoes water
> Au, au, dangi au
> chejhi aram-bekhshi au.
> The lips that tasted the wine
> tasted my lips.
> Al-rajul al-lathi qabalani
> kana waqifan hunak
> yuhibuni bi-samt!

She laughed at her own invention and then became aware of the woman sitting across from her on the other side, who looked up in surprise. She bit her lower lip; she was full of secrets. And no one knew that she was full of moonlight, full of colours wanting to invade the world. She felt that she was leaking words and she zipped up her cardigan.

She didn't know that the three-hour journey through the English countryside, lush and wet and full of promises, was taking her into total darkness. She'd received various emails about what would happen, what she needed to take for the duration of the week, and who the other participants would be, but she hadn't read them properly. She never readied herself for things, which is why she was utterly unprepared when she met Amer again outside the station. This derailed her optimism about the week.

'Charlotte told me you're going on the course,' he said. 'What a nice surprise!'

She realised he wasn't tall, but he would stand out in a room full of tall men. This made her stomach turn once more.

'Yes,' she confirmed awkwardly. 'It's a small world.' She was terrible at small talk.

Why was he so friendly, she asked herself, what did he want? Part of her was curious and another part was alarmed, even more so because she found him pleasant.

'So I was right… you come from my part of the world… I enjoyed your reading last night!

'Thank you,' she said. 'I didn't know you were a poet!'

'I'm sure there's a lot more you don't know about me.'

She gave him a quick glance, not sure if she wanted to know more.

The other participants had all gathered by the exit and they were introducing themselves to each other. Two large vehicles were ready to pick them up. She sat by the window of the bigger car, and he got into the other. She was anxious, this wasn't what she'd expected from the week.

Throughout the car journey she sat in silence next to a young Asian woman, grateful for the breathing space. She looked out from the clouded window as the minibus took them on a long windy journey through rain and trees. Two people talked behind her and every now and then she listened to them. One of them had an offer from a publisher and was preparing his manuscript for publication. The other man seemed interested as he had tried several publishers without much luck.

Lana found the first day of meeting new people the most difficult. She talked a little bit to everyone, doing most of the listening. It amazed her how much people loved talking about themselves and sharing their views and ideas. She herself had no views on western music, was not much of a theatre goer, didn't like any sports. At times she wished that she was interested in football as she felt left out when everyone got excited during the world cup. Her interests were limited. She could talk for hours about poetry, war, and patriarchy. She sometimes bored herself and admired those who were all-rounders and could talk for hours about nothing in particular.

The week rolled on full of reading, writing, editing, and passionate conversations. They gravitated towards each other without trying. Once she came into the workshop late and the only place to sit was next to him. Another time when she thought she'd found a quiet writing corner for herself, totally camouflaged in the shed overlooking the forest, he appeared out of the blue. He was startled for a second and then came forward and sat next to her. He laid down his notebook and pen between them. The woods opened in front of them; wet fir cones perfumed the air. The sky was blue with a few white clouds swimming freely.

'What an inspiring place,' he said.

'This is England as I imagined it before coming here.'

'When was that?' he asked.

'In 1997. I guess you were born here?'

'No, but I was young,' he said. 'My father was a member of the Communist Party. He left in the late '70s after his friends were arrested. Did you seek asylum?'

'No, I got married and came here.'

'Refreshing to follow the path of love!' he said smiling.

A romantic! she thought.

'Not really,' she said. 'I was a take-away bride.'

'It sounds like the title of another Julia Roberts film.'

She laughed.

'In the '90s men came home to the Safe Haven and found themselves Kurdish brides,' she said, feeling the need to explain herself. 'I never thought I'd be one of them, but he defeated me. He was kind and handsome. Everyone told me refusing him would be madness!'

'So what went wrong?'

I'm not going to slag off a Kurdish man to you, she thought.

'The usual stuff that goes wrong in a relationship,' she said. 'I guess I was disillusioned about the childhood myth. The prince came but happiness didn't. I was a cat and he was a dog. It wasn't meant to be.'

'I agree,' he said. 'It usually doesn't work out between cats and dogs.'

'No, it doesn't!'

'And good to realise that happiness is not given to us by others. I know a few people who still don't know that.'

'Hmm,' she said as she looked at the horizon. 'Me too!'

He took out a pack of cigarettes from his shirt pocket and started playing with it.

'I like what George said the other day.'

'What was that?' she said.

'That you should end with an image, not an idea, that when you are writing about a sparrow, everything should be sparrow.'

'That is poetic in itself!'

'He's brilliant, don't you think?' he said as he turned to look at her.

'It's great to have a poet as your hero. Others should learn from that.'

'Especially from our community,' he said.

She wanted to correct him and say 'our *communities*,' but was curious to know what he meant so she said, 'Yes! All the false heroes, confused causes, double standards.'

He played with his pack of cigarettes.

'Growing up is just that, isn't it?' he said. 'Realising that the group we associate with is far from perfect. We're not just victims but also victimisers, not just oppressed but also oppressors.'

She placed her elbows on her knees, looking at him intensely.

He raised a cigarette, 'Here is to honesty, to not hiding behind big words, to accepting the truth even if it's painful.' He lit the cigarette.

'I don't know,' she said. 'There are other nations who're the same but—'

'The same in what way?'

'In dividedness and self-destructiveness. But no one came off as badly as us.' She hoped he understood that the 'us' she was referring to didn't include his 'us.'

'Isn't it too early to determine that?' he said.

'How many decades of oppression should pass before I'm allowed to think that?'

'You're allowed to think whatever you like,' he said with a teasing smile. 'But the world keeps changing and at times it feels as if it's changing for the worse. I think this is just another phase and it'll pass.'

'An optimist,' she said, sinking back into herself, images of the gassed Halabja passing through her mind. Of course he is, she thought, he doesn't share my history.

'A rational optimist.'

'And confident, too!'

His hopefulness reminded her of Kawa. She didn't want to compare them and tried to pull away from these thoughts. She stared at a corner of the field, noticing the apple trees, frozen in thoughts she wouldn't share with him. After a moment of silence, he reached out and put his hand on her arm.

'I'm not the enemy,' he said. 'I hope you know that.'

I know you didn't do it, she wanted to say, but weren't you the silent bystander? Doesn't that make you some sort of enemy?

She turned away and he withdrew his hand. The light had changed. It was nearly four now, and the sun was golden. A few people were laughing loudly. She felt tired, aware of his presence. Her eyes were stinging.

He started whistling a song she knew too well, Abdulhalim's *Maw'ud*. She wanted to sing the words but didn't.

I know his music, she thought while closing her eyes, but he doesn't know mine.

CHAPTER ELEVEN

Hiwa

'I'm going to tell you a new story,' he said as he lay next to Shilana on the bed, 'the story of Kawa, the brave blacksmith, and the evil king.'

All Hiwa could see were her large eyes, the fire rings around her pupils, and how they merged with her green irises. She sucked her thumb, holding onto a piece of her blue comfort blanket. Every time she was angry or tired, a portion of the soft blanket soothed her and made her settle down. They kept each piece in a different part of the house to ease access.

'Many many years ago, in a land called Mesopotamia, there was a king called Zuhak. He wasn't a good leader.' Hiwa liked that his voice and closeness calmed his daughter. 'Good leaders make sure that their people have food to eat,' he continued, 'they protect their people from death. But he was a bad man, this Zuhak, so evil that...' He wasn't going to tell her that Zuhak had made a pact with the devil who kissed him on the shoulders and planted a snake on each one, making him sacrifice two children a day to feed their brains to the snakes.

Shilana released her thumb for just a second to say, '*Beele!* (Tell it!)'

He had to make something up quickly.

'Sometimes nature punishes bad people, and so it punished

this selfish king by making him hungry all the time. Every hour of every day his servants had to prepare a royal feast which made it impossible for him to think clearly. What he ate in a day was enough to feed a neighbourhood. All the farmers, the fishermen, the hunters had to give everything they grew and caught to the king. He ate and his people got hungry and so many families lost their children to hunger because of his greed. One of the families that suffered was Kawa's. All his children starved, except one.'

He skipped the part where the merciful royal cook used a sheep's brain instead of one of the children, to save a child a day. The rescued children, according to the legend, were smuggled to the highest and most distant mountains, where they learnt to fend for themselves.

One day you will learn that the surviving children were our ancestors, he thought, as his daughter opened her eyes and looked at him, as if the silence had woken her.

'Kawa realised that Zuhak would destroy his people if he continued ruling, so he rebelled against the king,' Hiwa continued despite thinking that Shilana would not fully understand everything. 'On March 21, more than two thousand years ago, Kawa killed the king and lit a fire on the mountainside to tell the people about his victory. Soon the news travelled, and more and more fires were lit to communicate the victory and celebrate freedom. That is why every year, we do the same. We light fires to celebrate the end of tyranny and the beginning of freedom. We celebrate the end of winter and the beginning of spring. We hold hands and dance around the fire. We jump over the fire so that it burns our sorrows away. One day, we'll go home during Newroz and you will see how it is.'

81

She was quiet, no longer sucking her thumb.

'Did you know that your uncle was named Kawa after the blacksmith, and so was your cousin? Do you know what that means? It means that we have fighters in the family who wouldn't accept oppression. In fact, your uncle died doing exactly that. He didn't sit back and let the bad people win.' Hiwa was whispering now, getting her used to the silence that would follow his leaving. 'So don't worry my dear. For as long as there is resistance, there is hope. For as long as there are people who are willing to sacrifice their own personal happiness for the greater good, it will be okay. I hope that you too will fight for your rights *baqurban*. I hope that if, one day, someone tries to dominate or hurt you, you'd be strong enough to walk away from them. And in case I'm not around to remind you, always remember that you were born free, and you should live as a free person who makes their own decisions. Don't let anyone take away your right to choose in the name of love or for any other excuse.'

He stayed for a few moments to make sure she'd fallen asleep. He then went to the kitchen, poured himself a glass of water, and joined his wife and sister in the sitting room. They were in the middle of a conversation, ignoring the silenced TV.

'I just told Shilana the Newroz story,' he said, 'without the snakes and beheadings.'

'Did she like it?' Lana said.

'She fell asleep, which is always a good sign.' He sipped his water and continued, 'We may have a real Newroz this year. It may be the end of his tyranny.'

'I hope so,' Sozi said. 'I hope his end won't be the beginning of another tyrant.'

82

'I hope not,' Lana reiterated.

'Anyone for tea?' Hiwa said, walking back to the kitchen to turn the kettle on.

'Yes please,' Lana said, then she turned back towards Sozi and resumed their interrupted conversation: 'Where was I? Yes, I tried to include him. I told him about our monthly readings at the Poetry Cafe and encouraged him to join Exiled Writers Ink, but he wasn't interested.'

'Is he depressed?' Sozi asked.

'Just arrogant,' Lana said. 'He's won a prize in Galawej Festival and thinks that our group, which was set up to support writers like him, isn't good enough for him.'

'He'll come around,' Hiwa said. 'It's probably a lack of confidence rather than arrogance.'

'Arrogance usually masks insecurity,' Lana said and then turned to Sozi: 'Next time Gara refers another person to me, please remind me not to waste my time.'

'If you're going to invest time in supporting newcomers, invest in the women, not in the male artists and intellectuals,' Sozi said.

'True! Men only recommend other men! No one talks about women's potential.'

'This isn't a feminist issue,' Hiwa said. 'It's just about who knows who.'

'It's very much a feminist issue,' Lana replied. 'Men recommend each other for prizes, open their networks to each other, back each other up, and side-line women. This is what patriarchy is about.'

'I like the way men try to make these things seem insignificant,' Sozi said, 'or accidental, or my favourite: "based on merit".'

Hiwa sipped his tea. He wasn't going to argue with them

because he knew he would lose. A part of him also recognised that what they said was true. On his visits back home, he'd noticed how most men didn't have personal relations with women beyond their own kin, they didn't have female friends, didn't talk to women beyond general civilities, didn't see women as human beings capable of doing good things. Even the more intellectual men didn't listen to women, not even to their own wives. They didn't read women's work, didn't invite women to participate in readings, discussions, and TV interviews, and didn't encourage them to submit their work for publication. All of that was true, but Gara wasn't a misogynist.

'I'll show you some pictures of Gara. You'll remember how innocent and good he is!' He immediately regretted saying this, worrying about ruining the mood of the evening, but his sister was now looking at him expectantly.

'Let's do that,' she said. 'Let's remember everyone's innocence.'

CHAPTER TWELVE

Lana

The house seemed like a maze now, rooms led to more rooms, doors opened to reveal closed doors, walls stood behind every window. A fine rain fell, as if the roof had been blown away. Lana's right arm stretched in front of her, opening doors as she walked through the damp space. She was interrupting the cobwebs and feeling guilty. They had saved the Prophet centuries ago when they built their web around the entrance of his hiding cave. She was certain that no spider would build a web to deter her enemies and nor would white doves build a nest in front of her house to protect her.

No, she thought. Such things only happen to holy men.

She reached the back of the house and stood in front of the wall which was bleeding. She could smell the blood that gently poured out. It mixed with the rain, creating thin blood streaks on the tile floor under her feet. She could hear Tara's weak cry behind the wall and her hands frantically moved up and down until she found the door. It was locked. Lana thought the key must be inside the house and went back through the closed doors, passing barred windows. She sensed that someone was following her, someone didn't want her to find the key, so she ran. She opened another door and saw herself standing there, looking back at herself. She screamed, her leg slipped, she fell backwards and woke up.

Her heart was pounding, the light from between the curtains was hitting her eyes, and she felt sick. She ran to the bathroom, making her way through piles of papers and boxes, and knelt before the toilet. She wretched, coughed but didn't throw up. Lana stayed on her knees for a few minutes until someone knocked.

'Are you okay?' Sozi said.

'Dada dada,' Shilana said as if repeating her mother's question.

'I'm fine, thanks.'

She heard Sozi walk away while chatting to her daughter and, a few minutes later, she joined them in the kitchen. They were listening to the news. Someone was talking passionately on Aljazeera TV. Hiwa's hair was a mess, he was in his pyjamas. He sipped his coffee and without turning to look at her he said, 'It's inevitable now,' and he turned the volume up.

Sozi had strapped Shilana up in her special chair and started putting breakfast on the table. Lana sat down, feeling unwell, the smell of coffee was nauseating.

'I had a nightmare,' she said without looking at anyone in particular.

'Tell it to running water,' Sozi said. 'It always helps.'

She looked at the kitchen tap and felt Sozi's gaze.

Is she worried about me? Lana thought. Do I look so bad?

'Coffee or tea?' her brother asked.

'Tea,' she replied, and he poured her a cup.

'Good morning *mallekem*!' she said to Shilana in a childish voice. 'Did you sleep okay?'

Shilana grinned, she understood that it was a friendly tone. Hiwa changed over to CNN, Sozi made a face and Lana smiled sympathetically.

'Can you just eat your breakfast and talk to us for a minute?' Sozi objected.

He turned the TV down. 'It's getting closer every minute,' he repeated.

'And there is nothing we can do about it,' Sozi said.

'I never thought there was, I just want to know,' he said, and with a sleepy movement he put soft cheese on his toast. 'So what was the nightmare about?' He turned to Lana.

'Our house,' Lana replied and sipped her tea.

Sozi was feeding Shilana something which looked like jam, it was all over her face. Shilana kept resisting and wanting to take over but Sozi persevered. She made faces to encourage her daughter to eat, opening her own mouth when she wanted Shilana to open hers and closing it when she wanted her to swallow.

'It's because of the photos,' Hiwa said. 'Images awaken more images, I'm sorry.'

'It's the war... everyone is on edge,' Sozi said.

'Everyone feels...vulnerable,' Hiwa watched Shilana take the spoon from her mother.

Yes, Lana thought, it takes us back to our nightmares, it hits us where we feel raw, it makes us feel guilty about putting salt on a slug when we were too young to understand, it makes us feel it's all ending.

'There're leftovers from last night if you like some,' Sozi offered, knowing she didn't like breakfast food.

'No thank you,' she replied. 'I don't feel hungry yet.'

She thought of Amer for a second. What is he doing right now? Taking a shower? Shaving? Listening to the news, to music?

Hiwa poured himself another coffee. He held his fingers together before his face, as if he craved a cigarette. For a second his back was hunched, his shoulders were sticking out, and he looked old and frail.

'Would you give me some of the tapes?' Lana said.

'Which?'

'*Daya*'s tapes. You've found them, haven't you?'

'Are you sure you want to listen to them now?'

'Yes,' she said. 'It'll give me comfort.'

He nodded and sipped his coffee once again. 'Remind me before you leave.'

Sozi silenced the TV and put music on. It was morning jazz, clean and gentle, easing you into the day.

Now what? Lana wondered as she started tidying up with Sozi.

After washing up, she declined Sozi's offer for a lift and decided to walk home, still full of sorrow. She turned left on Gayton Road, towards Northwick Avenue. The residential road consisted of large semi-detached houses which were divided into flats. The houses on the right cast their monstrous shadows on the road and Lana walked on the left side to catch the bits of sun that poured out from between them. The alternating patches of light and shadow reminded Lana of life's ups and downs. The dark patches had been periods of grief for her.

She became familiar with grief from an early age. She was eight years old when the oven in her father's bakery exploded in 1979, killing him instantly. At first, she couldn't grasp the finality of his death and expected him to give her *jazhnana* money on Eid or Nawroz, to give her a doll when she was the first in her class, to pick her up and comfort her when she fell, and to defend her if she had an argument with her siblings. It was a loss that grew over the years, confirmed by monotonous silence and dearth.

Tara's self-immolation in the old bathroom, two years after her father's death, was a different kind of grief. The weight of it was crushing, making her tongue-tied. Some days it manifested itself in a paralysing headache, other days through uncontrollable crying spells that made her convulse. She would hide in a corner and try not to make a sound, not wanting to make the others feel guilty. Then, over a period of years, the darkness lifted. Lana started writing, began her degree in English literature, and felt there was hope. Right then, Kawa's murder during the uprising threw her back into the depths of despair. She was twenty years old, and life seemed like an endless chain of misfortune and pain. She felt a defeating resignation when her mother died over a year later. It was partly this resignation that made her marry and come to England. She believed that what she did and where she was wouldn't make any difference, life would take what it wanted.

Lana crossed the road and looked up at the line of houses, imagining the large families that used to spread themselves here and the hassle of keeping a busy household. For a short time before her father, Tara, Kawa, and mother died and before Hiwa left, they too were considered a large family. Seven of them lived in their three-bedroom house. She shared a room with Tara, but spent most of her time, especially during the day, in the kitchen with her mother. She tailed her *daya* through many chores, prayers, conversations, decisions. She remembered the day when Ahoo decided to wall up the old bathroom to protect the rest of her children. Lana had been dreaming about walls since then.

Once, during the civil war between the Kurds in the mid-1990s she dreamt of the Berlin wall. Dozens of men and women on both sides were picking away at the bricks, but the pulled bricks flew into the air and settled at the top of the wall once again. The pressure from above meant that the missing bricks kept being replaced. In her dream she'd thought that it was the work of an evil magician and looked for him, but there was no one, just bricks rebuilding the wall as people tried to destroy it.

In another dream a doctor told her that her headaches were due to a wall that went through her brain. He showed her an image of her brain on the screen, and she was horrified by the tiny wall that went through her hemispheres dividing her brain from ear to ear. It cut through her grey flesh, dividing cells, and blocking neurons so that messages and information couldn't be delivered. She was told that if she wanted her headaches to go away, they must operate but that it was risky. There was a forty percent chance that she'd suffer from total amnesia if the wall was removed. She woke up in horror, sweating and trembling.

One night in 1997 when she newly arrived in London, she was woken up by her panicked husband: 'You're screaming.'

She dreamt of Tara's motionless and erect body in flames. Lana screamed and asked her brothers to extinguish the fire, but no one could see what she saw. It was as if there was an invisible wall between Tara and her brothers, a wall that only Lana could see through. Her brothers tried to calm her down, but Lana kept shouting, 'Please stop the flames.'

She traced her dreams back to her mother's wall, the one she built to save her children from remembering Tara's death, as if they could forget and move on, as if the brick wall would help them cope with what had happened, what could happen. She has carried the misfortune within her for years: that part which her mother tried to hide from them. But even if her mother built hundreds of walls around everything she wanted them to forget, the past never left her children alone. Whispers escaped the wall and leaked into their daily lives, echoed in their dreams, and contaminated their peace of mind.

Lana knew too well about walls of division and fragmentation that amputate lands and nations, detaching them from a part of themselves, making them bleed, leaving them incomplete. She knew about walls of denial and forgetfulness, depriving people of learning from their past, of not repeating the same mistakes, not being trapped in a vicious circle. She knew about walls of fear, immobilising people and not allowing them to take new risks. She knew about walls of apathy, preventing people from responding appropriately to crisis, injustice, and tragedy. She knew about walls of ignorance and walls of self-deception that left people less accomplished, less than a smooth history with a beginning and an end.

There were days when Lana had to avoid the back of the house because the smell of burning flesh drove her crazy. She tied a cloth around her head, stayed in bed, and cried. This was one of the reasons why she married Diyar. The first time he came to visit, the moment he stepped into the house, he said, 'Something is on fire.' Everyone was alarmed by this remark, and they reassured him that nothing was, but Lana knew what he could smell. Diyar smelt their past disasters which they were trying so desperately to hide. He could smell what she was running away from. Yet none of them thought about selling that place.

Why can't people let go of tragic places? she wondered. Maybe this is the problem with our lives, we can neither process the past nor leave it behind. We built too many walls between us and the past, but it keeps pulling us back, preventing us from building a different future.

And as she watched Kurdish news and read in the websites what her people felt about the war, she knew that they had the same problem as her family, they hadn't learnt a lesson from their past, they tried to forget previous misfortunes and hoped for the best. She knew that the psychological wall between past and present was strong enough to allow for optimism.

The realisation came to her one afternoon when she was walking up Oxford Street on a busy afternoon. For a few minutes she was the only one walking against the crowd. At first, she walked sideways to avoid bumping into people, but soon realised it was no use. She stopped trying to protect herself from the blows and started weeping. She understood that her people had gone against the strong currents at critical times. When the neighbouring nations were united to secure independence after the first world war, the Kurds fought amongst themselves and missed the opportunity. And now, when the world seemed to be anti-America and anti-war, they supported America and wanted the war.

Hiwa had once told her that the past was full of historical misfortunes and accidents that were to their disadvantage. Turkey was supported as a bulwark against communism, and Iraq was created around the oil in the south and north. The law of averages predicted better luck in the future, he argued. She found this hope irrational. She thought about the 1991 uprising when people were abandoned to be suppressed by the Iraqi army, the international silence that followed the Anfal genocide and the gassing of Halabja in 1988, the collapse of the revolution in 1974 in which America played a part, and the treaty of Lausanne in 1923, undoing the treaty of Sevres, after which the Kurds nostalgically named their daughters. She thought of all the broken promises and shattered hopes and found it difficult to be optimistic.

Why can't we learn from our histories? she asked herself. Why do we have such a short-term memory? Why do we keep making the same mistakes?

CHAPTER THIRTEEN

Lana

She turned right onto Draycott Avenue. A woman pushed her son's empty carriage as he walked next to her, close to the ground. Their dog walked ahead of them, panting, and swinging his tail.

The dog stopped, lifted his leg, and urinated on a tree.

'Why does Wolfie wee on the tree?' the boy asked his mother.

'Because he doesn't want to wee himself.'

'Why?' he persisted.

'Because he doesn't want to get wet and smelly.'

Lana had different kinds of pets as a child. Every spring her mother bought her five chicks to shepherd into adulthood. To identify them, she painted mathematical signs on their heads with her nail varnish. She then called them by the signs: Head-equals, Head-plus, Head-minus, Head-times, Head-division. The cat was always in ambush for her chicks and there was always disease. Only one or two chicks survived each spring and even those were killed by Ahoo when they were big enough. Lana cried after each death.

She had a similar experience with the fledgling sparrows which fell out of their nests on the mulberry tree. She fed them with her tiny fingers for as long as they survived. She cried for them, prayed that their parents would take them back, and buried them in the garden when they eventually died. For a long time, she fussed over a row of tiny graves where she had buried the dead birds. Each time she thought of the dead, she visited the graves and put flowers on them. That cold spring afternoon when, aged twenty-one, she sought comfort in the same spot in the garden, her ill mother watched her from the window and waited until she came back inside to confess about the empty graves.

'Every time you buried a bird, I secretly dug it out and threw it in the bin,' her mother told her, 'Burying dead animals brings bad luck to a house.'

At that moment Lana felt that she was being robbed of her earliest memories of the house. For her the story of the house began with the graves.

Maybe we hurt over empty notions, she'd thought. Maybe everything is an illusion and we're deceived about the smallest things that we're certain about.

She remembered her mother's desperate attempts to chase bad luck from their house, blowing prayers through the rooms and burning incense.

Poor *daya*! Lana thought. She tried so hard!

Thinking back, she felt the house itself was doomed to become a grave, a shrine for its owners. She wondered whether it was all because of *pura* Saleema's money. Her father bought the small house two years before his death when his childless aunt passed away. Saleema had been a stingy woman, 'not shitting so that she doesn't get hungry,' relatives used to say. She'd saved all her money for the troubles to come. 'White money for black days,' she would say. After her husband's death twelve years before her own, Saleema inherited his house and pension. Living alone made her even stingier; she stopped receiving people and kept complaining that because of her ill health she couldn't tend to guests.

The few loyal relatives who carried on checking up on the old woman knew that they would leave her house as hungry or as full as they'd entered it. She would serve them a glass of water and diluted tea with little sugar. Every time Lana went with her mother, *pura* Saleema asked after her father.

'Where is Akram?' she would ask them. 'Why doesn't he visit?'

Lana's father had stopped visiting his aunt years before, but her mother still went there out of loyalty. Going there meant that Ahoo spent hours cleaning the house which, if it wasn't for Sayran and herself, would become 'worm stricken.'

Lana wasn't allowed to touch anything in *pura* Saleema's house, her mother helped her drink in case her hands slipped and she broke a cup or a glass. Ahoo was always careful not to throw away leftovers and crumbs, not to anger the old woman. Sometimes she asked Tara to help clean the place. Tara hated going there, *pura* Saleema was rude as well as mean. When she was eleven, the old woman pointed at her breasts and said, 'They're growing.' Then she looked at Ahoo and continued, 'God help you.'

Tara's back bent in embarrassment and she swore at the old woman under her breath.

Lana was young when Saleema died but she had a clear image of the old woman squatting on her porch, wearing her black Kurdish dress as her grey hair whisked out of her white scarf. Her chiselled face was wrinkled and toothless. Her sharp nose was covered with blackheads. Saleema was found a day after her death, solid and dry in her old bed. Under her mattress they found ten gold sovereigns and her flattened jewellery. In her freezer, packed like meat, they found her money, coins and banknotes, some of them out of date.

Saleema's house was nearly rotting despite the two women's efforts to keep it going. Nothing had been touched up or fixed for twelve years, the window frames were seeping rust, the doors were hanging on to their hinges, the roof was leaking, and the walls were cracked. It was no longer useful, so Lana's father and uncle Hassan decided to sell it for what the land was worth and to divide the money between themselves and their sister. According to Islamic tradition, *pura* Sayran was entitled to half as much as her brothers, but she decided to give her share to Akram, the poorest of the two brothers. Years later she told Lana that she was worried about inheriting Saleema's fate with her money: to die a lonely and unloved woman.

Finally, Akram was able to buy a small house in Sabunkaran. Visitors walked across the front courtyard and stepped into the small entrance connected to the sitting room which was at the centre of the house. On the left-hand side the kitchen overlooked the front garden and was connected to it with a door. On the right-hand side and adjacent to the front garden, there was a large bedroom where the boys slept. Their parents' bedroom was behind the boys' room and was separated from it by the staircase that led to the basement. This bedroom overlooked the back garden which was much bigger than the front one. The girls slept in the smallest room in the house, right behind the kitchen and opposite their parents' room. They stayed mainly indoors. Their window opened onto the conservatory at the bottom. Because of being surrounded, their room had a desirable temperature throughout the year. In summer it was cooler than the rest of the house and in winter it was the warmest.

In the traditional manner, the bathroom and toilet were at the back of the house, behind the girls' bedroom and as far away from guests as possible. The sitting room and the kitchen were shared spaces where everyone spent most of their time. They were the only two places in the house which were always heated during winter. The TV, two sofas, and a mattress on the floor made the sitting room a welcoming place. For two years, before Lana's father died, her mother was the happiest in her life. She had her own home, her children were growing up, and they were living comfortably.

Lana knew what these things meant for a woman like her mother. After her parents had died in an accidental fire, Ahoo was raised by her uncle and his wife and grew up in a house next to Akram's family home. Ahoo's relatives didn't send her to school so that she could help in the house while her girl cousins were given this opportunity and they became teachers. Still, Ahoo always told her children how grateful she was to her uncle's family because they looked after her. She'd been a serious and hard-working girl, never sulking, and never complaining. It was her kindness and beauty that made Akram fall in love with her, despite being three years her junior. As a young woman Ahoo was envied for her good fortune. People told her that her husband would eventually get himself a younger second wife. This had been her fear in the early years of their marriage. Ahoo's second worry had been poverty. They'd lived in her mother-in-law's house for six years and when she was pregnant with Gara, her fourth child, they decided to move out and rent a place. Eventually, after ten years of renting, they managed to buy the small house in Sabunkaran, and this was enough for Ahoo.

Before they bought the house, it was inhabited by two unmarried sisters and their dead brother's wife. The three childless women were always in black and were supported by relatives and neighbours. The sister-in-law gradually lost her mind and was sent back to her family. The older sister passed away. The last old woman had become bedridden and was being looked after by her nieces. Then the house was put up for sale.

Was it to do with these women, Lana sometimes thought as she unlocked the door to her flat. Did we inherit their misfortune?

CHAPTER FOURTEEN

Gara

Gara was looking at his sleeping wife whose hand was under her cheek. Her mouth was slightly open, and he could see her teeth. On her other side, his son laughed himself awake. He rolled over to where his mother lay and touched her head.

'*Daya jwana*,' he said loudly, mum is pretty.

Aveen's lips moved, her eyebrows frowned a little, but she didn't open her eyes. Gara beckoned Kawa to come over to him. He stretched his arms out and picked up his son who was stepping over his mother. They lay down together. He looked into his son's large brown eyes.

'Yes, *daya jwana*,' Gara whispered and kissed his son's forehead. 'Kawa is also *jwana*.'

Kawa chuckled.

'It's too early,' Aveen said.

'No! It's cloudy.'

Kawa was resting between his parents' relaxed bodies, in the middle where the two mattresses met. He moved closer to his father to get more comfortable. Gara put his finger to his son's lips and then very quietly reached over Kawa and pinched Aveen's cheek. He quickly withdrew his hand so that when she opened her eyes and said, 'Who was that?' they both laughed. She then got up and attacked Kawa with kisses and little bites.

'*Hemm!*' she kept saying, 'delicious.' The two of them kissed and tickled Aveen back until she recoiled, and Kawa sat on her stomach. Gara quietly pressed his body against his wife's and stroked Kawa's bare ankle. The boy tried to tie a bunch of his mother's hair into a knot. He was intensely working on this, and you could hear his chest rattling.

'Brave little one,' Aveen said.

'He's brave like you,' Gara said remembering her in her black dress.

'I'm not brave,' she said.

He kissed her temple and said, 'You're practically my hero.'

Aveen laughed. 'Shame about the real heroes.'

'Yes, unfortunately,' Gara said, staring around him as if the past heroes were standing above their heads.

Sayran had already lit the *aladdin* heater in the kitchen and the kettle was whistling.

'Thank God there's another woman in this house,' Aveen said. 'Another person to light the fire in the morning, make food, clean the house, look after Kawa.'

'I feel bad now,' Gara said.

'But not bad enough to do anything about it.'

'I keep saying, tell me what to do and I'll do it.'

'Why do you need to be told?' Aveen asked, 'Dirt doesn't clean itself; dust doesn't blow away. Tidy up after yourself, at least.'

'I know I've said this before, but I'll really try. I'm sorry.'

He only started noticing how men felt entitled to be served and looked after by women, even if they weren't family, since Aveen pointed things out. Men ate their food and sat back expecting to be served tea, they left the sink, toilet, and shower filthy, stayed in friends' homes and expected their friends' wives, mothers, or sisters to cook, make the beds, and wash their clothes for them. One summer morning after a sandstorm, dust had covered everything in a yellow haze. Aveen and Sayran were vigorously cleaning together when Gara told them how his mother used to wash the house after a storm, making him feel that she could fix everything. He remembered the smell of wet dirt and the shining, slippery tiles.

'It felt festive,' he said.

The two women looked at each other and exchanged something he didn't understand.

'Did I say anything wrong?'

'It's easy to be romantic about dust when you don't have to clean it,' Aveen said.

Sayran had winked and they both laughed.

He knew that Sayran understood Aveen. She wasn't only an extra pair of hands, but someone who listened, someone to share jokes and grievances with. Since giving birth to their son, Aveen had often argued that humans were meant to live in tribes. Raising a child alone, without relatives, would be a nightmare, she thought. It was something some of their friends and relatives, who lived abroad, had to do.

'What do you feel like for dinner?' Aveen said, lifting him out of his trance.

'Anything,' he said, then turned to Kawa. 'What do you feel like?'

'Anything,' Kawa said.

'My son and I are easy to please.'

Kawa stopped playing with his mother's hair.

'Half of my brain power goes into making these banal decisions every day,' Aveen said. 'It makes me feel dumb.'

'Okay, red rice and chicken.'

'Will you get some chicken?'

'I will,' Gara said rolling over, 'I love Mondays.' It was the end of his working week, the paper was printed on Tuesdays.

He knew that days of the week didn't mean much to Aveen anymore. After Kawa's birth she'd decided to stay at home and look after him. Gara worried that she'd become too domesticated to go back to work, maybe she was scared.

Kawa got up and drew the curtain. There was no sun, but the room brightened up a little. He then walked towards the door: '*Hem-hem,*' he said, wanting his breakfast.

Aveen got up to open the door, but Gara pulled her back. She nearly fell onto the mattress. He sat right behind her, and she rested onto him and laughed, Kawa laughed too watching his parents play.

'It's been ten days,' Gara whispered to his wife as he kissed her neck 'How long will you make me wait?'

'You've been counting?' she said.

'I'm deprived.'

'I'm tired,' she said, making to get up again, 'Maybe tonight.'

'I'll be here,' he patted the bed. 'From ten o'clock. Don't be late.'

Aveen laughed. She opened the door and left with her son. Gara immediately felt guilty.

I'm just glad to have you, he wanted to shout after his wife.

Will you forgive me? he asked the ghost of the other man. I just wish I knew what you're thinking.

Aveen came to the door, 'Come eat with us.'

He was continuously surprised by how much he loved looking at her, at her oval shaped face, full lips, and smooth hair.

'Of course,' he said. 'I'm coming.'

He picked up the duvet and started folding it.

She stood watching him for a second and when he looked up, she blew him a kiss and whispered, 'I love you.'

'When did you start loving me?' Gara once asked his wife.

'I don't know,' she replied. 'Maybe after you kissed me that day.'

'But how could you start loving me just because I kissed you? What if I hadn't?'

'Well, maybe I started realising it then.'

'You mean you'd loved me before?'

'I don't know *gyanekem*; did you know that you loved me before?'

'No, I didn't, but when I kissed you, I realised I'd loved you for a long time. You didn't feel the same, did you?'

'Is this a competition?' she said. 'I love you and I'm happy. What more do you want?'

She was right, maybe he was asking for too much. After all, when she wasn't in love with him, she was in love with his brother Kawa, and he couldn't be annoyed about that. He couldn't feel jealous of a ghost, the ghost of his own best friend. Why did he always want reassurance?

When they decided to get married, Gara had written a long letter to Hiwa and Lana, trying to explain and justify their decision. He was worried that they would be angry with him. He'd written, 'We've been suffering for too long and we've decided to put a stop to that. Aveen and I have been living under the same roof for many years and it's time to put the past behind us, start again. You're probably wondering how long this has been going on without my mentioning it. I can't tell you when and how this started, we'd never spoken about it before. I think it was our bodies that told us the answer. We hope and believe this isn't betraying Kawa's memory, though this is difficult to explain.

Aveen has mourned for years, believing that there will be no one after Kawa, and I've never been keen on getting married as you know. For both of us marriage became conceivable only under certain conditions. For her it had to be someone who would respect her love for Kawa and accept it. For me it had to be a patient woman who would love me enough to put up with my depressive tendencies. But maybe I'm giving you the wrong impression, this isn't a marriage of convenience. I've grown close to Aveen over the last years, and it's taken us a long time to understand that what we feel for each other has changed shape and meaning. We're in love and quite happy. I hope that both of you will understand this and are not angry with us.'

Why can't I stick to what I had accepted then? he kept asking himself. Why can't I accept her love for Kawa?

Sometimes he wasn't certain whether it was Aveen that he worried about or himself. She never talked about Kawa, didn't tell Gara what went on between them when they were together, what they had talked and dreamed about, but he continuously wondered whether she compared him with his brother. He suspected that Kawa was a lot more fun than he was, probably a better lover, more attentive, a better listener, and he was, no doubt, the more handsome. She'd been able to produce her best works of art while she was with him and after his death, she hadn't been able to get back into it despite Gara's encouragement. Was she comfortable being a housewife? Was little Kawa just an excuse to stay at home and avoid the business of living altogether? Was Aveen depressed?

Sometimes he thought Aveen married him because she'd been yearning for love. After that night, when she told him that he misunderstood her, he noticed how she changed. Never again did she recite her memories loudly to herself, nor did she surround herself with Kawa's things. In the mornings when they all went to work, Gara to his school, Sayran to the Registration Bureau, and Aveen to the Printing House, she was friendly. In the past, she'd hardly looked at him. Sometimes he thought that she didn't even realise that he was a man who had thoughts and feelings. For the brief periods that they had looked at each other, her eyes registered nothing, they were completely empty of any feeling except for sadness. Then, after that day, he noticed that she dressed differently, lighter colours, more shapely clothes. Gara still hadn't dared to get close to her until she asked him to help her unroll the carpets for the Autumn, bypassing Sayran's and the neighbours' help.

The two of them carried each carpet, firmly rolled up and tightly bound, out of the basement. Aveen had already vacuumed the place and all they needed to do was to first move the small furniture out of each room and then unroll the carpets making sure the direction of the brushing was heading to the door. They lifted cupboards, chests, and beds to put the carpet underneath and then moved the rest of the furniture back on top. As they sweated together, bending their backs, pulling carpets, and lifting things, he felt her body brushing against his a few times.

He was still uncertain whether this was intentional. Each time he got tense, worrying that she may think he was getting too close. Finally, after finishing the last room, she straightened her back and looked up at him. He looked back full of confusion. She moved close, so close that he was bound between her and the cupboard behind him. His hands rested by his sides, his lips were slightly parted, he looked into her eyes. She hugged him tightly, her breasts squashed against his chest, and she kissed his earlobe.

'Thank you,' she said and held him calmly.

Did she really not love him?

CHAPTER FIFTEEN

Hiwa

The night before, the BBC had announced that Iraq was cooperating with the UN team and that the inspectors were 'making good progress,' searching for weapons of mass destruction.

'There may not be a war, after all,' Sozi told Hiwa while holding him from behind.

She was full of optimism, walking around the house tidying, cleaning, washing, and singing. Her hopefulness infected him. He promised to stay focused and efficient. In the morning, he kissed his wife and daughter before they left the house and went back to his room. He looked at the dishevelled books and papers and decided to organise the letters. Sitting on the floor, he placed his teacup on a book next to him and cautiously opened each letter, folded up to fit into small sized envelopes. The words were fading where the pages had been bent. Some of the pages were yellowing at the edges. Some were close to crumbling.

How touchy! he thought. How delicate and sore the past is.

Gara's letters were long. Hiwa felt that journalism was already happening to his brother in those early days, all those long reports, emotional and astute, addressing the family story alongside the Kurdish story. The women wrote fewer and shorter letters, sometimes just half a page of 'We're well, we hope you are too.'

Is it because they thought I couldn't relate to their problems, Hiwa wondered, or because they just got on with their lives and didn't feel entitled to complain?

The latter couldn't apply to Lana, she wasn't shy about speaking and challenging. Once Gara told him that in their family God had slipped up. While talking about Lana's sharp tongue Gara said. 'Just think about yourself, Kawa, and me, and then think about the girls, don't you think that we are the softer type?'

Hiwa laughed. His sisters had definitely been the more daring, assertive, and righteous. They both had clear ideas about right and wrong and were harsh with people who got it wrong. It was the boys who found it difficult to say no to people. They were the ones who found excuses for people's shortcomings and forgave them their faults.

His eyes landed on a sentence in the letter he was unfolding.

'What makes the past so dangerous?' Gara had written.

Hiwa stopped for a second and re-read the sentence.

Is it the past that makes the present unbearable? he thought, or is it just the way we live in the world? Is there a quota of misery that we must undergo even if there are no material reasons for it?

He knew that he'd lived a reasonably successful and happy life, despite the past. He'd managed to love and be loved, found computer programming and website designing satisfactory, married and fathered a girl, owned a home, and held a passport which opened borders to him. Yet he struggled sleeping through the nights and sometimes, when he was on his own, he felt completely desperate. His mind raced with memories, voices, and conversations which exhausted him. Some mornings when his wife and daughter left the house, he wanted to go back to bed.

Getting through such days was a struggle. The moments became unbearable when he felt Tara trespassing. Sometimes he felt her presence at the corner of his vision, as if she was watching him in silence, but when he turned to look, she wasn't there. Other times she whispered things he couldn't understand. He'd try talking to her, asking her questions, begging her forgiveness, but nothing made her leave his mind for long. Sometimes he felt exhausted, couldn't focus, and found life a struggle. The past was dangerous, his brother was right. It had the potential to spill into the present at any moment and create havoc. He bit his lower lip and, despite his promise to Sozi, he started reading the letter:

23/4/1992

My dear brother,

I keep asking myself, what makes the past so dangerous? Why do past events become so destructive when we remember them years later? Or were we destroyed long ago, when it all happened, without realising it? How else can you explain all this rage? Stories of pain creep into our dreams and haunt us. It's the small things that keep me awake, the minute details that are what the story is all about. Last week, I bought a loaf of bread on the way to work, and offered a piece to *baji* Pertaw, the cleaner. She burst into tears.

'How could I have warm bread?' she said. 'My two-year-old begged for bread till he died.'

The boy had starved to death in Dibs camp where the women and children were jailed during Anfal. A piece of warm bread will never be the same for *baji* Pertaw. She worked in a bakery before working here and left it because the smell reminded her of her son's suffering. In this place, the basic, simple things have been tainted with memories of violence. We got used to the blood-stained roads, the burning forests on summer nights, the pockmarked walls covered with pictures of him, the women who strolled the streets in black, those whose brothers were hanged, whose husbands were killed in battle or tortured to death, whose sons fled to exile. Violence was a normal occurrence, and it now continues through its constant relaying. The videos of interrogation and torture, seized during the security building raids in the uprising, are now for show everywhere. Even children can watch them, as if they are entertainment. People seem to think it's necessary to see, to know what happened to people's bodies and lives, to remember what was done to us.

We obsessively keep the memories of violence alive, and end up reproducing them. Such things don't suddenly disappear, they just change shape. And when you see them, all the young armed men, hungry and insecure, you think it's just a matter of time. It's happening already. Women are getting killed under the guise of treason and dishonour, and no one gets investigated or punished. It's always been painful to be a woman in this place (our beautiful sister!), but things are worse now. The same revolutionaries that the women supported are turning their backs on them. The legends are being put to the test; let's hope they won't fail.

I keep thinking of the children, growing up in this chaotic era of freedom, in a place where violence, hunger, and insecurity occupy a large part of their days, where they are expected to do their homework by the light of lanterns. What will become of them? In this place where past collaborators are now woven into the fabric of society, where the victims will get neither justice nor a proper

111

hearing, where there are many armed men and no law and order, how can we have hope in tomorrow?

The first Kurdish elections will be held next month, and we're taking steps to detaching ourselves from Iraq. Could this be our new beginning, something to look forward to? A better system of governance? Will the heroes remain heroes after they become rulers? The anticipation is creating so much hope. Couples have planned their weddings on that day; they want to vote in their wedding outfits. If her health allows, *daya* is planning to vote while holding up a picture of Kawa. Many survivors of violence are planning to line up and raise pictures of their murdered relatives. I imagine there will be tears of joy, of relief, of dreaming big. The hope infects me, too, I must admit, though I'm probably less optimistic than others.

I wish Kawa was here to see this. Everyone keeps telling *daya* that she should be proud he didn't die in vain, that his dream of freedom has come true. Of course, this is no consolation for a mother who's lost her son. Grief has aged and weakened her. She was planning to record a tape for you, but she's not feeling well. She wants you to know that she misses you very much and wishes to see you before she dies. I hope that you can come home in the summer.

I embrace you and leave you in peace.

Your brother,
Gara

Hiwa never made it back to see his mother and didn't remember being warned about her death. Reading his brother's letter nearly eleven years after it was written, it was as if he was reading it for the first time. He kept wondering whether he'd forgotten to read the letter after receiving it all those years ago. Maybe it had just fallen behind a desk. Maybe it slept in a book for years. Maybe it had been accidentally put away before being read.

The letter was in a blue envelope, posted to him from Paris. The back of the envelope had the name and address of a woman, Layla Ibrahim. The name sounded familiar, but he couldn't remember who she was. He imagined a round hipped woman who has four children, lots of dyed brown hair, and deep laughter lines. Maybe it was another total stranger who visited the No-Fly Zone in the 1990s and posted the letter to him upon her return to Europe. People did that for each other then, replacing the destroyed postal and communication services. The letters, photographs, and tapes were carried by people who themselves were full of stories of love and loss. They posted them to strangers they would never meet across Europe, America, and Australia. Sometimes the letter-posters included a short note saying something like 'I never met your family, but a friend asked me to post this to you. I hope it contains good news.' Or: 'Your brother is an old friend of mine and I've heard lots about you. I hope you're well.' But Layla Ibrahim had said nothing. Hiwa shook the empty envelope, and nothing fell out to help him identify her. Who was she, he wondered, how was she living?

He went to the kitchen, lined up some of the rubbish bags by the wall, and made himself a coffee. The quietness was only interrupted by traffic noise—cars that broadcast radio stations, lorries that made a big fuss as they passed, and urgent sirens that seemed to boast of saving lives. The sky was opaque white, and it took him a while to realise that it wasn't raining. He sat on a chair and started drinking his coffee. The kitchen was tidy, the cushions were in the right place, the papers were in order, but it was as if something had been violated.

Is it possible, he suddenly thought, that he'd read Gara's letter and then perfectly calmly ignored its content? Could he have done that, refuse to respond to the small details that his brother had written about? Had he just read the letter, felt a little anxious, and pushed it aside in his mind? What was he doing in the spring of 1992? The thought stabbed him in his stomach. He remembered waking up in a single bed, in a house-share in Kilburn where people played loud music through the night and left the toilet and kitchen filthy. He remembered missing Sarah's smell in the mornings, missing turning over and finding her there, her skin all moist and warm, her curls flattened by the pillow, her arms opening to embrace him, her eyes closed, her lips seeking his forehead.

The breakup and subsequent financial hardship overshadowed that year and the next one. In the last months of that relationship, when it became clear that they couldn't accommodate each other anymore, he was informed by his boss that they would let him go. Being a proud Middle Eastern man, he never told Sarah about losing his job. He took the cheapest accommodation he could find and moved his stuff to that damp room in the shared accommodation in North West London.

When he went to view the room, he was horrified by the state of it, the black fungus growing on the interior walls, the yellow stained wallpaper, beige with pink and green flowers, the old toilet and older bathtub. He had two months' salary to survive on and he immediately started looking for another job. In the meantime, he worked in a postal company, sorting envelopes and loading the company vans with the large sacs that travelled in different directions. The company staff were young. Many of them were immigrant students who studied full time and worked part time to pay their bills. Throughout the four months he worked there, he didn't go beyond general civilities with anyone. He kept quiet and did what he was supposed to do. To the rest of them he looked like a serious older man who was mysterious and sad. One of the managers, a young black man in his late twenties, was the closest he got to calling anyone an acquaintance. Daren was tall and wide, he had the most cheering smile, and he regularly laughed at himself. When Hiwa left that place to start as an IT assistant in a small company, Daren shook his hand and told him, 'Look after yourself man. Whatever it is, it will pass.'

Hiwa hadn't looked after himself that year. As far as he was concerned it was all over for him, he'd blown his chance at happiness. He knew there were no shortcuts, no bypassing the grief he felt, he had to endure it. He hoped that time would heal him from the strong pangs of longing and regret which woke him in the middle of the night, as if thirsty or in pain. Some days he felt that there was a hole in his heart, he could feel the sting, and saw everything through a curtain of tears. Other times he felt completely numb and walked around as if in a dream, nothing seemed real anymore. It was during this period, eleven years after her death, when he felt Tara's presence for the first time. Unable to sleep or to open his eyes, he lay in bed feeling heavy and tired when he heard Tara laugh at him maliciously. It was a loud and cruel laughter, as if she was saying, 'see how

115

you like it!' It made him shiver. Another day he thought that she sat beside him in silence, enduring the pain of lost love, lost opportunities, and wasted potential.

He tried to spend as little time in his room as possible, but he couldn't escape Lucy's regular fits of crying, her loud telephone conversations with her boyfriend who was a 'bastard' and an 'asshole,' and her attempt at killing herself by slitting her wrists in the bathtub. He found her there and felt certain that he would be blamed for her death, the blood trickling down her thin white wrist as her breasts floated lifelessly in the water.

He couldn't escape Tom's rock and roll music and his loud one-night stands. The squeaky bed kept Hiwa awake and amazed. He felt sorry for the young women who came home with Tom, not knowing what awaited them there. He thought that his flatmate tortured these women and was always surprised to find them unbruised and uncut the next day. Some of them looked at him shyly, knowing that he'd heard them scream, others just ignored him as if he didn't exist. During this time, when living in that flat, being away from Sarah, and worrying about money had taken so much out of him, he was told that his mother had died. He didn't cry. He didn't have flashbacks about her. To him she remained in the kitchen, her back to her children, cooking and washing as she sang the old, sad lullabies.

Some days he had an image of his mother sitting on the floor and baking bread in the courtyard as the *paramez* howled under the convex *saj*. Sometimes she was just praying while counting with her prayer beads, the *tasbih*. In his mind she never became a cold, dead body that was buried deep in the ground, she never had a grave. Even two years later, when he visited her grave, he felt no connection to it. He couldn't believe that the silent mud mound was what she'd become. He never mourned her death.

Was it because of this, he wondered, because he couldn't believe that his mother could die that he didn't remember the letter? Maybe he just lacked clarity of mind at the time, maybe he'd been so self-absorbed and self-obsessed that he couldn't realise the importance of what his brother was telling him. Or maybe he'd blocked all of that because he couldn't handle it, because he didn't have the money to travel. That summer when Ahoo was living her last weeks, he was too caught up in his own pain to feel anything.

Was it time, he wondered, did he have the time and space to mourn his mother now?

When Sozi and Shilana came home, Hiwa was taken over by daydreams. He absent-mindedly took Shilana from his wife and started to take off her shoes and coat, didn't speak back to his daughter, and didn't fully notice Sozi, who was watching him. He was starting to grasp that the past he'd wished to categorise and move away from was threatening. 'Don't fix it so that you don't make it worse,' the old proverb said. He'd acted against common wisdom and made everything worse.

'Are you okay?' Sozi asked him as she rubbed his back. 'Do you want to stop working on this? We can watch a movie if you like, or we can do it together. I can help you after work and we can sort things quicker.'

'I need to do it myself,' he said. 'It's okay, I'll do it slowly.'

Sozi was preparing food and then, out of the blue, Sarah called. It was as if he'd conjured her up by remembering her. This hadn't happened when he'd desperately thought of her for years. After they broke up, Hiwa wished that Sarah would find him and call him, just to meet for coffee or a drink after work, to sit across the table from her even if they didn't say much. He'd imagined being face to face with her again, watching her sip her coffee as the sun was reflected in her eyes even when there was no sun. He'd wanted to browse her ageing hands, the slightly swollen joints, the blue-green veins. He'd imagined seeing her again until he didn't anymore. He gave up visiting the places they'd inhabited together and gave up scanning faces during London's rush hour. The hope and desire gradually waned, getting covered up by new images and memories. He was certain that he was finally free of her and then, just after thinking of her, she called.

He heard the phone ring and heard his wife answering it. She then came to his room and said, 'It's Sarah Hyman, she wants to speak with you.'

He raised his eyebrows for a second, not understanding who it was. Then he jumped. 'Oh,' he said and walked to the phone, having come out of his dreamy state.

'Hello,' he said.

'Hi Hiwa, it is me, Sarah. It's been a long time.'

'Yes!' he said. 'Too long. How are you?'

'I'm well, thank you. I've been thinking of you with the news and all, just wanted to see how you are.' She paused for a second. 'I hope that's okay.'

'Yes of course,' he said, 'nice of you to call.'

There was silence for a few seconds. Hiwa knew that Sozi was listening.

'So, is everything alright with you and your family?' Sarah asked.

'Yes, thank you. There won't be another post-war uprising and flight this time,' he said. They both remembered the last war and how desperate he'd felt when the news of Kawa's death reached him and when the short-lived uprising was crushed, followed by the exodus. Sarah had lived through those moments with him when they were transfixed by the images of Kurdish refugees walking the mountains to Iran and Turkey in April 1991, oppressed by the rain and hailstone.

'Good,' she said. 'That's good.'

He turned around and looked at his wife's back and turned away again.

'So, what are you doing now?' he asked.

'The same as before,' she replied. 'Listen! I was just wondering,' she paused for a second, 'Would you like to meet? I would love to catch up.'

'Yes,' he replied, 'that would be nice.'

'Great!' she said. 'When are you free?'

THREE WEEKS BEFORE THE WAR

CHAPTER SIXTEEN

Lana

Keeping in mind the poetry reading in the evening, she chose a brown midi dress with knee-high boots. She'd learnt to lead a double life in exile, splitting her wardrobe between conservative and relaxed clothes. She wore Kurdish clothes for Newroz celebrations, travelling long hours to hold hands and dance around the fire with Kurds from Iraq, Iran, Turkey, and Syria. She dressed modestly for the community parties, seminars, exhibitions, and commemorations, and was well behaved in Kurdish restaurants: no alcohol, no revealing clothes, no singing, no dancing, no laughing too loudly. The open collar and bare back dresses she wore only with trusted friends, dining in expensive Iranian or Lebanese restaurants in Great Portland Street and Knightsbridge where they could request Kurdish music, sing along, and dance. The rest of the time she listened to poets and novelists in quiet cafés, sheltered from community supervision.

She'd managed to avoid nasty confrontations and rumours by being careful, but her situation aroused suspicion. She was a thirty-two-year-old divorcee, living alone in a place with many opportunities to break away from tradition. One of the women in her circle of friends, who worked at a community centre, was once caught out and stigmatised. Tanya was a cheerful young woman who believed that things weren't as bad as her friends assumed and people were more open-minded. She made the mistake of having a brief relationship with one of her colleagues who fell in love with her. It became so tense that she had to resign when everyone sided with him against her.

Normally, Lana didn't hold Amer's hand and didn't hug him outdoors; it wasn't worth the risk. But interpreting had taken too much out of her during the day and she wasn't thinking straight. She'd watched a caseworker bully a young asylum seeker who looked as if he had the dirt of a century on his skin.

'Goddamn it!' the woman said. 'Why do they all stink so bad!'

Lana knew this remark was intended for her and not for the asylum seeker, but she decided to interpret a milder version of it, to give the man a chance to explain himself and to embarrass the caseworker. He looked puzzled for a second and the woman asked Lana in surprise, 'Did you just tell him what I said?'

'I was trained to interpret everything,' she replied.

The caseworker shook her head and muttered something that sounded like 'outrageous'. Lana ignored her.

'Because of the lorry,' the young man said. 'I was in the closed space for four days.'

As the interview progressed, the woman asked him questions about his journey, how many lorries, how many days in each, where he'd changed from one to the other, the names of the agent and the people who travelled with him.

She kept telling him, 'You're a liar!'

Lana regretted what she'd done because the woman was taking her anger out on the man and there was nothing she could do to help him. Her day went on from one bad interview to another. A woman who was having her asylum interview kept crying, refusing to answer questions, repeating that she didn't know anything. This frustrated the caseworker, who was generally better behaved. By the time Lana left work she could hardly talk any more. She didn't get a seat on the tube which was overcrowded with tired faces. Some women looked elegant in their high heels, effortlessly standing straight. Others looked as if they were about to cry.

Maybe it didn't feel so bad in the morning, she thought, or maybe they thought that looking good is worth the pain.

Most of her life Lana had defied beauty standards, wearing little makeup, not styling her hair, not buying expensive clothes, and not following fashion trends. As a teenager she'd traded with God and asked for knowledge in return for becoming less attractive. She wanted to learn, create, and experience things, to not be reduced to a pretty object who looks after others.

The tube jerked forward after a long stop in Baker Street station, and Lana held the bar above to steady herself. She looked at her elbow and remembered a school friend had once said, 'If a girl manages to kiss her own elbow, she will turn into a boy.'

The girls had spent their break time trying to kiss their elbows, hoping to become boys. They wanted to be valued like boys, to be spoiled and praised, and to have more freedom. Some people described girls as 'oil barrels' that have the potential to explode and dishonour their families. At best girls were seen as 'guests' who would be given away to men. Women greeted each other by saying, 'may your son not die' and 'may your brother not die,' no one said, 'may your daughter or sister not die.' They told each other 'may you become a mother to boys,' no one said, 'may you become a mother to girls.'

Lana arrived at Swiss Cottage station, passed through the crowded barriers, and found Amer waiting for her, hands in his pockets, wet from the rain.

He's such a lovely man, she thought. Why does he like me?

She opened her arms and hugged him, a long hug, enough time for her to inhale him, her hands tracing his shoulder blades over his damp woollen coat. Amer kissed her head gently and asked whether she was alright.

'I am now,' she whispered.

She sensed something around her, a little change, barely detectable. People were still leaving the station in large numbers, high heels were rapping on the tiled floor, men in suits and thick overcoats were carrying black bags. She opened her eyes and above Amer's shoulder, as if out of nowhere, she saw Khalid's puzzled face across from her. He seemed to have stopped to make sure. She let go of Amer who hadn't noticed the change and was about to say something. She moved him away so that she could see what was behind him, but Khalid had disappeared.

'Who was it?'

'Khalid!' she said. 'Hiwa's friend, the one who lost his ex-wife and children to Anfal.'

They stood for a few seconds scanning the crowd of rushing people. No one was looking back at them. He touched her back.

'Let's go,' he said. 'At least he's a friend.'

They made their way to the venue without a word. Amer knew the organisers of the reading, so he stopped to have a chat with them. Lana found the toilet where she put on some blusher to hide her tiredness and tried to tame her frizzy hair with wet hands. She wondered what Khalid may be thinking of her and whether he would tell others about what he'd seen.

Maybe it's time to speak with Hiwa, she thought.

People were arriving to listen to the two Arab poets from Iraq and Egypt. Lana had once met the Iraqi poet who lived in Sweden and was widely translated into English. Nibbles and drinks were laid out on a long table: falafel, humus, tabouleh, soft drinks, and red wine. A handsome young man who was part of the organising team invited them to have some food. A woman who assumed she was an Arab, started speaking to her casually. After a couple of sentences Lana got stuck and switched to English. The woman asked her where she was from and before she had a chance to respond, Amer answered for her, 'Kurdistan.' The woman smiled, but Lana sensed a change in her, a change that could only be detected by people who shared a history of conflict. Amer called her attention away, his friend had just got engaged. The young man had a huge ring on his finger.

'His fiancé wants everyone to know that he's been taken,' Amer said.

He'd met his fiancé in the Senate House library, the man said. 'On the sixth floor, the philosophy section, to be precise.'

While listening to him, Lana forgot about her tiredness, about what Khalid may be thinking of her, about being on Arab grounds. The place was getting crowded now and they had to pull back and stand by the wall while eating. The falafel had a herb in it which gave it an extra kick. She sipped her red wine and scanned the room. There were a few familiar faces, some English poets who were interested in poetry in translation. Charlotte waved at her from across the room, accompanied by an attractive older man who looked wise.

'Hello Lana,' Charlotte said while giving her a hug. 'This is Ali.' Then Charlotte was hugging Amer and talking to him. The minute Ali opened his mouth Lana knew he was Persian.

What is it about these charming Iranian men? she thought. They could win over women of any age.

Charlotte told them that Ali Hassanzadeh was a famous artist who'd come to the UK in the aftermath of the Iranian revolution. He lived in Hampstead where he hosted 'lovely cocktail parties' and where he painted.

'Would love to know about your next exhibition,' Lana said. Ali raised his glass and Charlotte promised to send an email. The poets had walked in with the host who was an elegant English lady in her early fifties. When she introduced them, it was obvious that she had read both of their works and was good friends with the Iraqi poet, Husam Ahmed. The Egyptian poet seemed much younger and his voice was timid. The poets read in Arabic and the English woman read the translations. Husam even sang one of his poems upon request. He had a dedicated group of fans that clapped after each poem. In the interval people got up to refill their glasses. Amer was catching up with some old friends and he kept introducing them to Lana, trying to get her involved in the conversations.

'I met Muhammad at university,' he told her. 'We became friends because no one else befriended us.' They both laughed heartily.

'That's not true actually,' his friend corrected him. 'Some of the girls did, didn't they?' They laughed again.

'This man is trouble, I'm telling you, watch out for him,' Muhammad said to Lana.

Amer kept explaining things to Lana until she whispered in his ear, 'Don't worry about me, I'm happy to listen.'

He briefly put his arm around her and Lana noticed the man across the room who was staring at her. She knew him from previous events. He was an Arab nationalist who believed the Kurds did too well under Saddam Hussein's government, they had their ministers, representatives, and regional autonomy.

'What about the gas attacks?' an English man once asked him.

'That was US propaganda, the government used flour to scare the people who rebelled against their own state.'

Lana had never talked to this man personally; she knew that his cold-hearted and dismissive attitude would only hurt her and cloud her judgement. And now he was looking at her with a smirk on his face, a look that Lana understood very well. He said something to the person who stood next to him and nodded in Lana and Amer's direction. His companion turned around and inspected Lana from top to toe. He then looked away and said something back to his friend and they both laughed. Lana turned towards Amer and said, 'I'm going.' He looked puzzled for a second and looked at her as she walked across the room to get her coat.

The two men then approached him with a grin, 'Your Kurdish princess seems to be upset, my friend!' One of them said and Amer looked at them angrily. He apologised to his friend and left.

'Lana!' he called out after her. 'Can you wait and tell me what happened?'

She turned around and stood there for a few seconds. 'I should've known,' she said. 'I shouldn't have come!'

'Don't let them think they have won,' he said. 'You should've stayed to despise them... this is what they wanted, they wanted you out.'

'No, they didn't want me out. They wanted me to stay... they wanted to make me feel cheap.'

'Let's forget about them, they aren't worth it.'

It was before 10 pm but they both looked tired.

'Stay with me!' he said as she looked up at him with eyes full of thin red veins. They walked to the station in silence and remained silent throughout the journey. She leaned on his shoulder and stared at the dark window opposite them. Their heads touching, they fit together like two pieces of a puzzle, the puzzle of love bloon' '~ '~ ~~~flict She looked at their intertwined fingers and their   olive skin. She thought about the harmony betw   hair, the contrast between his black eyes and I   How could we look so good together, she thou   perfect match?

A   from a nightmare where she lay in a mas   ife and children. They were all alive, wait   was crying and it felt normal to lie dow   to expect to be covered with dirt. Out   uting orders in Arabic. She could hea   alid's youngest daughter, the one wh   held Lana's index finger.

                         girl whispered to Lana. 'I don't

lik   face; she could only see her

clo   bright blue flowers, and an

or   ͼ   of black hair, but her face

was invisible. On eit   eople were lying down and waiting. At the bottom end of the grave, by their feet, soldiers started to appear, their weapons pointing downwards.

'Ask him,' the little girl pleaded once more. 'He's your friend, isn't he?'

Lana saw the soldier's shaking hands, and when he pushed his helmet back from his face, she realised that it was Amer. A man with a big voice shouted 'Fire!' and hundreds of bullets were fired into the wide open grave.

'Amer!' Lana shouted. 'Don't shoot!' And before her heart started aching, she saw him cry.

He cried and shot and shouted, 'I'm sorry. I have to.'

She woke up thinking she was dead; her heart had just stopped beating in her dream. She sat up in bed feeling sweaty, shaky, and thirsty. She turned around, Amer was just waking up, his eyes refusing to open. His lips looked a bit more swollen and his eyes were two shivering slits.

'What time is it?' he managed to say.

'Too early,' she said. 'Sleep! I'm going to the loo.'

He went back to sleep, and she went to the bathroom, ran the tap, and told her dream to the running water.

'Water will take your worries away,' she heard her mother say. 'And water cleans, and water heals, and water cancels the evil that goes lurking around.'

CHAPTER SEVENTEEN

Hiwa

The pub hadn't changed much and entering it was like going back in time. The smell of burning wood in the open fire was welcoming. He scanned the room for Sarah, and then walked over and dropped his scarf and jacket by the fireplace. He liked the carved wood and high ceiling, the mirrors behind the bar, and the golden letters that announced a large selection of whiskeys, brandies, and wine. He ordered a pint of beer and was tempted to get Sarah a dry white wine, but he knew he shouldn't make assumptions about what she liked or disliked now.

They used to love coming to The Pineapple for sausage and mash, chicken and mushroom pie, homemade burger with chips, and the Sunday roast. It was still the kind of place where people read a book over a glass of wine and where others were catching up on years of gossip. He sipped his beer, feeling nervous. Sarah had been the first woman he'd really loved. Never before had he woken up next to the same woman every day and felt grateful that she was his.

From the early days he was amazed by her ability to go beyond anger and frustration at the world, and by how she managed to be successful and happy. She understood pain. Her mother had survived Bergen-Belsen as a child and managed to form a family of her own only to kill herself when her son and daughter were in their twenties. Sarah had explained to him that as a teenager she read about the Holocaust obsessively because her mother wouldn't tell her anything about it. And despite her parents' subtle discouragement, she decided to learn Polish, her mother's first language. She'd never heard her mother speak it except when she thought she was alone in the kitchen, and she swore in her language.

Hiwa tried not to disappoint Sarah and throughout their four-year relationship he stayed loyal to her. This was something he hadn't managed with other women. Sometimes, he felt alienated amongst her friends and didn't understand their cultural references. He didn't know the music they talked about, the directors, artists, plays, films. Once, one of her friends talked about Vivaldi's *Four Seasons*. This was the first time he heard of the composer and first time he heard the words concerto, cuckoo, and trotting. He couldn't remember why Tom called Vivaldi the Red Priest, nor could he remember the details of what he said but Hiwa was intrigued by the idea of music telling the story of seasons. If culture shock and envy hadn't clouded his judgement, he would've been impressed by Tom. Instead, he found him pretentious and annoying as he went on and on about why the violin concertos were so great.

That evening when their guests left, Sarah played the *Four Seasons* for him. He grudgingly admitted that Tom's lecture helped him understand the piece and draw more pleasure from it. Soon they set up their own tradition of music and film nights where they listened to Schumann, Chopin, Bach, and watched *Casablanca*, *To Kill a Mockingbird*, *Westside Story*, *Sophie's Choice*. She taught him how to dance and gave him novels and

132

history books to read. She encouraged him to do a vocational course in computing when she realised that he was good at it. He managed to hold down a job. Eventually, however, things became complicated again and his depression recurred. He couldn't take her to his country, show her the places he loved, teach her his language, and watch his favourite films with her. He was overwhelmed by her success, her good friends, and her clear perception of tomorrow. He couldn't do it anymore and when they decided it wasn't going to work, he moved out.

'So nice to see you,' Sarah said.

'And you,' he said as he helped her take her coat off. 'You look really well.'

She sank into the old leather chair opposite him. She had thin wrinkles around her eyes, a sign she'd kept her hearty laugh, and seemed more beautiful to him now, maybe because she was more confident and relaxed, maybe she was happier. She was wearing a black jumper and a large-beaded turquoise necklace comfortably settled over her breasts. Her curly hair, streaked now with grey, was short, brushing her jawline. The bluish-charcoal eye shadow made her eyes look bluer. The veins on the back of her hands were more pronounced.

She filled him in, told him she'd changed jobs a few times, continued to write, was working as a freelance journalist, and she sometimes wrote for the radio. She'd published a book about Tibet which had been well received. She'd moved to West End Lane, to the house she'd aspired to own when they were together.

'All good news,' he said. 'I'm glad things are going well.'

'Not everything,' she said. 'My dad passed away last year.'

He'd liked her father. David Hyman was a shrewd philosopher

who quoted from Descartes, Wittgenstein, and Kant and knew what they'd said and on which page of each book. He had curly brown hair and a full beard, and he wore a thick pair of glasses. Once he'd explained to Hiwa how boring the English Empiricists were and how, as an undergraduate, he'd dozed through those lectures in Oxford. David had introduced him to Sherry, a drink that he continued to enjoy. The generosity and supportiveness of this man went against all the stereotypes that Hiwa had heard about Jewish people in his community. His encounters with individuals from different backgrounds in London made him rethink many old beliefs he'd accepted as truths.

'I'm really sorry. He was a great man.'

'Yes,' Sarah said as her eyes teared up. 'I miss him. I can't believe he's dead, still think he's in his study, reading.'

'I know what you mean,' he said, 'I also find it difficult to believe that my mother is no longer here.'

'Ahoo!' she said. 'I've often thought about her.'

He gave her a silent look. There was a time when he wished so much that Sarah and his mother could meet. She'd once told him that Ahoo was like a character from a novel, kind and generous despite the heartbreak and disappointments thrown at her.

'How are your siblings?' she asked while sipping her wine.

'Lana lives here. She married someone and came over.'

'Oh, that is good, I hope.'

'She is divorced now, but seems happy. She writes poetry in English!'

'Impressive!' Sarah said. 'I must check her out!'

'Yes, she's a good writer,' he told her. 'How is your brother?'

'He's moved to the US with his family.' Then after a moment's silence she asked, 'Married?'

'Yes, I have a sixteen-month-old daughter.'

'How lovely! What is her name?'

'Shilana!' Hiwa said. 'She's already a dictator. I'm having to give her my room… things to throw away, letters to read, photos to sort.'

'Careful there,' she told him. 'That can be a dangerous business.'

He nodded silently. She was always fast and noticed things before he did.

'What do you think of the war?' Sarah asked.

'It's difficult to say! Change from within isn't possible in a country where the opposition is either destroyed or forced into exile. But the way these guys are going on about it… I don't know.'

She said she was glad that he didn't give her a straight answer. 'The way things are developing, I don't have much hope!'

'But I couldn't join the anti-war protest,' he said. 'Because that would mean campaigning for him to stay in power.'

'I know how you feel. I've been thinking about you and your family, about Kawa, the gassing, the exodus.' Sarah looked away and into the fire, as if she saw something there.

'How is your sister-in-law, by the way? Did she manage to rebuild her life after Kawa?'

'Yes,' he said, 'she married my brother Gara. They have named their son Kawa.'

Sarah's eyebrows were raised. A combination of surprise and horror flashed in her eyes.

'I know,' he said. 'Don't ask me questions about that. I have no answers.'

135

They ate and had more to drink. Over the course of the evening, he became so comfortable that he felt as if they'd never parted. It was just like old times when they ate and talked and laughed. He was surprised to find that they communicated more easily than before, maybe because all these years of living in London had finally made him a Londoner with similar standards and references, something which he'd never thought possible in the past.

'We must do this again,' she said as she put her coat on.

'Yes,' he said without much thinking. 'That would be nice.'

Early the next day he woke up on the sofa when his wife walked out of the bedroom. The sound of her footsteps dwindled as she walked towards the study and stood there for a few seconds, as she did every morning. He knew she would be pleased to see space showing up on the floor and the red carpet becoming visible again. He imagined her inspecting his desk where the letters were muddled up and the photographs were gathered in separate piles. She would note the large pile of tapes, CDs, and books. He heard Sozi walk back and check the kitchen before turning around to see him on the sofa. He was half sitting up and squinting. The TV was still on and silent news was being broadcast.

'What is it?' he said innocently. 'What time is it?'

'Why didn't you come to bed last night?' she asked as she sat on the edge of the sofa next to him.

'I wasn't sleepy and didn't want to wake you.'

He pulled her towards him and her breasts fell forward, nearly out of her dress. He pressed her against him.

'Ouch,' she said as she kissed the tip of his nose.

'Got time for a cuddle?' he asked, guiding her hand under the blanket to where he was hard and ready.

She gently squeezed him and shook her head, 'Sorry my love. I must get ready.'

She had often rejected his offers in the mornings and argued that the morning was about rushing to work, to continue life, day after day.

'How was last night?'

'Good,' he said as he played with her hair.

'What does that mean?'

'It was good to see her, she hasn't changed much.'

She blinked. He guessed that that wasn't what she was hoping to hear.

'There's no need to worry,' he said and kissed her cheek, the corner of her mouth. 'I'll make you breakfast then.'

'That will be great.'

Sozi went to the bedroom and started singing to Shilana who needed to get ready to go to the babysitter. There was a long process of cuddling to ease her into the day, changing her nappy, washing her face and hands, and dressing and feeding her. He put the kettle on and took out a banana, two eggs, a piece of broccoli, and some cheese from the fridge.

It'll be a grim day, he thought looking at the dark clouds.

While his daughter was being dressed, he mixed a handful of oats with a cup of milk, boiled it until it was soft, added a mashed banana, and left it to cool down. He sat Shilana down in her chair and started feeding her. After wiping her face, he gave her milk in a sippy cup. She grabbed it with both hands and started drinking as she lay on the sofa.

'No garlic,' Sozi called out from the bathroom.

He put on *Anta Umri* (You are my life) and cut the broccoli florets into thin pieces. After frying them until they were soft, he added two eggs on top, and sprinkled them with salt and parmesan cheese. When she came into the kitchen all dressed up, the pot of tea was brewing on a tealight candle. The toast jumped out of the toaster as if to say good morning. The omelette was sizzling. The table was laid. Umm Kulthum was singing about love in the background. Sozi sat down and watched her husband walk around the kitchen in his T-shirt and shorts.

'How are you all so comfortable with yourselves,' she asked him. 'How come you never worry about how you look?'

'We're not the objectified sex,' he said as he turned around to look at her. 'That works in our favour, don't you think?'

'Hmm,' she said, 'so unfair!'

She poured the tea and started sipping.

Hiwa brought her toast and half an omelette on a large plate. His wife was wearing black corduroy trousers and a thick burgundy top. She never went out without her mascara; it highlighted her eyes. She seemed happy and calm, looking at him with love.

It was nearly 8 am when he kissed his wife and daughter and saw them off. All the while he kept having flashbacks of his conversation with Sarah. Before their meeting, he'd refused to admit to himself that he was excited about seeing her again, curious about how he would feel after all these years, what she looked like, and what she was doing. He'd spent all of that day working hard, moving things, reading things, and throwing things away, not wanting to think about seeing her. He passed the corridor mirror and realised that he was smiling. He wondered whether he was happy because he'd found an old friend or because he still loved her. Umm Kulthum made it all seem alright, love was never wrong the way she sang about it.

CHAPTER EIGHTEEN

Lana

The cramps were like period pains that wouldn't stop. She wondered if this was a reaction against the war. War destroys what the womb creates, cancels the body's precious fruit. Her body was protesting against the meetings and discussions, fighting against the war and its possibilities. It kept demanding her attention. This part of her body which she'd learnt to ignore and forget, was saying, there is this place, this dark and moist space inside you that booms with possibility and protest.

But why now? Why with Amer?

The body doesn't listen to reason! It makes its own choices, desiring one person and rejecting another, oozing for one person and drying up for another. The body has its own understanding of love and sex, it has its own memories, its own pace, and it always tells the truth, without pretence. Growing up, everything she learnt about sex was from the stories other women told her. A friend's cousin had been shy on her wedding night, not wanting to undress and have sex immediately, but her new husband ripped off her underpants and forced himself on her as she cried. A relative went against her family and married the man she loved only to have him spit at her after sex. 'Now I've fucked you,' he'd said, 'there's nothing they can do about it.' Once, at a neighbour's wedding in Sarshaqam, the women were talking about their first time, and one of them said it felt like hammering a nail into a wall.

A woman shouldn't be a man's wall to pierce, Lana had thought.

Some of the women laughed uncomfortably, others seemed to recognise the feeling.

An older woman scolded her, 'Don't scare the girls, you're just trying to hide the fact that you enjoyed it.'

Lana had learnt that men enjoyed sex, wanted it, expected it, demanded it, and got what they wanted from women. Throughout her three-year marriage, she believed she was frigid and didn't like sex, and she struggled to have an orgasm.

The social world doesn't prepare women for enjoyment, she thought. It prepares us to shun or endure sex.

But her body had chosen Amer to enjoy sex with, to climax with, to make a baby with. Her body had its own logic and tempo. It responded to the fact that he didn't push her or make demands on her, he didn't enter her before she was ready. Sex was part of a larger relationship where there was conversation, laughter, and empathy, and her body liked this.

They were silently leaning on each other on the sofa in her sitting room. She was breathing quietly. Everything seemed forever still. Papers and books kept a low profile on the tea table in front of them. A block-heeled red shoe pointed towards them from the door, the other was pointing away. Coats, his and hers, were hanging on the back of a chair. Cups stood guard on the windowsill, on the bookshelves, the desk in the opposite corner, even on the floor.

'Let's do it,' he whispered, and she turned to face him. Strands of her fuzzy hair were caught in her scarf, and some fell around her cheeks. He held her gaze, his fingers stroking the back of her hand until she got up and went out of the room.

'Are you okay?' He asked her after waiting for a few minutes.

When she came back, she was holding the white stick that made all the difference to their lives, raised it for him to see. There were two clear blue lines through the white. A quick smile brightened his face, he hugged her gently, and stroked her hair until she asked, 'What shall we do?'

'I'll make some tea,' he said.

He sat her down on a stool in the kitchen and put the kettle on. Lana watched him wash two cups, place the tea bags inside, and turn around to look at her. He leaned on the sink, his fingers tapping a happy tune on the edge. He placed a steaming cup in her hands and sat on the stool next to her.

'What are you thinking?' his voice was calm. 'What do you want to do?'

'I don't know...' she said.

Her seat was too high, she needed to lean on something, she leaned on him.

CHAPTER NINETEEN

Hiwa

From the study window he watched how the streetlamps illuminated the rain, highlighting its vigour and determination. He was alone in the house. His friend Khalid was in Hull and Sozi and Shilana were spending the night with Khalid's wife and son.

After packing for the night, Sozi had become reluctant to leave him. 'I can tell Rozhin I can't make it,' she said.

He knew she was worried about the study and the reappearance of Sarah. 'What about the *dolma* she's made you?' he said. 'She'll be disappointed.'

'She'll understand.'

He hugged his wife. 'Don't worry and enjoy your time,' he said in a reassuring tone. 'Khalid will be pleased, but I just hope she won't go into labour tonight.' He raised his eyebrows in dread.

'She still has a few weeks,' Sozi said. 'Will you call me if you feel down? We can talk later in the night.'

'I promise that if I need to talk, I'll call you, but don't wait for me.'

Sozi had left him after wrapping Shilana in her raincoat, hat, and gloves. He watched from the window as his wife drove into the rain, her windscreen wipers hectically moving back and forth. For a second, he felt regretful for letting them go when the rain was so fierce, and the wind was reigning the night. He knew, however, that his daughter would enjoy the experience. She had no fear and a lot of greed for new experiences. She happily went with her mother, not even glancing back to say goodbye to him.

He resumed reading another letter by Gara, dated 02/09/1994.

'Everyone is still in black,' Gara had written. 'They are making an art of suffering, finding novel ways to mourn.' A flash of lightning made Hiwa look up. It was followed by a loud roll of thunder. 'Aveen takes refuge in Kawa's belongings and Lana refuses to throw *daya*'s clothes away.'

Hiwa read a few more lines about the grieving women and felt Tara's presence close by. He put the yellowing pages back in order and added them to the file entitled 'Family Letters.' He walked into the kitchen; his head was heavy with Gara's regrets. He took a bottle of red wine from the top of the fridge, the label said Chateau Margaux. He poured himself a large glass, sipped it, and sat down. The dark ruby colour and the black cherry finish on his tongue fit the heaviness of the evening.

He imagined himself walking home every day to a household full of heartbroken women – a widow, another who was a widow without ever marrying, and a young woman who'd never been loved, all united in grief. Maybe they mourned for their own lives. He sipped his wine and thought of a country where women grieved for the dead men until they died. He was a teenager when Abah *chaw-jwan* (Abah the beautiful eyed) was shot dead in front of his house in Sabunkaran. In the 1980s when the Kurdish parties were fighting each other in the mountains, each of them carried out 'purging' assassinations against members of the other party in the cities. Abah had been a brave fighter in the previous revolution of the late sixties, but after disillusionment, he left the mountains and was living with his mother and five sisters, working as a labourer. The atmosphere of those years was permeated with fear and suspicion. Neighbours and family members with different political views didn't trust each other and every sudden move could signal the presence of an assassin. The morning Abah was killed, Hiwa noticed the two men who stood by a pole near his house. Everyone else, Hiwa later found out, had noticed them, even Abah's sisters, yet no one warned Abah about them. Later his sister wept and said that God had made her speechless.

Abah was already dead by the time the neighbourhood gathered around him. His pierced and bleeding figure was later washed in the small mosque down the road where the men gathered and offered condolences to his old uncle. Hiwa remembered Abah's sisters who remained in black for years. Their faces and legs covered with hair; they were the constant picture of grief. The eldest three, Zara, Nawroz, and Layla refused all the good suitors and never got married. They said that they didn't feel entitled to enjoy life when their brother was deprived of it at such a young age.

'I can't be the man who brings life back to this household,' Gara had written. Hiwa wondered if any man could bring life back into such a household. How could a man change things, he thought. How could he compensate women for all the things they are robbed of in their lives? A man could love and support a woman, but he couldn't remove the barriers she faced, couldn't stop people staring at her, couldn't provide opportunities. 'It should've been the other way around that day... it should've been the other way around... the other way around.' It was typical of

Gara to think that and feel guilty about things outside his control.

Another thunderbolt brightened the kitchen. Hiwa looked out the window and thought of the people who were stranded in the rain. He imagined those who had no umbrella and no hood, running for shelter. For a while it seemed that his family and his nation were stranded in an endless storm. Suffering had rained incessantly, and they'd given up seeking protection or running for shelter. They just learnt to endure. Everything felt like a metaphor, a window that took him back to places and people from the past. He knew that even if Gara had been killed instead of Kawa, the family would have suffered the same. His mother, sister and aunt would've turned Gara into a legend just as they had done with Kawa. The dead are more valued than the living, and even though he tried to value and care for those who stayed behind, Hiwa too was guilty of glorifying the gone and the dead.

He finished his glass of wine and, feeling the urge to do something, moved three piles of books from his study to the sitting room, putting them down before the empty bookcase. The dusty books agitated him, and he scratched his nose. Since he'd stopped working in an office, he shaved twice a week and let his hair grow long. He remembered himself in suit and tie, taking the busy London transport every morning and arriving home exhausted at the end of each day. He enjoyed having a stable income and having the evenings and weekends to himself. Now that he worked from home, it was difficult to set a boundary between working time and private time. He also found it difficult to turn down a project because of the uncertainty of freelance work.

Hiwa crouched before the bookcase in the sitting room, organising the books into groups and stuffed them into different shelves. He filled two shelves, and the phone rang.

'*Gullekem?*' he said, thinking it was his wife.

'Hello kaka *gyan*,' Lana said. 'It's me.'

He could hear the rain through the phone. He could sense it from his sister's voice that she was shivering.

'Are you outdoors? Where are you?'

'Just finished interpreting at the South Harrow police station,' she said. 'What are you up to?'

'I've opened a bottle of wine,' he said. 'Come over!'

In the last months Lana had looked beautiful and relaxed. There were mysterious phone calls that she'd leave the room to answer. Once, he heard the man on the other end of the line, speaking English with an accent. Occasionally she was gloomy, slow at responding to questions, as if she was absent or far away. Her visit was perfectly timed, he thought, they could talk without interruption. He fine chopped onion and garlic and started frying them on the fire. The blue flames, he believed, were necessary for making good food. Fire made him feel alive and he didn't mind, occasionally, burning his fingers; it was about being connected to the four elements. He felt sorry for his daughter who was growing up in a flat without a garden, without any contact with earth, water, and fire. Getting his hands and clothes dirty in the garden as a child had been an essential part of forming an attachment to the place and the people. He and Tara built houses from mud and cooked soup on the little fire pit that their mother made for them. Most of the time the soups tasted terrible, but they enjoyed eating them anyway. Once,

147

Tara accidentally sprayed the food with paraffin, but they ate it nonetheless, burping petrol and feeling nauseous for two days, and not telling their mother for fear of being scolded.

He stirred the browning onion pieces until they were evenly mixed, then added the chopped tomatoes and black olives. He cooked the pasta without giving it any thought, poured himself another glass of wine, and sat opposite the TV screen. The anti-war protests were continuing in different parts of the world. He wished to see the same energy and mobilisation when dictators massacred their people and genocides took place. Non-violence was a noble concept, he thought, but a luxury that oppressed people can't afford. What do you do when all means of peaceful resistance are destroyed and the only option is armed conflict? What do you do when you are attacked?

The bell was pressed twice, his sister's signature ringing, and he went to open the door. She came in wet from the rain, her hair dripping, and her coat smelling like a wet carpet. She hugged him; her right shoulder weighed down with the laptop bag. Her body was shaky, and her breath was hot on his neck. She hung her coat by the door and took off her shoes before coming to sit down in the kitchen.

'Where are they?' she asked.

'They're staying the night with Rozhin. Khalid is away,' he told her as he stirred the sauce one last time. 'We have pasta,' he added and poured the sauce into a large bowl.

'I ate something a couple of hours ago.'

'Okay,' he said while walking towards her, 'just have a little.' Not eating at all wasn't an option in his house.

He served her pasta and poured her a glass of wine, but

she looked at them with no interest. He noticed her pale skin, the dark circles under her eyes. She was wearing no make-up and had made no effort to hide her forlorn state. Realising he had to be gentle, he didn't push her to eat, didn't ask her questions. He ate quickly and in silence while she stared at the window absentmindedly.

'Let's move over,' he said as he put the plates in the sink. 'I'll do the dishes before Sozi comes back, I promise.'

After shuffling through various CDs, he put Kemal Mihemmed on. His sister liked this music.

'The 1980s,' Lana announced. 'He captures those years for me.'

Maybe that is why I'm not keen on him, he thought, I missed that period.

'I remember first hearing *Ba arami wa aroyt* (You're leaving calmly) in a taxi. *Daya* and I were going to help *pura* Sayran pack a few weeks after grandma's death. When we got there, she was crying on her own. The house was a mess and *daya* immediately started helping, but I was frozen in my place. The song was replaying in my head, and I wanted to sing it out loud. I was sad that *nana* had died but happy that *pura* Sayran was moving in with us. So silly! I didn't understand that *nana* hadn't just been her mother but the pillar she'd built her life around. Everything turned upside down for *pura* Sayran after she was gone.'

This was often Lana's way, he thought. She talked about something to avoid talking about something else, or maybe to talk about the other thing indirectly. She hadn't talked about her ex-husband, not even when things were going badly between them. She didn't talk about her sadness, her new love, or her troubles at work. For all her courage, his sister couldn't talk about

149

her worries, maybe that was why she wrote.

'And I remember the day when I was out shopping with *daya*,' she went on. 'We passed by the pickle-sellers. Ahh, that smell! How I miss it.' She closed her eyes for a second, then went on: 'One of the shops was playing *Minim badbakhti sharan* (I'm the unfortunate of the cities). *Daya* was negotiating prices when suddenly a disruption started down the bottom of the square and people started running. Two trucks full of soldiers had arrived. They were jumping out, straight into beating and arresting the men. *Daya* grabbed my hand and pulled me without looking back. I kept turning around but couldn't see anything except for people running in the same direction as us. We left behind all our shopping that day—the vegetables and my brand-new red slippers which were never replaced.

'And the young boy,' she said with a quiet voice, 'who used to follow me after school for a while. He used to sing *Tu aw chatray* (for the sake of the umbrella).'

'What happened to him?' he asked, glad that finally a happy memory had come up.

'He got killed during the Iranian bombardments in 1986.'

Hiwa raised his glass and stared forward. Gara had been right, all their memories were contaminated with violence.

Lana tapped her fingers on the sofa and started singing *Akh shirine* (Ah sweet one) with Kamal.

'It was Kawa's favourite song when he was in love with Aveen,' she announced. 'He was always murmuring the song as he walked around the house. Occasionally he would sing a part of it at the top of his voice, surprising everyone.'

Hiwa laughed. He could imagine Kawa doing such things,

suddenly raising his voice in the shower, in his room, in the kitchen and then lowering his voice for the rest of the song. He did whatever came to his mind.

'He had a short time with his *shirine*,' Lana said and her voice broke, 'two years, just two.'

She started shivering in the warm sitting room. Hiwa covered her with a blanket but could still see the goose pimples on her neck every time she remembered something.

Sometimes it's best not to look back, Lana *gyan*, he wanted to tell her. Sometimes what keeps us going is a version of the past that we can live with. Don't go down that road, don't open the door to the past. We're living in this day and there are enough things to try to understand.

She started telling him about Kawa's arrest in 1982, a year after Hiwa had left the country. The student demonstrations started as a commemoration of the Qaladze napalm attacks eight years earlier when many students, professors and civilians were killed. That warm afternoon when Kawa shouted the slogans, the soldiers attacked from three sides. He ran through the alleyways of Sabunkaran taking shortcuts only he would know. When Lana opened the door for him, he was sweaty and breathless.

'I'm being followed,' he said.

It took their mother a few seconds to give her son pyjamas and hide him away, praying that no one would knock on the door.

'He was shaking,' Lana recalled. 'I'd never seen him so scared.'

Hiwa wanted to stop her again, why was she telling him this after all these years? But she kept going, not even looking at her brother anymore, as if she needed to tell this story to herself.

'The soldiers banged on the door a few minutes after Kawa

was out of sight. *Daya* opened the door, trying to seem calm. "Where is he?" they asked her in Arabic. "Who?" she replied in Kurdish. There were five of them. Five tough Arab men searching for a seventeen-year-old Kurdish boy.'

The soldiers started beating her mother and kept asking her where he was. Lana started crying, just as she had done all those years ago when they beat her mother. Hiwa held her in his arm as she carried on telling him, as if her life depended on it.

'He came out when he heard them beat *daya*, and they grabbed him and dragged him out. *Daya* begged them not to, she tried to kiss their boots, but they kept kicking her... and I just stood there crying like an idiot... not able to do anything.'

Hiwa was finally able to open his mouth: 'It's okay, it's all okay now.'

She ignored his remarks and carried on.

'For the next four days, she just cried and cried and sang mournful songs about him. She would sleep an hour and would wake up crying, she prayed and cried, sat at the *sifra* and cried, never comforted by anyone or anything. "Don't take this one away from me," she prayed to God, "You took Tara, don't take this one!" Poor *daya*, she didn't know that they would spare him this time only to kill him nine years later.'

Hiwa gave his sister a glass of water and a tissue. He knew the rest of the story. Kawa was released one evening, barefoot and in his torn pyjamas. He'd been blindfolded and taken in a van, dropped on a side road, not knowing where he'd been. A taxi driver took pity on him and gave him a lift home for free. That year it wasn't uncommon for young people to be dropped on the streets, some dead, some mutilated, and others terribly swollen and broken. Kawa was hospitalised for a few days and kept some of his scars for good. But the moment he arrived home he made a joke: 'If they'd beaten me one more day, I would've named you all as collaborators.'

Lana blew her nose then paused and rocked herself like a chair. Her eyes and nose were red, her face was swollen.

'Have you ever felt that by loving someone you're betraying your past?' she said.

He looked baffled for a second.

Is he an Arab? he wanted to ask. Is that what this is about?

He wanted to tell his sister that love was no betrayal. But instead, without thinking about what he was going to say, he said, 'Nothing you do is as bad as what I've done. I killed Tara.'

'No,' she said shaking her head. 'That's not true.'

Her eyes teared up again and he wasn't sure if she was crying for herself, for Tara, or for him. He was surprised at his own response, but Kawa and Tara had always been connected in his mind, how close they were, how they died so young, how lonely they left them each time.

Lana cried her tears in silence and he brushed her head until her breathing slowed down.

'Don't be so harsh on yourself, Lana *gyan*,' he managed to say. 'Fighting yourself isn't going to make it easier.'

She was quiet now, as if listening to him, or maybe thinking of something, someone else.

'If you want to know my opinion, I'll tell you this: Don't rush. Don't feel that you have to make important decisions too quickly... and as long as you're honest about your dilemmas, people will forgive you for them.'

She was staring forward.

'Stop analysing things,' he told her. 'Don't miss the chance of loving and being loved. Some people are never given the opportunity.'

His voice dropped towards the end of the sentence. He wished he'd thought like this when Tara was alive. He wished he'd told her the same thing.

Have I learnt my lesson? he thought. Have I really changed?

He watched Lana consider his words in silence. She then took a sip of water, put the glass down, and started mumbling along with Kamal.

'*Biryari chi bam? Chon khak jebellim?* (What decision shall I make? How shall I leave homeland?)'

CHAPTER TWENTY

Hiwa

He said good night to his sister and lay still in bed as his thoughts raced. He'd obsessively thought about the chain of events on that mild spring day in 1981. He thought about it so much that things escaped him, zoomed into the moments so closely until nothing meant anything anymore. His brain retained a word here or there, a voice, a scream, a colour. He would never forget the colour of Tara's top to toe home dress on that day, dark green with bright blue flowers. Later he would realise that it was made of the cheapest kind of nylon, so vulnerable and so tough.

He and Tara were inseparable when they were young, synchronised in their feelings and actions. Once they sat on the dusty bazaar floor in protest, chanting, 'ice cream, ice cream,' until their mother gave in and bought them some. They hid from her if she threatened to beat them, and if one of them took a beating, the other came to take a few of the blows. At times, without involving a third party, they fought each other with passion—he kicked her, she bit him, he pulled her hair, she scratched his face. He was strong, she was fast.

His mother never realised that her eldest two stopped believing in God when they were ten and eight years old. For a long time, she'd told them that if they were good, God would protect them from evil and send them a sweet each.

'Close your eyes,' she told them at the end of each good day. 'Pray to God!'

They covered their faces and prayed excitedly. God's sweets were always the same: gooey toffee which stuck to their teeth. They loved it and they loved God for prizing them like this. The continuous sweets were a reassurance that they were in his good books, that he would watch over them.

They stopped believing in God on the day that Tara climbed on top of the cupboard and found the bag of toffee there. From then on everything about God seemed dubious and whenever someone said, 'God willing' or 'God is mighty' they looked at each other and smiled. That God was dead was their little secret. They were now on their own and needed to watch over each other because no God would shield them. Once as they played in the garden, they promised each other that they would die to protect each other. They both spat on their favourite pebble, a round greyish-blue, and buried it in a corner of the garden as a sign of this pledge. The two of them remained close until their bodies betrayed them, until Tara suddenly grew tall and beautiful. Her body went through mysterious changes at the age of twelve, and she started hiding things from him. Every month she fell ill, and she told him, 'It's just a tummy ache.' But he didn't believe her. He felt that he was no longer her best friend because she was shy around him.

Tara had been a pretty child, 'pretty for misfortune!' some said. But when her body rapidly transformed into a woman's body, everything intensified. Her childhood puffiness receded, and her cheekbones became more pronounced. To make her look less beautiful, *daya* cut her straight black hair which came down to her waist. But the new haircut made her look more like a woman, her hair had more volume, and her long neck was more noticeable.

She was prevented from going out and playing with Hiwa. Instead, she had to help in the kitchen and clean the house. He helped her wash up, wipe, and sweep because he didn't feel entitled to play when she was doing housework. Everyone seemed worried about how close they were. One day after they moved to their new house, their father came home and said that Hiwa would start working after school.

'I've spoken to *wasta* Ali,' Akram said. 'He's willing to let you learn under his instruction.'

Hiwa looked at his mother all worried and Tara mirrored him.

'What will he do?' Tara asked.

His father looked at her for a second, about to lose his temper, but he merely replied, 'He'll help fix cars.' He then looked at Hiwa: 'It's a very good skill to have... you may become an engineer later, this will help you.'

Hiwa had seen the young boys who worked at such shops, they were always covered in grease, their hands looked awful, and they smelled of cars. The matter wasn't open for discussion. He was fifteen years old, and he needed to start working. Later, when his father had gone to bed, his mother told him, 'It'll be good support for *baba* too. You'll help look after your siblings.'

That night Hiwa cried in his bed, but Tara didn't dare to come and comfort him because they were no longer allowed to sleep next to each other. The new house meant the loss of childhood for both of them. She was constrained at home while he had to work and fell behind in school. *Wasta* Ali wasn't an abusive

157

boss, but he made Hiwa work hard. A fat man who regularly needed things fixed gave him dirty looks when his boss wasn't looking. Once when *wasta* Ali was at the back of the shop, the man looked at Hiwa all flushed and breathless and tried to touch him from behind while he was checking the bottom of the car. At the last second, Hiwa turned around and hit him with a large screwdriver. The man doubled over and started swearing, he'd been hit under his left ribs. After having an argument with *wasta* Ali, he left the store and never returned. Hiwa was grateful that his boss didn't report the incident to his father.

Tara's life also became more difficult in the new neighbourhood. She was incessantly watched and talked about. One hot summer afternoon a blind man came and said, 'I've been told a houri lives here, I've come to see if she can cure my eyes.' She was fourteen when they noticed an increasing number of people knocking on their door; some claimed to be beggars, some were thirsty and asked for a glass of water, some said they were lost and asked for directions. Soon Ahoo forbade her from opening the door to anyone.

A man who wore military clothing kept standing by the pole opposite their house. He was clearly a member of the Ba'ath Party, and he carried a gun. Most of the time, he was drunk and sometimes he sang old love songs and burst into tears. He used to follow Tara at every opportunity, write letters to her which she never accepted, and sing songs about her. The neighbours worried that one day he may get fed up and kill one of their sons in revenge. He loitered for a few months, singing into the night, until he suddenly disappeared. Some believed he'd been killed by the *peshmarga*, others believed that he was a member of the underground movement, pretending to be a Ba'athist, and the government tortured him to death, shredding his body.

Tara's movements were restricted, she had to rush home from school and not leave until the next day. At this time, when Hiwa wasn't around or was too exhausted and self-absorbed to talk to her, she announced that she'd fallen in love with the theatre. Her best friend's father was a play director and he'd become the source of this newfound joy. It had all started innocently when Layla Ibrahim secretly brought one of her father's scripts into school and read a part of it to Tara in the break. They'd huddled together in the back of the classroom, reading the play, both excited and terrified. Tara had then asked her friend to lend her some of the play scripts and she started reading them at home. Their mother seemed pleased about this hobby which kept her daughter busy at home. Hiwa knew that being illiterate, Ahoo didn't understand what the texts were about and how dangerous they could be. She didn't understand the liberating potential of words, how they helped Tara imagine another world, one that was radically different from her own. She naively accepted Tara's explanation and believed that the stories would help with her Kurdish and Arabic literature lessons.

Tara's fascination with words and stories made Hiwa envious. He had to work hard while she sat at home reading and enjoying herself. He felt that he alone was carrying the burden while the rest of his siblings studied and played. He became reserved.

'What's wrong?' she asked him once. 'Are you angry with me?'

He shook his head angrily and said nothing, annoyed that she even had to ask. She should know what is wrong, he thought. She'd escaped into this other world where characters could do things:

159

they lived, took risks, made mistakes, had regrets, fell in love, were heartbroken, and could, if they lost hope, kill themselves. She'd told Hiwa that she imagined herself part of that world one day, a world where even though people suffered, they were free to experience everything and to make choices. She took notes of these scripts and copied paragraphs and dialogues. She read and re-read them until she memorised them, elaborated on them, until she was the hero, suffering, crying, and loving.

Once she gathered her siblings in a room and recited a few passages to them. At the time Hiwa was sixteen, Tara was fourteen, Kawa was thirteen, Gara was eleven, and Lana was seven years old. Lana was too young to understand what her sister was saying but was mesmerised by Tara's performance and passion. It was the heroine's last reflection before she killed herself, and Lana cried her eyes out. Despite himself, Hiwa was amazed by his sister's ability to bring the words alive. It was as if these were her own words, originating from her own daily suffering. Kawa and Gara sat through the performance wide eyed, unable to escape their sister's grip on their imagination. She was eloquent, passionate, beautiful, and natural. When she finished, they clapped for ages while she bowed to them again and again, crying from joy.

In his memory, this was the moment when Tara realised that she wanted to act in front of an audience. Soon after this day, she started talking about studying drama in the Institute of Fine Arts. But when she eventually met Layla's father after school, she was tongue tied. He picked up his daughter from school and they were going to a play that afternoon. Layla 'liked to see the play,' Tara told him, but she herself would die to see it. She wished that she could trade passing her end of year exams with going to the theatre on that day.

Hiwa remembered how she repeatedly complained about her school and wished to complete her schooling quickly so that she could go to the Institute. This hope kept her going in her hard-going lessons. She particularly disliked two of her teachers. One of them was the Maths teacher, Ms. Raana who kept picking on her. Ms. Raana once told her off for wearing blusher to school. Tara swore that she wasn't, but she was forced to stand before Ms. Raana who wiped her face with a handkerchief in front of her classmates. She wiped Tara's face until her cheeks were red and burning hot. When she relayed the story to her family, she was crying and shaking with rage. Once she hadn't done her homework and Ms. Raana told her, 'Of course you don't have time to study, you spend all your time styling your hair.' Tara never styled her hair.

She also hated the Religious Studies teacher, Mr. Osman who gave her extra work to do and was particularly harsh with her if she couldn't interpret a verse from the Qura'n. To Mr. Osman she was the seductive female who would corrupt good men and take them off the path of God. As far as he was concerned, she was already guilty of all the crimes she would commit in her life, there was no way back for her, she couldn't be salvaged.

Hiwa didn't understand the pressures his sister was put under. He didn't see how theatre had become her saviour, her means of escaping the suffocating confinement and surveillance. In a manner typical of insecurity, he read her notes aloud and laughed about them one day. He teased her about 'the silly books that were full of daydreams.'

161

'Real life isn't like that,' he told his sister. 'In real life people just get on with things, no one kills themselves for love.'

Tara gathered her books and stood up angrily to tell her brother, 'No, of course not. Not everyone has the courage to do that, especially not you.'

He was furious with her, and he attacked his sister who was ready for him. She'd acquired more strength since the last time they fought. This puzzled him for a second, he lost his grip and she managed to get on top of him, slapping and boxing him. Years later he could only explain her triumph over him in terms of her newly found clarity of mind, the strength of finding new passions. He was beaten and instead of getting up and fighting back, he started weeping under his furious sister's fists. It took her a few seconds before she realised that he wasn't fighting back. She stopped and looked into his eyes, all confused. She hugged his face, and he hugged her body while weeping silently.

'Don't cry,' she told him softly. 'It's okay, I'm not angry.'

He kissed her temple gently as she stroked his head. He kissed her hair, her neck, and shoulder. She let go of his head and wanted to get up. He held on to her and begged, 'Don't go.'

CHAPTER TWENTY-ONE

Gara

When he was a boy, he watered the garden, cut the grass, and weeded with his mother. None of the others were interested in Ahoo's roses, morning glories, portulacas, and marigolds, her mulberry, pomegranate, and fig trees, her seasonal vegetables. He loved the smell of freshly cut grass, how it promised peace and purity. He loved the neatness of the newly mowed lawn and could weed for hours, putting his head down, forgetting to drink or go to the toilet. All he thought about was uprooting the unwelcomed shrubs that fed off his mother's good greenery. He didn't notice his tiring knees and hurting back until he finished and felt pain in his limbs before blood returned to his unfolded arms and legs.

Gara longed for those carefree days of small goals and easy satisfaction. He drank the last drop of his cold tea which was sickly sweet and wished he could solve today's problems through a similar process of mental and physical dedication. He had to finish his column by tomorrow, but he couldn't concentrate. The official discourse of the Kurdish leaders was that of non-interference in the war, but unofficial sources seemed to suggest otherwise. Lack of transparency and unwillingness to provide information by the authorities was one of the major challenges that he and his colleagues faced on a day-to-day basis.

He leaned back and rested his head on the back of the chair. The spotless white ceiling made him happy. They recently moved to this new building which to him meant that they'd made it. After years of reporting the news to his brother, long dissatisfaction with the party publications, and lengthy discussions with various people, he left his teaching job and founded an independent weekly paper with his friends. He wanted a name 'that would reflect the current reality, and not dwell on the past!'

'How about Sacrifice?' Dara had said in his usual sarcastic manner, making them laugh.

At the time, the Kurdish rhetoric revolved around victimhood and heroism. Victimhood was highlighted through the yearly commemorations of the gas attacks and the Anfal genocide, and representations of destroyed villages, mass graves, deportations, Arabisation of the oil rich regions, torture, death squads, and gallows. Heroism was highlighted through the hymns and documentaries about the revolution, the uprising, the martyrs of guerrilla warfare, the members of the underground movement, and the tales of survival and solidarity.

'How about *Emro*—Today?' Rebwar had eventually proposed. 'It'll critically appraise the performance of yesterday's heroes and become the space where facts are presented as they are, without political agendas.'

'We need to break the traditional divide between the political and social,' argued Hanar, the only woman in the group. 'Just as it's important to talk about corruption, nepotism, and mismanagement, it's also important to talk about domestic violence, "honour" killing, women's rights, conservativism, and radicalisation.'

'I'll come as far as the gallows,' Dara responded, 'and will wave you off from where I am.'

Their marketing slogan was 'Speak today, learn from yesterday!' They imagined it as a platform for marginalised perspectives and an exercise in free speech. Years ago, Gara had written to his brother about the increasing number of publications in the aftermath of the 1991 uprising. He'd expressed his happiness about the plurality of the newspapers and newsletters when dozens of political parties emerged. Some of these were splinter groups from previous parties that vanished as quickly as they appeared. Each party, from the extreme right to the extreme left, including the Islamic parties, had its own publication. It was difficult to keep up with all the new publications and the diverse political perspectives. He'd called it 'the euphoria of ideology and opinions' which he'd liked at the time. It all seemed like a healthy exercise in democracy after decades of silence when every publication had to be approved by the Ba'athists. As years went by, however, Gara became less optimistic about these publications, less hopeful that between them they may cover the truth. They were the preaching organs of the parties that supported them, creating different versions of the same reality. Each of them was skewed in one way or another, each claiming to represent the people, and they were full of silence about their own party's disastrous political decisions and corruption. While *Emro*'s team included people from different ideological backgrounds, they agreed that consistency was the key: no party or ideology would be immune from criticism.

'When injustice happens,' he'd said, 'neutrality means complicity.'

To do it right, they knew, they would have to counter the polarisation created by the political parties —each with their own women's rights organisations, students' groups, writers' groups, and workers' unions— and to foster a sense of citizenship, regardless of political or religious affiliations.

From the first day, *Emro* faced disapproval and backlash. It was attacked by all the different sides, each accusing it of being a secret organ of the other. The first three years were full of suspicion, pressure, and lawsuits. Finally, Gara felt that they had come through all of that, that despite all the attacks and attempts they'd managed to stand their ground and be accepted. All sides had gradually recognised that this weekly paper wasn't the hidden instrument of some new party, it was just what it claimed to be: an independent paper.

Outside, Gara's colleagues were having a laugh. They were a young and enthusiastic group, most of whom had learnt on the job. Sometimes journalists visited them from abroad and provided workshops, training, and support. There were also opportunities to go abroad for training and studying. Many of the ones who left, however, tried not to come back. Homeland had become a sad place owned by the political elite, a place full of injustice and inequality, a place where there was little opportunity to move forward. The young graduated only to find unemployment, poverty, and waste awaiting them.

Gara checked his email. No one had written to him. He went on to the BBC website. Somebody walked towards his room. There was a knock and Dara put his head through.

'Have you heard? Ihsan Noori's had a heart attack.'

He last saw Ihsan six months earlier when he accompanied *pura* Sayran to the Rheumatologist. The waiting room was crammed full of pained people who waited impatiently. Sometimes they took their anger out on the secretary. 'When is my turn?' they asked him. 'Why is it taking so long?' Everyone was convinced that the secretary was messing up the queue, putting 'important people' first. Every now and then the man swore by God, opened his book, and showed them the line to prove that he wasn't messing up the order.

A woman was crippled by her knee pain and moaned every time she moved. A man's back curled around a stick. A well-dressed old woman, who was on a wheelchair, looked at everyone with acute eyes. She had an air of authority about her, Gara thought, she could have been a leader in another world. Two women with three children comfortably occupied a sofa to themselves. They were both drowned in gold but had come to the clinic in their home gowns, wearing old, torn slippers. They kept whispering to each other and covering their mouths when they talked even though no one was listening to them. Gara was sitting at the edge, next to his aunt. The woman who sat on the other side of his aunt asked her what she'd come for.

'Arthritis,' Sayran answered as she touched her knotted fingers.

'Ah,' the woman said, 'I'm here for my knees. They tell me the gooey stuff is disappearing and my bones rub against each other.'

'I hope you'll get better,' Sayran said.

'This doctor only cures the people he knows,' she whispered.

'I've told a relative to put in a good word for me.'

'I hope he'll cure you.'

'Last time,' the woman continued, 'he gave me an injection which was very good... but it didn't last. They do it on purpose, don't they? To keep you coming back.'

It was clear that *pura* Sayran had run out of words to console the woman with and she turned away from her. At that moment Ihsan walked into the waiting room with a younger man whose arm was plastered. Neither Gara nor his aunt recognised him at first. He had grown completely grey, and his face had lost its sharpness. His petite figure was still shapely. If you saw him from the back, you would think he was younger.

'*Slaw* to you, Sayran *khan* and *kaka* Gara, how are you?'

They got up and shook his stretched-out hand and then Gara recognised him. *Pura* Sayran became emotional, she used to see Ihsan every day at work when she was a young woman. Ihsan turned back to show them his son with a nod, he'd broken his arm falling from a ladder to the upper roof.

'The satellite dish,' Ihsan told them.

'Unfortunate,' Gara said.

'I'm so grateful for *Emro*, *kaka* Gara. You're doing a great job, we have faith in you.'

'Thanks so much,' he responded, 'We're grateful for your articles.'

'So what do you do now, Sayran *khan*?' he said.

'I've retired,' she told him. 'It's difficult to write anything with these hands.' She lifted her hands up for him to see. 'I'm okay though. My nephew and niece send me medication from abroad, I just need to be careful.'

He patted her on the shoulder and said, 'I still don't understand why bad things happen to good people even though I've lived much longer than you.'

That was the last time they saw him. Gara was surprised at how empty the *pirsa* was. His sons, brothers, and nephews were standing to receive people but there were few consolers. He looked around to find a familiar face, then turned back towards an old acquaintance.

'Why are there so few people?'

'Haven't you heard?' the man whispered back. 'His own party did this to him.'

'What do you mean?'

'They faked a Ba'athist file for him… Imagine! They created a file for *kak* Ihsan who spent his life supporting the party!'

Gara remembered the day he met Ihsan after the uprising, when he was all optimistic and full of praise for the new leaders. After his disillusionment, he'd resigned from the party and started criticising them. His last articles were a harsh appraisal of the Kurdish government, full of disillusionment and anger.

'Anyone would've had a heart attack!' the man said. 'He knew that enough people would believe it. And look at this! He deserves a better wake.'

CHAPTER TWENTY-TWO

Hiwa

'Hello,' he said as Sarah opened the door. 'I was in the neighbourhood and thought you may be in.'

'Hello,' she said with surprise in her eyes. 'Just got home, do come in.'

She looked pale but smiled warmly. It reminded him of the way he used to surprise her. Once she got home to find a candle path that led her straight to the sitting room where he awaited her with a glass of wine. She led him to the sitting room.

'Is everything okay?' she asked him as he sat down.

'Yes, I hope I'm not disturbing you.'

'Not at all. I was just making some tea. Won't be a minute.' And she walked out.

He slumped on the sofa that wasn't his. He felt its welcoming embrace as it kindly accepted his shape without putting up any resistance. He was comfortable, resting his head on the back and looking up at the calming apple white ceiling. The place smelt of coffee and a soft perfume, the same scent that she'd always worn. It was fruity and mild, not intrusive, not sharp, not in your face, just a gentle sweet smell that had become a part of her. When they lived together, even their bed smelt of it. Later when she was out of his life, he'd smelt this perfume on women who rushed past him on streets, platforms, and escalators. He always turned around after them hoping to see her. No one carried it off as she did. To him this smell was fully hers and it suited no one else. Now he was surrounded by it again, it soothed him.

He could hear her making tea in the kitchen but didn't get up to join her. He wanted to remember her place, to take it in, to feel that he was part of it, even if just for a short while. He wanted to feel that he was okay there, that he had the right to be there. He looked around him and noticed how a spider had knitted a web in the left-hand corner of the room. The bookcase opposite him was well organised by subject. The novels occupied the top two shelves, the non-fiction another two, and the rest was history and philosophy. Her taste in books hadn't changed much; *One Hundred Years of Solitude*, *The Sound and the Fury*, and *Grapes of Wrath* were still at the top. She wasn't playing any music, but he felt he could hear something. Maybe the upstairs neighbour's music is leaking down, he thought.

She walked in with a tray, tall in her lean blue jeans and grey T-Shirt. The blue stripe that went across her chest was demanding his attention. She poured him amber tea in a large glass, remembering that he liked to see his tea, didn't like the opaque cups. He brought it close to his face and smelt her tea. For a while he just wanted to stay there looking at her as she sat next to him, he didn't want to talk, didn't want to drink, didn't want to touch her. He just wanted to keep everything still, the silver strands of hair spiralling in her curls, the blue turquoise earrings, her long bony fingers curling around the cup.

'So how are you?' she said.

He closed his eyes for a few seconds and tightened his fingers around the glass, not wanting to lose the moment.

'Fine,' he said, smiling at her.

Her hand came to him, her index finger nearly touched him, his shoulder imagined the weight of her hand, but she pulled her hand back and turned away. He pulled her hair the way he used to when he was teasing her.

'I was thinking about you,' she said.

'Let's not ask why you're thinking of me and why I'm here.'

She turned around and looked at him with raised eyebrows. The room had a high ceiling and the crystal chandelier with six lights dangled above the coffee table.

'We don't have to know everything,' he said. 'In fact, we can't, even if we want to.'

'Things happen for a reason,' she said. 'Even if the reason isn't clear, there is one.'

'There's enough absurdity in this world to prove that some things can't be explained, there's no logical reason for them, but they happen anyway.'

'I've been reading my mother's diary,' she said after a pause. 'I don't think I knew her really. It's very strange.'

'Why do we keep going back to the past?'

'It's absurd, isn't it? But the past doesn't leave us alone, it catches us unawares. After my father died, I realised there were many things I'd never asked him about. We spent many of our years trying not to talk about mum, and then when he died, I thought I can never have this conversation with him. It's too late now. So, I dug out the old letters, the photos, the diaries... it's a discovery.'

'I didn't want to read the letters again,' he said. 'I didn't want to find the photographs. I just wanted to clear the room for my daughter. But it's like an ambush. We leave the old country, detach ourselves from its smells, sounds, and colours. Then, years later, something completely unrelated forces us to open an old box. At the bottom we find the image we've run away from for many years. After that nothing can stop the forces that unleash. Once you open the door to the past, you cannot hold back from going through it all over again.'

Sarah was tearful now. He didn't want her to cry, that wasn't why he'd come. For him this was all about not regretting. He gently touched her arm.

'I'm sorry, maybe I shouldn't have come. Do you want me to leave?'

'No,' she said as she wiped her tears. 'I'm sorry... don't know why I'm crying.'

'Maybe you're starting to mourn your parents... trying to understand.'

'Ahhh, family!' she said. 'We'll always try to understand, and our understanding keeps shifting. Some things discovered and others forgotten, some things highlighted, and others ignored. It seems that we'll never understand the full truth, never know exactly what happened and why. But we keep trying.'

She looked at the bookshelf for a second and back at him. 'But suicide! She was only a few years older than I am now when she did it. I was only twenty-two at the time. Some days I feel angry with her for leaving us like that. It's selfish, I think. Other days I completely understand and respect her choice. Sometimes I'm glad she refused to suffer, other times the thought of it kills me.'

'I think I know what you mean,' he leaned back into the sofa and finally came clean about a lie he'd told her many years ago. 'My sister's death wasn't an accident,' he said calmly, staring at her.

'What?' Sarah looked at him with raised eyebrows.

'No, it was no accident,' Hiwa confirmed again. 'She too killed herself.'

Dealing with suicide had been another issue that made him feel close to her.

'She set herself alight in the bathroom,' he carried on. 'She was a roasted piece of meat, but she survived for two days. And when I went to see her in the hospital, you know what she did? She didn't look at me. That's how angry she was. She never looked at me again, never said a word, never forgave me. I'd promised to protect her, but I didn't.'

He wanted to tell her the whole truth, to say that he'd been in love with his sister and lusted over her like everyone else. And worst of all, she knew it, that's why she was so disappointed in him. But he couldn't admit this to anyone. He knew that no one would see him in the same light again if they knew. He looked at Sarah and continued. 'Maybe this is why I'm here, so that I can finally tell you that I killed her.'

'You can't...' she said in a quiet voice.

'Yes, I can blame myself,' he interrupted her, 'and no matter how many times you tell me it wasn't my fault, it won't help. I know it was. I can never forget the smell, you know. That sickening smell is what I remember the most about it, the smell of burnt skin, hair, and blood mixed with the smell of a burnt nylon dress. That's my last memory of her.'

Sarah was weeping now.

'I don't want to remember her like that, I don't. It's horrible.

She was lively, she was clever, she was funny, but I keep remembering her last days.' He started crying, his body was radiating heat. 'My beautiful sister, she wasn't beautiful anymore... she was no one's problem. It was over for all of us.'

'Shhhh,' she said while hugging his head, as if soothing a baby. 'She's beyond all of that now, at peace. Shhh!'

She kissed his head, his ear, and his temple.

'It's okay now,' she said, 'It'll be okay.'

'I have to go,' he said.

'Don't go,' she said, just as he'd said to Tara that day when she was on top of him. And just like that her voice came back to him in all its force as she pushed his body away. 'Animal,' Tara called him. 'You disgusting idiot!'

CHAPTER TWENTY-THREE

Lana

Lana felt guilty about love. She knew that women were killed for lesser crimes; she'd loved a man outside marriage and created life with him. This other life that lay inside her made its presence strongly felt. It made her feel nauseous and exhausted every morning, confused about all the things she was certain about. She needed to talk about this new confusion to another woman and arranged to meet Nazah after work.

The Victoria train was brimming with asylum seekers who looked defeated by their immigration interviews. The wagons gracefully carried the exhausted people, their sorrowful stories, and various languages. Lana sat by a window and looked out, avoiding face to face contact with everyone. She caught fragments of conversations in Kurdish, Arabic, Persian, Dari, and other languages which she couldn't understand.

Sometimes when she sat in the interpreters' room at the Immigration House, the mix of all the languages became an unbearable hum. The large room contained more than one hundred interpreters, divided by a few tables around which the different language communities sat. The Kurds shared a table with the Persians at the top left corner. The Turks sat opposite the Kurds. Between the Kurds and the Turks there was a buffer zone; a group of Eastern European women sat together around a table in the middle of the room. They were a quiet group, and they ate small portions of food, each on their own. The Arabs were at the other end. They were a large group from the gulf, the Middle East, and North Africa with their various cultures and dialects.

Lunchtime was the busiest time when the smells from all the different cuisines mixed. The Kurdish interpreters ordered meat with rice and stew, kebab, or shawarma from the two Kurdish restaurants, and ate together. Sometimes, even though everyone had breakfast at home, they ate a second breakfast together. Rolls of bread were brought with yoghurt, cheese, honey, walnuts, cucumber, and olives. Every day there was an argument about who pays for whom. Lana could get away with free food every day if she wanted to. Being the youngest and a writer gave her an elevated status in the group. She had to fight to pay for herself and others. It was a continuous dispute.

At Clapham Junction several people got off the train and some got on. A young couple came in and sat opposite Lana. They were already in the middle of a kiss and Lana noticed two young Middle Eastern men curiously looking at them. When Lana saw young couples talk in cafés, kiss in public, and stroll the streets hand in hand, she remembered her sister. In her country love had no public space, was forced to go underground, and had to be experienced in silence. There was no space where lovers could meet, let alone make love. Young people lived with their families and there was nowhere for them to experience each other.

When Tara was in love, young couples were lucky if they could speak on the phone without their families finding out. Those who were braver communicated through lengthy letters that were decorated with dry flowers, written with feverish fingers late at night, before a candle when no one was watching. The blank page was the space where lovers poured their hearts out to each other, where they talked about their dreams of being together, fleeing to a distant land where no one knew them, and where there was no fear of dishonour and death. People weren't supposed to fall in love until they were at university and when they did, they were supposed to get married. Sex outside marriage was a punishable sin that led to loss of face for the families involved, but particularly for the girl's family. Young pretty girls bore the brunt of surveillance. It was believed that more men would be interested in them and therefore there would be more chances of them rebelling and loving back. Lana wondered sometimes if Tara would've suffered less if she had been less beautiful, or if the family had lived in a less communal neighbourhood like Aqari, for example, where rich families managed to have some space and privacy. She wondered whether Tara's life would've ended the way it did if they were rich.

Rich people got away with things. They could buy their reputation back or go abroad for a while if there was a social crisis. They didn't need the approval of the community to survive. When *pura* Maneej, a poor woman who was beaten by her husband for twenty years, had a nervous breakdown everyone said she'd gone mad, whereas when a rich distant relative had a similar breakdown because her husband cheated on her, they said she was tired and in need of rest, so she went abroad on holiday. Poverty contributed to it, Lana knew. The people around them were caring, but they were also too involved in each other's lives. At times they took small stories and blew them out of proportion, making every little divergence seem criminal. How strict they were, how efficient in their watchfulness!

The train unpacked itself in Victoria. Lana was surprised at the number of people who kept leaving the train, as if an army had been packed into the long vehicle. She took the District Line to Hammersmith. She spent the seven stops standing amongst a crowd of people who looked exhausted. Some of them seemed excited about the prospects of the evening. A few women were already making themselves up for the night. She was glad that despite everything, people didn't give up on themselves; they tried to look their best and to have fun no matter how complicated it was.

At Hammersmith station she took the Hammersmith Line to Latimer Road. She turned out of the small station and crossed the road into the small lane that took her to her friend's block. She took the lift to the 13th floor where the door was already open and waiting for her. She walked through, inhaling all the good, nourishing smells. Nazah greeted her with a big hug. She'd cooked pilau rice with beans and chicken. Lana loved her friend's innovative way of cooking, like adding ginger and chillies to the beans. 'The Indian influence,' Nazah called it. The chicken was roasted in pomegranate syrup, it was dark brown and mouth wateringly delicious. She'd put a thin layer of bread around the rice before steaming it and it came out of the pot like a cake. Lana loved cutting through the crusty bread to get to the rice.

'It suits you,' Nazah said as she took a mouthful of rice. 'You look good.'

'I don't feel good though,' Lana replied. 'In fact, I feel awful.'

'But is that because of the pregnancy or other things?'

179

Lana was eating fast, as if she hadn't eaten for days. 'Both, I guess. Didn't you feel like that?'

'I was only nineteen,' Nazah reminded her. 'Too young to even understand what it involved. We didn't question things then, people just had children when they got married and that was that.'

'Yes, when they got married,' Lana emphasised. 'Look at me. What am I doing?'

Nazah laughed and put her hand before her mouth. 'You sound like your mother, a decent God-fearing woman. You can always get married, can't you?'

Lana wished she'd been a bit more like her mother, so graceful and accepting of life, so un-rebelling, so rational. Her life had been so different from that of her mother and sister. She'd experienced things that her sister had no chance of experiencing. She'd gone against tradition, made choices, made mistakes, and learnt from her mistakes without paying a heavy price. She'd grown, gained confidence, learnt new things, and acquired skills. But some choices were difficult and costly.

Maybe this is why it's difficult for women to free themselves from patriarchy, Lana thought, maybe women aren't taught the things that would help them handle the responsibilities and stigma that come with having agency and decision-making power.

The phone rang and Nazah answered it.

'*Gyan*, I'm good *basaqa*, how are you?'

Lana heard the voice of a young woman on the other side.

'Yes of course! You're here tonight. We are eating pilau and beans, don't worry. You have to tell me all about it later.' After laughing and saying goodbye she hang-up and came back to the table.

'Who was it?' Lana asked. 'Is she coming here?'

'No, no.' Nazah said. 'She's going to the theatre with her friends, but she's told her mother that she's visiting me.'

'And why is it okay to come and see you but not go to the theatre?'

'Who knows,' Nazah said. 'Maybe they think the theatre is dangerous, but a Kurdish woman is not?'

Lana knew about the subversive power of the arts. She remembered Tara and felt concern for the young woman.

'And what if her mother calls you?'

'I'll just say that she's in the bathroom, call and tell her to speak with her mother.'

Lana smiled, impressed by her friend's resourcefulness.

'You have to find a way around the system.' Nazah said. 'At least you can do that here.'

Yes, Lana thought, at least you can make the system work for you.

Nazah cleared the plates, dimmed the light, and lit the candles which were all over the room. Omar Dzayi sang about searching many cities and never finding anyone who was as beautiful as his beloved. The song ended with him remembering all their good times together and feeling "wounded, wounded!"

'I dreamt of Kawa last night, he had a long beard and looked heartbroken. I asked him what's wrong, but he wouldn't talk to me.'

'You feel guilty, and you think he's heartbroken,' Nazah said. 'This is about how you feel, it's not about how Kawa feels.'

'I shouldn't have got back in touch with Amer,' Lana said

with a quiet voice. 'I should have let the silence between us continue. Sometimes silence is the best option, the most peaceful relationship. I should've let him go.'

'You couldn't do that,' Nazah reminded her. 'You didn't want to be an old woman, sitting in a wheelchair, looking out from a window, and regretting not making that phone call.'

'I don't know what to do,' she said between her tears. 'I really don't.'

'You don't have to decide anything just yet!'

TWO WEEKS BEFORE THE WAR

CHAPTER TWENTY-FOUR

Hiwa

The anti-war campaigners were demonstrating in Europe, America, and the Muslim world. The Kurds were campaigning against Turkish intervention. Prime Minister Blair and President Bush were trying to prove the necessity of the war. They evoked images from the 1980s gas attacks to justify their position. The picture of the gassed Omari Khawar, who had clutched his baby boy and fallen facing down, flashed across the TV screens once again. He'd become the prime example of Saddam's cruelty.

The majority of civilians everywhere believed that Saddam Hussein imposed no threat to the West. What he did to the Kurds was considered old news. Most people didn't want the war. Everyone, including those who had slept through the previous wars and major political disasters elsewhere, even those who still didn't know where Iraq was on the map, were politicised. They all had strong views and for them things were black and white—the war was bad, it shouldn't be waged, and Iraq should be left alone.

A minority of people wanted the war and many of them were from the country itself. A larger group didn't know what to think and they were angry with everyone. They weren't represented in the dominant discourse, everyone wanted a 'Yes' or 'No' answer. The heated situation and debates reminded

Hiwa of the period before the civil war in 1994 which lasted for four years. He remembered feeling the same powerlessness and desperation when the war was imminent. His brother had written to him then. He remembered the letter very well. It captured the emotional tone of the time for him. He opened the folder, found the letter, and started reading it.

13/3/1994

My dear brother,

They're rolling out the carpets for this coming war. It's on our doorstep and after each pause, you can feel the heat of it coming, you can smell it. It smells like the butchers' alley in the bazaar. All those years of enmity and competition are leading to a disaster. Sometimes I think that we have no future, that it's just a long and hopeless anticipation. Maybe we've already lived our glorious futures. The revolution was a beautiful past which will not be followed by a beautiful future. When we were united in fighting a common enemy, everything made sense, but now when brothers are sharpening their knives to kill each other, what can you expect?

I was speaking to Ako yesterday, he too is pessimistic and is thinking about resigning. Probably the most honourable choice for a politician is to quit any party that engages in civil war. Families want to protect their sons from death, so they sell their homes, land, and jewellery to get their sons to the West. In the past, people got their boys out to protect them from the Ba'ath government, now they worry for them in the new era of Kurdish rule.

We're left with a mass of confused people who've lost the

conceptual difference between right and wrong, good and bad. It's heartbreaking to see the struggle end like this. I must warn you that I've become like *daya*, I cry often! I think of the young people who're leaving this ruin in search of a better life. I think of those who sacrificed their lives for this land. I think of Kawa who does not deserve this. I cry because I feel old, as when you live long enough to see the deaths of everyone and everything you loved, because at this moment, I can't see how things could get better.

What can we expect from the children who grow up without toys, games, and bedtime stories, who sell underwear, birth control pills, plastic bags, and water on the streets, and who worry where their next meal will come from? All those families who have no breadwinner and no compensation, no roof over their heads, if their children don't end up being cleaners, waiters, car-mechanics, and porters, how can they survive?

People ask me, why don't you leave? The truth is, it no longer matters to me if I'm here or there. Maybe I won't be hungry, and I'll have a warm home, but I won't be able to escape this circle. I know that twenty-seven years of being subjected to these uncertainties cannot be forgotten, there is no other place for me. I'm not playing the hero who doesn't want to leave no matter how difficult things are. The difference between me and the scared masses is that I've learnt not to mask my fear. I'm just a shadow who talks and criticises, as if he himself can do better. I'm witnessing the decay and collapse of what I hold dear.

Since *daya*'s death, the women in this house visit the graveyard regularly and try to comfort each other, but I cannot do anything to help any of them. They get on with their work and come home to cook and clean while I lock myself in the room or go out looking for familiar faces on the streets. My presence here is symbolic, I know, but I can't walk away from these women, I can't leave my students behind. I have no greed for anything better, so I will stay here, and I won't get married either. Now that mother is dead, this seems even less necessary. She was hoping I'd have children, but I don't want a pregnant wife in the next exodus, another dead baby in the rain. Our unfortunate mother! Three sons and two daughters and she never had a grandchild. Here death is so closely tied up with life and I don't want to add another widow to the world. Am I just making excuses for my meekness as I watch and cry for this place?

With much love!

Your brother,
Gara

CHAPTER TWENTY-FIVE

Gara

Some nights he felt hours of his life were slipping through his fingers into the darkness. The blackouts had become a permanent part of their lives, dating back to 1990. Everything had been rationed since: water, electricity, food, and sometimes Gara thought even love and rationality. There was shortage of all the good things, the basic things that made a community, a nation, a country. Most families had their own private generators that gave them a few extra amperes but with the coming war and the high oil prices it wasn't possible to use them every night, so he just waited his life out in the dark.

Little Kawa was falling asleep in his mother's lap as she told him a story. He couldn't help listening to the stories Aveen made up for him. She had been dissatisfied with her childhood stories where the boys did everything; they were courageous, they went out and changed the world, they fought with the beasts, and they won the wars, while the girls waited for a man to rescue them, love them, give them a purpose, make them happy.

In Aveen's stories both boys and girls were capable of being brave, they made decisions, they followed their dreams, and if they were good, they got what they wanted. Sometimes she modified an old story for her son. She told him about Rezan Khatoon, the little girl who went after the treasure her grandmother told her about. In the original story, Rezan Khatoon was warned by her grandmother, and all the creatures she met on her way, that she would never succeed because an evil monster guarded the treasure. She ignored all their warnings, pursued her dream, and found the treasure. At the end, however, she was enslaved by the male monster and her bravery ended in her demise. Unlike Gurnatalla, the little boy whose adventures and bravery —going to the mountains and beating the female monster— ended in becoming a hero. In both stories, Aveen explained to Gara once, the males win, both as humans and as monsters.

In her version of Rezan Khatoon, the young girl found the treasure, fooled the monster by telling him that she will marry him if he gives her the moon, sending him off to hunt the moon, and came home a grown and wise woman who used her money for doing the right thing. She became the ruler of her land by popular vote. She was fair, supportive of the poor, and a defender of the good. She was renamed Rezan the Fair.

'And when the time came,' Aveen told her son, 'she fell in love with the baker's son who made golden bread from brown flour. She loved him because despite his own poverty, he gave bread to the poor in the neighbourhood.'

Gara looked at his aunt and they both smiled about the reference to the baker's son.

'He was a kind young man who supported her. He knew about hardship, and he helped Rezan help people who were usually forgotten, who worked the hardest and got paid the least, who never had a full stomach, whose children worked because they couldn't afford to go to school. The baker's son became her first minister and together they built many schools for poor children and gave their families plenty of golden bread to eat.'

Kawa fell asleep as Aveen stroked his head. She then gently picked him up and said goodnight. Gara held his palms up to the Sopa heater and stared at the fire inside.

'Are you alright *basaqa*?' *pura* Sayran asked him. 'Are you worried about the war?'

'You can't not worry about it, can you?'

'No, you can't. But if you have to flee, you must leave without me.'

'We won't have to flee,' he said. 'No one will be left behind.'

'Do you think it will have a good outcome?'

'Iraq may fall apart,' he replied. 'Countries that are held together by force, where there is no natural affiliation between citizens, can disintegrate when the pressure is lifted. It may be a long and bloody process.'

She gently massaged the joints of her fingers.

'Do you still think of him?' he asked her out of the blue and she looked surprised for a few seconds before showing signs of recognition.

'Yes,' she told him. 'Not a day passes without—' And she seemed to immediately regret what she said, so she changed her tone.

'How can I not think of him?' she asked him. 'I had no one else to love. The men of my generation were either killed or fled the country.'

Gara wanted to put his arms around her but didn't.

'Aveen has you and Kawa,' she said.

Again, his brother Kawa was there, listening to this conversation, Gara felt.

'Are you unhappy? Is Aveen unhappy?' Sayran asked.

'I don't know,' he replied. 'What is happiness?'

'You're a beautiful and healthy young couple,' she told him. 'You have a lovely son and a roof over your heads. You love your job, you're not poor, you have lots of people who love you. What more is there?'

'You're right, what more?'

'You have to let Kawa go,' she told him.

'But he doesn't want to let go.'

'No,' she said while shaking her head. 'He wouldn't do that. This's about you, not him.'

Gara looked at his aunt who had lived with the memory of a man for twenty-five years. He looked at her greying temples, her prematurely dull brown eyes, her stooped back, and wondered if she had ever been loved. He remembered her when she was young, wearing little skirts and high heels. She had been petite and beautiful, straight backed with a tiny waist. After her mother's death and aged twenty-five, she chose to move in with Gara's family, rather than uncle Hassan's, to support them.

The least I can do for her, he thought, is to be happy, to provide her with a warm and loving place for all that she did for us, all that she's been through in her life.

Sayran had often told them how happy and anxious she was about starting work at eighteen. She was of a generation whose mothers repeatedly told them, 'don't touch your hair on the street,' 'don't smile,' 'don't look into men's eyes,' 'don't look around or point at anything,' because all of these could be misinterpreted by men who may feel encouraged to follow them, harass them, or try to court them. Gara remembered the way his young aunt walked the streets, frowning, and her gaze directed at the floor or the sky. To strangers she must've seemed arrogant and gloomy, but these were lesser crimes than accusations of 'asking for it,' and being 'easy.'

When Gara's grandfather passed away, his aunt took a job to support herself and her mother. She'd been the first in her family to work in an office, and she had no one to advise her about what to expect and how to behave. She ended up sharing a room with Jiyan *khan* and *kak* Ihsan, both of whom were a lot older. Their manager, *kak* Mistafa, whose office was next door to theirs, and who was eighteen years her senior, would become the love of her life.

According to custom, she wore mourning clothes for over a year after her father passed away. Black didn't suit her, it brought out the golden shade of her skin and made her look ill. She gradually started wearing blue, green, and sometimes purple. She became more confident at work, less reserved, and more cheerful. She'd once told Aveen that things changed between her and Mistafa during a picnic when he got drunk and sang his heart out. He nodded in her direction and told one of his friends, 'Look at her, she was a shy child a year ago, just look at her now.' Then he looked at her and said, 'How did you grow up so quickly?' But it was months of teasing before Sayran realised that Mistafa liked her. Once he picked up her cup of tea and turned it around, putting his lips on where her lipstick had stained the cup. She looked around fearing someone else may have seen it.

'Shall I make you tea?' she asked him.

'No,' he said. 'I just like yours.'

He started leaving messages in the documents and files that he passed on to her. 'Wear blue more often!' he wrote to her once. Another time when she was looking pale, he doodled a picture on a lined piece of paper, it was a little face with frizzy hair saying 'Akh!' She didn't know how to respond to him. He seemed to enjoy putting her in a difficult situation and waiting to see what she would do.

Sayran planned to tease him back. One morning she walked into his room when his back was to the door. His palms were flat on his desk, he was reading something and whistling. His spine was sticking out of his shirt, staring at her. She approached him quietly and ran her index finger over his spine, slow and gentle. He froze and stopped whistling while enduring her touch. She reached his waist and waited a second before moving her finger away and walking back out. Ten minutes later he came out and looked at her desperately. They weren't alone; it was his turn to suffer in silence.

Mistafa was shot in the chest with a silencer in the middle of the night. It had missed his heart, but he'd fallen out of bed and after some struggle, bled to death. In between her tears, his aunt would tell them how he hadn't made it to the phone, how the floor was covered in blood, and how slow and painful his death had been.

'If only somebody was with him,' she said, 'maybe he would've survived.'

She never saw his body, but his sisters sang in his *pirsa* about his cold figure and his purple lips as he lay in his own blood. They sang about his unfulfilled and childless life, his broken heart, his seriousness about everything.

A few months after his murder, Gara's grandmother started worrying that Sayran was still in black and asked Ahoo for help.

'She's not his widow,' the old woman said. 'We can't even take pride in her loyalty to him.' She then pleaded to Ahoo to speak with Sayran. 'Every time I try to speak to her, she cries and doesn't respond.' His grandmother thought this devotion to a man who wasn't even her daughter's fiancé was shameful and unjustified. People may think that she'd slept with him and even if this wasn't true, the whispers would ensure that her daughter would never marry.

'He's dead,' Sayran responded to Ahoo angrily. 'You can't worry about a dead man.'

Many years later, Sayran told Gara that Ahoo changed the way she behaved when she told her, 'But you don't have to exhibit grief. You can still quietly remember him and cry for him without letting the world know.'

Years passed before Sayran realised that Mistafa was, and would remain, the only man in her life. She wrote letters to him in her diary. She described the rain, told him the latest jokes, and complained about daily struggles. Once, when Gara asked her about the year when the four young men were publicly executed, his aunt opened her diary and told him not only the year, but also the details of how it had happened, she'd narrated it to Mistafa. They'd brought everyone from the government offices and shops nearby, telling them that there was an important event they needed to witness. The four young men were lined up by a mud brick wall. They were blindfolded and handcuffed. The people were forced to gather in a half circle and clap when they were shot. They had to sing praises to the leader while the thin, bleeding bodies fell like leaves: 'With our souls, with our blood, we serve you, O Saddam!'

Gara saw the many notebooks filled with letters to Mistafa. 'But why?' he'd asked her. 'Why did you write to him all these years?'

'I was lucky to have found love,' Sayran told him.

'Doesn't it bother you that he doesn't respond?' he'd asked.

'No,' she said. 'I feel alive for as long as I miss him.'

Gradually, as his aunt's health deteriorated, she stopped writing letters. But when she seemed absentminded, confused, or withdrawn, Gara knew that she was speaking to Mistafa, just as Aveen spoke to Kawa for many years.

Does she still talk to him? he wondered. Is Kawa hanging on because of this?

CHAPTER TWENTY-SIX

Lana

People were blocking each other, the old men and women who at first stood at the front, got tired and went to the back to squat. All morning, a group of young men and women were directing people from the station, giving them letters to sign and post to their MPs. Kurds from all the different parts, and residents of different UK cities had come to Downing Street to participate in the demonstration. Children had the flag painted on their foreheads and cheeks. Some young men were wearing the colours of the flag on their foreheads. Lana saw a glimpse of Khalid and wanted to go and say hello, but she was interrupted with every step and had to stop to talk to people. A man in a wheelchair who was at the front and had a big voice kept shouting, 'No Turkey, no Saddam, *Fedrali bo* Kurdistan.' Lana shook her head at the irony of rhyming Saddam with Kurdistan.

The noise was becoming a hum in Lana's ear. People's faces, the colours they wore, and their bodies became blurred objects that rubbed against her and prevented her progress. She felt as if she was dreaming or drunk. Someone screamed next to her but although Lana turned towards the noise, she couldn't see who it was. Drops of rain were falling on her face, further disorienting her. She kept thinking: If only I could get to the other side... if I could get through... I'll be okay.

She tried to move forward although she wasn't sure where she was trying to get to. Something moved her heavy body forward. She stopped for a second, wanting to sit down but there was no space. She was dizzy and the sharp perfumes were making her sick. She stumbled and nearly fell but a man held her up. A man whose face came close to hers, made space for her and asked, 'Are you okay?'

She thought she knew this man, she smiled at him, and moved into the space he'd cleared for her by the wall. He gave her a pat on the arm before turning away and disappearing. Lana lost sight of him, there were many men of similar height, in black coats just like his. She gave up looking, took a bottle of water out of her handbag, and Khalid came to say hello to her.

'How is Rozhin *khan*?' she asked.

'Good,' he said. 'She wanted to come but the baby is due in three weeks.'

'It's not safe for her,' Lana said, looking at the thousand plus crowd.

Khalid started talking to someone else. Lana wondered if he was angry with her, if he would question her about what he'd seen, but he wasn't betraying any signs. She looked through the crowd and thought everyone seemed to be talking to dozens of others at the same time.

How do they manage? she wondered.

Twana, who she'd been seeing more of in the committee meetings, came towards her: 'We were wondering where you disappeared to… a good crowd, isn't it?'

'Yes,' Lana replied, 'despite the short notice and despite Friday.'

Lana noticed him looking at her.

'Good job,' she said. 'Everyone must be pleased.'

'Yeah!' he replied while looking at the crowd thoughtfully. Then he turned around: 'What are you doing afterwards?'

'I think I'll go to bed, too tired.'

'Not coming with us for a drink? A short break?'

'I wish I was up to it,' she said and looked away.

Twana was good looking and over the past few weeks he'd tried to get close to her. She thought that if the world was better organised, she would be in love with him, and things would be simple.

If only, she thought, if only things could be less complicated.

Gradually she felt better and started moving through the crowd, she met people she hadn't seen for years. There were hugs and kisses, exchanging new mobile numbers. But all through her tour she searched for the man who held her up and patted her on the arm so kindly. Two young women who Lana had seen before approached her and she stopped to talk to them.

'We expect more from you Lana *khan*,' the younger one told her. 'You did nothing for Nigar.'

Lana's mouth opened in surprise. Nigar was the seventeen-year-old girl who was stabbed to death by her father because she had a boyfriend. Since living in London, Lana had regularly spoken and written about patriarchal violence, worked on campaigns that connected diaspora activists to those at home, and organised events and conferences. It seemed to her that her community was divided into those who acted and those whose vocation was to criticise those who acted. She felt angry, exhausted, and fed up with these expectations.

'Something should be done about all of this,' the other young woman told her.

'Why don't you do something then?' Lana asked them. 'Why do you always expect others to do it for you? You are both young, you obviously care, you have the energy for it.'

'You're a writer,' the younger woman said. 'You can write something, we can't.'

'I already do it but you don't even read what I write,' Lana replied impatiently, 'and if you are so angry you should start something and maybe I can support you.'

She walked away from the two of them full of rage. She knew they'd become her enemies now and would probably badmouth her for a long time. Having spent the last weeks working so hard, she was fed up with their lazy expectations.

You must be everything, she thought, and nothing that you do is ever enough.

The day ended sooner than planned. The rain was pouring and two young men climbed one of the statues on the pavement, trying to put a Kurdish flag on it. The police weren't pleased, and people were getting restless. As the rain was beating down, the crowd dispersed. Lana went to the station alone. She put her head down and walked fast, hoping that no one would stop or accompany her. When she got through the barrier of the underground station she saw him again, the man she'd liked so much. He was accompanied by a woman and two little girls. Earlier, she hadn't noticed that he was bald. She stood in a corner pretending to search for something inside her bag as she kept an eye on him. He was squatting, fixing his younger daughter's shoelaces. His wife was pretty and pregnant. He looked happy. Soon they had gone down the escalator without noticing her.

She felt sad. There was something about him which made her sad. She slowly walked down to the platform, got on the train, found a seat, and looked at the person opposite her without seeing him. Suddenly, her heart clenched, her throat tensed up. Her eyes remembered him before she did, tears clouded her vision. It was him, that man from all those years ago, that beautiful man who seemed much taller than he is now. The one who gave her the precious sweets each time they met him in an alley. It was Azad, the man Tara loved, the one who delivered the last blow.

Although summer was ending, the steady heat parched the land, dried the leaves, and kept people in their prolonged siestas. The curtains were all drawn, and people slept in the cooler rooms in the back of the mud brick houses. Lana watched her sister keep an eye on Hiwa, praying that he would wake up and go back to work. Then she convinced her mother that she needed to pick up a book from a friend's house. She took Lana with her, as a guarantee for her mother that nothing dodgy was going on.

Lana was aware of the detailed planning that went into each of these outings. She was happy to follow Tara and to keep a secret. It made her feel grown up and important. Although her sister had asked her only once, her instinct told her that she must keep quiet about the young man they met each time. Tara thought she was too young to understand but being a quiet child, she knew more than others assumed. She still whispered to her dolls and fell asleep in boxes and cupboards, and her presence was largely ignored. She also became Tara's messenger a few times. She took letters back and forth between them. She kept this secret for years, even from herself. She'd forgotten about it until a year earlier, when she was reading a novel, and it came flooding back.

She liked the young man whom they secretly met that summer, he was kind to her and gave her chocolate and ice cream. She liked his clean looking face and dark forelock that rolled backwards above his big forehead. He had light brown eyes and a thin nose that fitted his face perfectly. She liked the way he would lean forward a little to say hello to her, as if trying to reach her height. The three of them sometimes walked in the late afternoon heat, choosing remote roads in areas where no one knew them. Other times they just stood in the shade for a few minutes, when Tara and the young man talked quietly and exchanged sighs.

Lana stood beside them, munching away at her chocolate or ice cream, and quietly following their whispers. They talked about missing each other, about not living the moments they were apart, they talked about getting married, but how? She was seventeen and he was eighteen. He was supposed to go to university, his family thought he was too young to get married, none of his older brothers were married yet. Together they went through these scenarios, and they found no way out. They just had to wait, wait until they both went to university and could meet away from home.

But Tara was under pressure, Hiwa was strict, and her mother was suspicious. She was giving up on being able to choose, on being able to act. Azad promised that he would look after her and help her to follow her passion and fulfil her dream. Tara talked about her misery in those narrow roads, about having enough of being watched by everyone, being restricted by everything, being perceived as a threat, as a bomb that would go off at any moment. She told him how her mother began restricting her from the age of eleven and she couldn't stand it any longer. Each time she made an excuse and came out to meet him, she was terrified that someone would see them together, that someone would tell her family, and it would all get worse.

One rainy October afternoon, Azad picked them up in a car and took them to a house to which he had the key. Lana was given fascinating toys to play with, toys she couldn't dream of having herself, tall blond dolls that had a change of clothes and cupboards and chairs. She was also presented with a quick snapshot of a Disney video which delighted her. They didn't have a video player at home and although Lana wasn't able to watch the film to the end, she ended up imagining different endings for it. Many nights she was awake in bed, thinking of how the prince could wake the beautiful princess and marry her.

During this brief time when she was glued to the TV, absorbed by the film, she was partially aware of the absence of her sister and the young man. She knew, in a way that only children can know, that some sort of bodily thing was going on, not being able to imagine what it really was. She was happy being left alone in a room full of everything she ever wanted: expensive toys, biscuits, and cartoons.

She never knew where that big house was with its huge garden, which neighbourhood, what road. Golden cushions were neatly arranged on the light turquoise sofas; a large crystal chandelier was hanging from the high ceiling; a glass vase full of fresh flowers was placed on the wooden coffee table. As a grown up, she understood that Azad's family would've never agreed to his marrying a dead baker's daughter, even if she was as beautiful as a mermaid.

She always remembered Tara the way she looked in those last months, her straight dark hair reaching her waist and shinning when she bent her head, looked away, or turned around. There were always strands of silky hair falling on her face and she would pull them back gently, bending her lovely head. Her lips were ruby, she had an oval shaped face and a small nose. Tara wasn't tall though Lana thought she was. There was nothing in the world that she wanted more than growing up to become like her sister, so beautiful, so talented, so much in love.

The happiness that Tara experienced, and Lana experienced second hand, lasted for a few months. On a cold December day, the spell was broken. It was an unusual stint of dry cold, a cold that went through chunky soles, layers of clothing, and thick hair. It penetrated bones, making them brittle. The slightest bang on hand or foot became a lightning of pain, heading straight to the heart. The wind starting from Goyzha mountain and heading to the centre of the city added to people's sense of fragility. Faces were numb, breathing was difficult, and only by watching others, would people suspect that their own nose was streaming. Eyes were burning, glazed in a warmth that felt like an illness. The frost carried on for two days and on the third morning people woke up to white roads and houses. The snow had started in the night, falling silently, landing on the frosted grass, trees, roads.

Lana had spent the day in bed, consumed by fever. That morning when Tara drew the curtains and shouted in excitement, she opened her eyes for a few seconds, wished she could get up to see the snow, and then closed her eyes again. Somebody had said, 'The cold spell will break.'

She was feeling weak, one side of her face was swollen, and she slipped in and out of strange experiences. The next time she woke up no one was in the room, and she started crying. It felt as if someone was strangling her, her throat was painfully swollen. She tried to scream for help and only managed a weak moan. Her mother rushed in with a mug of water.

'Take me to the kitchen,' she whispered, knowing that she would be close to her mother there. Ahoo disappeared again and Lana closed her eyes, too weak to feel angry at being abandoned. She was nearly asleep when her mother's hands went under her body. '*Bismil-lah*', her mother whispered, 'in the name of God,' and picked her up with care. She was taken to the kitchen, wrapped in her moist blanket, and was laid on a small bed in the top left corner of the kitchen, near the *aladdin* heater. Her mother checked on her regularly.

Lana woke up when her mother's cold palm rested on her forehead, she opened her eyes and saw her mother blowing prayers all around her. Once she opened her eyes and saw her mother's body topped by a goat's head. She made a weak noise and started weeping. '*Bismil-lah al-rahman al-rahim*' her mother's voice started, she recognised the sura from the Quran, she'd just learnt to recite it herself. The next cool palm was Tara's who shouted, 'Take this heater away, her temperature is too high.' And then came a freezing wet cloth on her forehead. She started shivering again but Tara's hand prevented her from moving the cloth. The pressure cooker was echoing in her head. She felt her head was getting squashed by a large stone. When Kawa and

Gara came home, they brought the smell of snow with them, and this made her shiver. She had no appetite, but Tara raised her head with a few pillows and started feeding her a diluted soup.

'She doesn't want to eat', Tara said.

'She has to,' *daya* said. 'She's not eaten since yesterday.'

Lana started weeping again but Tara said gently, 'Just eat a little so you can have your pills.' Lana managed to swallow a few spoons with difficulty. Kawa bent over her and said something. She looked up and saw that Tara and Kawa were whispering. Gara was standing above their heads. She took her medication and closed her eyes again. She heard Kawa say, 'Maybe we should take her to the hospital.' Her mother said something in reply. Tara's shadow was still landing over her, blocking the white light from the opposite window which hurt her eyes. The shadow suddenly lifted, and she opened her eyes to see her father looking anxious.

He came forward, bent over Lana and whispered into her ear: 'Look after your sister.'

'How?' she asked.

Her father got up and the light hit her eyes again.

'Don't leave her alone,' her father said, and walked away.

Lana started crying. Some argument started at the bottom left corner of the kitchen, by the door to the courtyard. Somebody had come in; somebody was making a fuss about something. She lifted her head and saw Uncle Hassan standing with his shoes on, the door was open behind him, letting in a breeze which made her shiver once more. She moved her head in his direction to hear him better.

He said something like, 'I knew it, I knew this would happen—'

Her mother looked shocked, her hand was covering her mouth, her white scarf was nearly falling off her head. Kawa came into the corner, trying to say something to his uncle.

'You shut up,' he shouted at Kawa, 'Hiwa needs to deal with this, otherwise I will—'

She could see Kawa's back and didn't hear what he said, but it managed to make Uncle Hassan furious. He started taking God as his witness, saying some things which sounded threatening and turned away to leave. Lana closed her eyes; she could hear Tara crying but couldn't see her. She lifted her head from the pillow but all she could see was blinding white light and all she could hear was Tara sobbing. She closed her eyes again and her father whispered once more, 'Help your sister'.

'She doesn't regret it,' Hiwa addressed his crying mother. 'She never admits her mistakes.' He then turned towards Tara: 'Since father died, everyone was scared of this, but I thought you had more sense than that. I thought you cared about everyone enough not to do such a thing.'

'I've done nothing wrong,' Tara shot back at him in a firm voice.

'Nothing wrong? What is wrong enough for you?'

'I love him,' she said, 'and you can't prevent me from loving him.'

'Does he love you?'

'Yes.'

'Then why doesn't he propose to you? Why don't you marry him and leave? Everyone will be happy.'

Now Tara was quiet.

'He won't propose, will he?' Hiwa said. 'We're not good enough for his family, are we? Is this the man you love, a man who wants you as his girlfriend but not as his wife?'

'Can't you see what you're doing?' *daya* asked. 'You'll dishonour us... you'll lower our head before people... you'll—'

'He'll lose interest in you, Tara,' Hiwa interrupted his mother. 'You're just another pretty girl from a poor family.... and he'll meet many.'

Daya sat down, rocked her body, and started to whisper to God.

Lana raised her head and looked at her sister who refused to speak.

'You can't see him again!' Hiwa said in a calm voice and Tara finally looked at him.

'You can't prevent me,' she said.

'Yes, I can... and you won't see him again. If you do, you won't be allowed to leave this house again until you get married.... not even to go to school.'

'I think you're all over-reacting... Tara won't see him again; she's just saying that because she is angry,' Kawa tried to intervene, but Hiwa cut him short: 'You shut up!' Then turned back towards Tara. 'I'm warning you,' he said, 'be careful.'

'For the sake of your father's grave, don't shame him,' their mother cried out. 'Don't give people an excuse to laugh at us.'

Suddenly Tara addressed Hiwa in the sharp, daring voice which was typical of her when she was angry. 'You're just jealous,' she said.

Her remark made him angry. 'Jealous of what?' he was now shouting. 'You are my sister.'

207

'You're jealous that someone loves me... because no one loves you.'

'Shut up,' their mother said. 'He's your older brother, don't talk to him like that.'

Hiwa had taken two big strides towards her, staring into her eyes. Tara stared up at him, as if she was daring him. Their mother stopped crying, but she didn't intervene. Lana whined standing up. Holding on to the wall, she wanted to walk to her sister, but she was too weak.

'Don't get up,' Tara said, helping her back into bed. Hiwa's fist had relaxed now but Tara looked up at him, she wasn't going to make Lana an excuse to hide away from him. Hiwa walked back to the door and talked in a firm voice without sounding angry or emotional.

'I won't repeat it again, it's your choice.' He walked away, his footsteps echoing in the house, the floor conveying the vibrations.

Tara defied everyone. She saw the young man again, not knowing her uncle had sent someone to follow her. Then one day Hiwa came in and without arguing with her he stated that she could no longer go to school because she'd broken the agreement. For the first week Tara fought with her mother every morning but still went to school. She got there late, after arguing and being pursued by her mother. Once, unknown to her, her uncle was waiting for her on the road. The moment she walked out of the house he grabbed her by the hair and pulled her back into the house. Some neighbours saw her, and she was humiliated. After that she stayed at home.

Lana watched Tara clean and tidy up in silence, scrubbing

the carpets, walls, and windows every morning. She didn't look up at anyone, and, despite her mother's pleading, she didn't eat with the family. Some days she refused to eat altogether; other times Kawa took food to her room where she spent most of her time. Lana went to her regularly and one day she drew a picture of a mermaid swimming towards the image of the moon.

'This is for you,' she said to her sister.

Tara hugged her and wept, struggling to breathe at times. She managed to go out twice after shouting and arguing with her mother but had come home crying. Lana thought that she was trying to meet Azad and failing. In the afternoons, when everyone else slept, Lana would walk into the room and see Tara staring out the window without movement. She only spoke with Kawa and sometimes while fixing Lana's hair, she would mutter something. No one else heard a word from her that winter. Lana got close to her sister at times, putting her arms around her neck or hugging her from behind. She responded to these hugs with a brief smile, a smile that reminded Lana of the summer breeze, too short and light to make a difference to the heat.

That afternoon when Hiwa walked in with Azad, she was drawing next to Tara, who paid no attention to Hiwa and his guests. Lana heard her brother usher his guest through, so she went to find out who it was, and nearly screamed from joy when she saw him. 'It is him,' she wanted to shout. He patted her head as he passed her by, following Hiwa into the sitting room. Ahoo welcomed the guest without knowing who he was, and Lana ran to tell her sister. Tara rushed into the room, not believing what she heard. He was unshaven, wearing a black jumper with his blue jeans. He sat across the room from Hiwa. Lana and Tara walked into the sitting room as their mother was giving Azad a cup of tea. Tara started weeping then, as if that was all she ever wanted: having him in the house and her mother serving him tea on a cold afternoon. He got up when he saw her, and her mother looked at him.

'This is Azad,' Hiwa said to his mother without moving. 'He came to see me at work, he wants to talk to us.'

Tara kept on weeping, one hand on her mouth. Her mother kept staring at the man her daughter loved.

'Come and sit down *daya*,' Hiwa told her. 'Come Tara.'

Ahoo did as she was told but Tara stood for a bit longer looking at Azad who stood, looking back at her. Lana quietly sat at the bottom corner, close to her sister, in fear of being asked to leave the room. Fortunately, no one thought of excluding her from this negotiation and she was able to observe it all, leaning into the corner and keeping still.

Tara was sitting down now at the bottom of the room, neither next to her family nor next to him. She was drying her tears when Hiwa spoke.

'Okay, we're all here.' He said as he looked at Azad expectantly.

Azad cleared his throat for a second and looked lost for words.

'I first want to say… I'm sorry if I've caused you problems,' he said as he steered his gaze towards Ahoo. 'I love Tara and I never wanted her to suffer because of me.'

Ahoo looked angry now, but Hiwa looked at his mother, urging her not to say anything.

'I've come to ask for her hand. I want to marry her, and I am happy to do whatever you require of me.'

Ahoo looked at Tara who was still looking at him and crying, ignoring her mother and brother. Lana saw pity in her mother's eyes, as if she felt sorry for her daughter, as if Tara was deluded or unwell.

Hiwa lit a cigarette and looked at Azad. There was a bit of silence before Ahoo spoke.

'Good man, you say that you love my daughter, and you want to marry her. She wants to marry you too.' Ahoo paused and looked at her daughter who didn't seem to be listening. 'You've created a problem for this family. Maybe no one will marry my daughter now because of all the rumours.'

Hiwa kept inhaling the smoke and looking down at his ashtray as Azad listened to Ahoo and nodded to what she said.

'Still,' Ahoo went on, 'I would be happy for you to marry her but what about your family? Would they be happy for you?'

Azad bit his lips. It seemed that he both expected but also dreaded this question. 'No,' he said as he shook his head sadly.

Lana looked at Tara who was smiling now, maybe because of what they were talking about or because she was happy to see Azad.

'How old are you, my son?' Ahoo asked, sounding sad when hearing what she already knew.

'I'm eighteen, turning nineteen in four months,' he said seriously.

Ahoo's face blushed, as it usually did before she cried, but this time she didn't cry.

'So how will the two of you live? I don't think you've ever worked in your life.' She looked at his clean white hands. 'How will you support the two of you? Where will you live?'

211

Tara looked happy. Nothing else seemed to interest her, not how they were discussing her future and how her beloved was struggling.

'I'll get a job,' he said keenly looking at Ahoo and then Hiwa. 'We can get engaged and I'll start looking for a job.' His voice dropped as he went on as if he himself was thinking about how difficult that would be. Hiwa was stubbing his cigarette now, exhaling smoke.

'What kind of job can you do?' Ahoo pressed on. 'What about going to university? Will your family be happy for you to work?'

'No, they won't be,' he said more energetically, 'but I'll do it anyway.'

Ahoo looked at Tara one more time and saw that melancholic happy smile as if she was listening to music or watching young children play. She turned towards her son who looked at her with raised eyebrows, at a loss to say anything. Azad was waiting expectantly, almost not breathing. He wasn't even looking at Tara anymore, just staring at Hiwa and Ahoo as if his life depended on them.

'Why don't you start looking for a job now?' Hiwa finally said to him. 'Once you're settled in your job, I think *daya* won't object to your marriage. We just need to see that you can do it.'

Tara looked at her brother sharply as if telling him he had no right to set conditions. She kept his gaze for a few seconds before she looked away from all of them, taking in a deep breath.

'I will,' Azad said enthusiastically. 'I'll be back very soon.'

He got up and went to Tara without looking at Hiwa and

Ahoo. She stood up to face him. 'You came!' she whispered.

'I'll be back,' he said to her. 'I'll come and see you very soon.'

Lana's journey back from the demonstration was painful. Her body was invaded by the past. She was ten years old when Tara killed herself. It was an ordinary spring day. The weather was cool, and the mountains were light green. It had rained in the morning and the fresh air was full of the season's assurances. Tara seemed to be recovering from the initial shock of finding out that Azad had abandoned her. She'd spent the first week in bed having no will to get up, no will to open her eyes, to eat or talk. Hiwa went to see her twice, but she never lifted her eyes to look at him. Kawa and Gara put together a little play for their sister, a funny play about twin brothers who mirrored each other in their movements. It brought a weak smile to Tara's face.

Despite her mother's encouragement, Tara refused to return to school after recovering. She resigned to staying at home. No one knew that while spending long hours wiping the old, stained walls, hand-washing the curtains, the sheets, pillows, and mattresses, and moving furniture around to make more space, she was preparing the house for her own wake, for the consolers who would soon flood the place. She knew that everyone was watching her as if she was mad and tried to show them that she was fine. Gradually, everyone thought that things were back to normal until that afternoon when she put out fresh clothes and went to have a wash. Lana was playing with her doll. She hoped that her sister would offer to wash her hair like she used to, but Tara didn't. No one realised that she'd taken a bottle of Kerosene into the bathroom with her.

The first scream made Lana jump and drop her doll. She ran towards her screaming sister and was the first to get to the bathroom. The door was locked, and Lana started banging and shrieking. Her sister's excruciating voice terrified her. She could smell the burning skin and hair. Her mother arrived, screaming, and tried to open the door, but she didn't manage. Her brothers weren't in the house.

Ahoo pushed Lana towards the door and shouted, 'Tell *kak* Ahmed to come and help us.'

Lana ran to the neighbours, but *kak* Ahmed wasn't home. She knocked on several doors, crying and talking hysterically before she found a man. All the women and children were already in their house, each trying their hand at unlocking the door. Lana kept thinking that she hadn't listened to her father's advice, she'd left her sister alone, she hadn't saved her. By the time the door was broken down Tara was beyond rescue. The way she looked when *kak* Muhammad wrapped a blanket around her was something that Lana dreamt about for years. The raw flesh, the burnt blood, the bleeding bald head, the blackened face and skin, the way her dress stuck to her body, melted on her skin, and wouldn't part from it.

Lana arrived at the tube station, dragged herself to her flat, and fell onto the untidy bed. She had stomach cramps and a cold sweat was dripping down her spine. As she retched, she remembered her sister secretly giving her money to buy tamarind in the last few weeks of her life. She wondered if Tara had continued seeing Azad after that visit when she accompanied her to that house.

Was she pregnant when he abandoned her, Lana thought. Did he know that she was? Is that why she had to kill herself?

Lana couldn't move. She was certain that she would die but couldn't call anyone, she didn't want to. She completely understood her sister's resignation to die. Sometimes the burden of living from one moment to the next was too much. Sometimes she couldn't be bothered to live, to endure the hours. Like her sister, she felt ready to die, to let all of it go, to rest in peace, and leave the struggle to someone else.

Two hours later when Amer let himself in after failing to contact her by phone, he found her on the edge of the bed. Her right arm was dangling, her left cheek was resting on the edge, and she'd thrown up, making a mess on the floor. She opened her eyes and saw panic on his face. He called an ambulance, cleaned her up, and embraced her from behind while rubbing her arms. He tried to talk to her, to bring her back from the dead.

'We'll move to the Highlands,' he reminded her of their dream to live up there, 'We'll fly to Inverness and buy a cottage near a forest or a lake. We'll have more time together, more time to just sit in silence.'

Amer's voice was shaky. 'It'll all be okay,' he told her. 'We'll go for long walks, we'll write, we'll have children. We deserve to be happy, *habibti*. We will be happy.'

CHAPTER TWENTY-SEVEN

Hiwa

Shilana tried to force a Barbie on Dilan who put his hands behind his back and shook his head. She dropped it on his lap and started undressing the other Barbie, hoping he would join in. Dilan pushed the doll away and poured the Lego pieces out of their plastic bag. They were playing alongside each other now: she dressing the doll and he building a house.

How early children learn about which toys are appropriate for girls and which for boys, Hiwa thought.

He was glad that his own daughter wasn't restricted; she had access to dolls as well as cars, dresses as well as trousers. Hiwa knew that Khalid, who valued tradition and norms, would be pleased that his son was interested in 'the right things.' Backing his daughter and wanting to show Dilan a different example, Hiwa picked up a Barbie and started combing its hair. Dilan laughed, as if saying that it was inappropriate for a man to play with a doll.

The TV was trying to communicate progress. An Arab intellectual was debating with an English politician. Hiwa wasn't listening anymore. He left his friend's side and started making tea in the kitchen. Everyone was full of *kifta* and they were waiting for tea. Khalid seemed to be still preoccupied with the young men he had met in Hull. He'd told

Hiwa that they reminded him of the warm-blooded young men alongside whom he fought years ago when he was a *peshmarga*. All that passion, he stressed, if only it could be utilised well.

There were plenty of clattering noises from the kitchen, water was running, and the kettle was boiling. The women were washing up and putting things away. He brought the tea tray in, gave Khalid his tea, and sat down next to him.

'Waste of time,' Khalid said, flicking his head at the TV.

'Yes,' Hiwa said while sipping his tea. 'They could spend their energy on how to do it well instead.'

Sozi stood in the door and looked at the TV for a second.

'There is no doing a war well,' she said. 'You can't control things; it'll be a mess.'

'They could try to make it less messy.'

Sozi shrugged: 'Not when America is involved.'

'Look at these communists,' Hiwa said, nudging Khalid. 'They're left behind in time.'

'Nothing to do with communism,' Sozi said. 'Just common sense.'

Sozi walked back to the kitchen irritated. Her father had been a member of the Iraqi Communist Party and he believed in the ideas long after his disillusionment with party politics. Sozi had grown up thinking everyone understood that the best outcome was when everyone did well and when there were no major disparities of wealth. She'd told Hiwa that growing up consisted of one disappointment after another when she realised that the world was 'dominated by greedy and selfish people who were obstinate about simple facts.'

217

From where he sat, Hiwa saw how Rozhin looked over her shoulder at Sozi. He knew that she'd noticed the change. Sozi was talking as usual, but something was different. She was less easy going, less tolerant with him.

'What is it?' Rozhin asked. 'Is something wrong?'

'Nothing,' Sozi said, 'Hiwa doesn't know when to stop teasing sometimes.'

Rozhin said something which he couldn't hear, and she finished washing up. In his mind, he saw the plates standing on their sides, the cups and glasses turned upside down as drops of water trickled down them.

'You really shouldn't have washed up,' Sozi told Rozhin. 'It was Hiwa's turn.'

'I heard that!' he said. 'I tried to, but she wouldn't let me.'

Rozhin laughed. 'You know me, I don't like sitting down with this big bump. It makes me sleepy.'

The two of them walked back into the sitting room where the men had taken over the sofa. Hiwa recognised the look Sozi gave him. She'd often expressed her annoyance with the way men occupied too much space without thinking of women and children.

'Can you move up a little please?' Sozi said as she touched his shoulder.

He quickly moved up to make room for Rozhin. Sozi put the cake on the coffee table. Shilana came forward for her slice as Dilan watched shyly.

'Come on,' Sozi beckoned him, 'have some cake.'

He came and sat by his mother's side, she still helped him eat.

'How was Hull?' Sozi asked Khalid as she turned the

volume down.

'A mess,' he replied. 'I tried to talk some sense into them, but it didn't work.'

'How did it start?' she asked.

'A group of drunken locals attacked a bunch of Kurdish guys on Saturday night. Two days later, Kurds from around Hull came to help their friends. It was a massive knife-fight. Dozens were arrested on both sides.'

He swallowed a piece of cake, then continued, 'I told Hemin and his friends that they should stop acting like a tribe. But they think the tribe protects them.'

'The tribe,' Hiwa said. 'The avenging, self-destructive tribe in this day and age.'

'Just because you've moved on,' Sozi argued, 'it doesn't mean that the nation has.'

'I know,' Hiwa said in a more sombre voice. 'Sometimes anything to do with the Kurds is heart-breaking.'

'Sometimes you just don't want to know,' Rozhin said as she fed her son another mouthful of cake. 'Sometimes it's all just bad news.'

'You can't hide from it,' Khalid said looking at his piece of cake without enthusiasm. 'I always want to know.'

'So did your visit do any good?' Hiwa asked.

'I don't know. I met a Kurdish caseworker who was optimistic. He said that once they realise that things are different here and that not everyone hates them, they'll calm down.'

'Do they think everyone hates them?' Sozi wondered.

'Yes, at least the young men I met believed that. Apparently, people aren't friendly.'

'It's as expected,' Hiwa said. 'This immigration thing is new up there.'

'Yes, and most of the new arrivals are young men who hang around in groups. They must look frightening,' Khalid explained.

'And they themselves are scared,' Rozhin pointed out.

'Many will be deported when the war ends,' Khalid said.

'The war again,' Sozi said as she wiped Shilana's mouth with a wet tissue.

'Khalid had a go at an anti-war campaigner the other day,' Rozhin said, while fanning herself with the handkerchief.

'Well, we were getting home in the rain,' Khalid said. 'We'd done some shopping, I was happy, and then out of the blue, just round the corner from our home, this guy shoved a leaflet into my hand.'

'You didn't beat him up, did you?' Hiwa said in a mischievous voice.

'No, but I wanted to,' Khalid laughed. 'What has awakened all these people, you think? I asked him how come they now care about Iraqi people? How come they didn't demonstrate when he was killing us?'

'And what did he say?' Hiwa asked.

'He said, "even if what you say is true, that's no excuse for keeping quiet again this time." Imagine, he told me, "even if what I say is true," he wasn't sure.'

'We were outside our door when he read the leaflet,' Rozhin said, 'and he walked all the way back to talk to the young man. I waited for ages and then I walked back to get him.'

'Perfect timing!' Khalid said sarcastically. 'I'd just told the guy that Saddam Hussain shot down my wife and four children in a mass grave and there Rozhin came with a bump, holding Dilan's hand.'

They all laughed.

'At least you told him what you felt,' Hiwa said.

'Yes, but he couldn't care less about what I told him, and I was angry for days after seeing him. Can you turn that up please?'

There was another debate about whether Turkish troops would enter Iraqi Kurdistan in return for providing access to American troops. Sozi went to wash her daughter's mouth at the sink. Hiwa knew that she was tired of listening to the news. Maybe she was tired of him, pretending that everything was okay. The evening before she'd told him that he smelt different. He didn't smell of Sarah, he was sure, but maybe he smelt of his stirred up emotions. He was convinced that women could smell love, whether a man had fallen in love with them or another woman, they could feel it. Sometimes Hiwa caught himself walking around the house with a smile. He knew that his wife had noticed and was looking for an opportunity to talk to him. She returned to the room and sat next to Rozhin.

Rozhin was looking at a framed picture of Hiwa and Sozi on the half empty bookshelf opposite them. Hiwa was standing behind Sozi in the picture. She was covering his left shoulder and her right arm was raised, touching his neck, as she looked into the camera and laughed. Hiwa's lips were kissing her head, he'd lowered his eyes. His long fingers were holding on to her bare shoulders. Her eyes were at the centre of the photograph. She was wearing a turquoise dress and large red earrings dangled from her ears. It was a perfect moment, they looked young, strong, and very much in love. The photo reminded Hiwa of Rozhin and Khalid's wedding day, where they had met. His mother was right, happiness could be contagious, creating more happiness.

'That's beautiful,' Rozhin told Sozi quietly, trying not to disturb the men. 'When did you get that framed?'

'Years ago,' Hiwa said. 'I found the photo recently; we'd forgotten all about it.'

'Can you believe that?' he said to Sozi. 'It was four years ago.'

Sozi looked at the picture and turned the wedding ring around on her finger.

'Everything was beautiful and clear like glass!' he imagined Sozi thinking, 'how fragile it all is!'

The good thing about lunch invitations, he thought, was that when the guests left, there was still time left in the day. It was eight pm and Sozi took Shilana to bed. While washing the last round of dishes Hiwa remembered Khalid's wedding five years ago. It took place in the Kurdish Cultural Centre on a cold Saturday in October. The rectangular tables were laid around the edges of the hall to leave enough space for dancing in the middle. The metal chairs with red cushions were arranged around the tables. The place was decorated with golden balloons and red tablecloths. There were no flowers on the tables but there was plenty of food. The band played enthusiastically despite being occasionally out of tune and people danced to digest the *dolma*, stuffed lambs, and *kubba*. Rozhin was glowing, with glinting black eyes and ruby lips. She wore a long ivory dress, and a pearl crown encompassed her gathered black hair. Halfway through the party she changed into red Kurdish clothes and let her hair down.

Hiwa disliked parties but he dragged himself up there for

Khalid's sake. When he got there, he thought just seeing his friend happy, after ten years of grieving for his lost family, was worth the hassle of putting up with a noisy crowd full of gossipers. He found some old friends and acquaintances to sit with and noticed Sozi soon after arriving. He later found out that she'd come to the UK to visit her sister in 1990 but when Iraq invaded Kuwait and the gulf war began, she became a refugee. Two years before coming to London she'd completed her degree in Economics and Administration and was working in an office. Her baccalaureate grades weren't high enough to study Arabic literature which was her passion.

In London, she'd completed several training and vocational courses and ended up working in a computer company, this was something she shared with him. There were many parallels between their lives: places they'd lived, and friends they had in common. Yet despite living in the same city for eight years as members of a small immigrant community, they'd never met. This may have been because they'd both lived on the fringe of the community then.

When he first told Lana about Sozi, he said, 'She doesn't put up with bullshit.'

'So she'll put you straight,' Lana teased him. 'You won't get away with things.'

'Yes,' he'd said. 'She stood up to her controlling brother-in-law and lived alone a year after she arrived.'

'I already like her,' Lana said.

It was tough for a young Kurdish woman to live alone in 1992. Sozi's sister didn't talk to her for a few years and the community sided with her sister. Moving out was against all traditions of staying at home until one gets married. It also made it possible for her, they whispered, to become sexually active. To avoid gossip and confrontation, she decided not to mingle with Kurdish people. She hired a studio in Kilburn, worked at a company in Baker Street for a while, went to the gym twice a week, and kept herself busy.

Hiwa heard the bedroom door open, but Shilana started crying, forcing her mother to go back inside. Putting her to bed was his least favourite part of being a parent. Shilana made them stay until she was fully asleep. He smiled in sympathy with his wife and started cleaning the greasy cooker. He knew that it worked between Sozi and him because they'd met at a good time, when they were both ready to start a Kurdish family. They missed the affectionate words in their mother tongue, the words of love and passion, the generosity, the sense of humour and community.

That day, for Rozhin's party, Sozi had put on a green fringe dress with golden beads. The dress was three quarter length and fitted perfectly around her thin waist and broad shoulders, it also showed part of her plump lower legs. She wore a cherry-red flower in her hair and had painted her lips the same colour. To him she stood out from everyone else; there were some young pretty girls, but she was different. She was warm but not overwhelming, beautiful but not full of herself, elegant but not over the top, youthful but not too young. Her dress, her short straight hair, and her dark lipstick made her look like a woman from the 1920s and he loved that look.

Hiwa didn't dance at parties but when Khalid came and asked him to join in, he went straight to Sozi and introduced himself.

The semi-circle of people holding hands and dancing was getting larger and larger, curling inside itself twice. Sozi smelt of spring, her skin and hair were fresh. She had long dark eyelashes, large brown eyes, and a clever looking round nose.

They exchanged a few words, but the music was too loud to attempt a conversation. A young man who danced energetically stepped on Sozi's foot and she let out a little scream. Hiwa whispered in her ear, 'Shall I beat him up?' He gave her a wink and she laughed. He danced next to her until the music stopped and he felt full of energy and joy.

After the dancing, he picked up his beer, left his own table, where he was sitting with a family, and joined hers. He pulled the chair slightly away, trying not to make this too vulgar for the community. They talked about where they lived, what they did, and how long they had lived in London but avoided talking about family. Later, when she trusted him, Sozi told him about her father's gambling and how her mother learnt many techniques to get some money from him before he lost it all. Her mother continued to love him even when her two daughters grew up to dislike their father. For many years Sozi and her sister were embarrassed by their father who came home in the middle of the night, a drunken loser who sang badly and woke the neighbours. But their mother never gave him up.

'"You will understand when you are older," she told us. "He really is a good man."' Sozi said. 'The only thing we understood was that despite his hopelessness in everything else, he was good in bed.'

'That's an important quality, don't you think?' he said. 'You too will find it difficult to give me up because I know how to please you.'

'Don't flatter yourself,' she said, 'so does a vibrator!'

Hiwa smiled remembering his wife's comeback. He dried his hands on a towel, opened a bottle of wine, and sat at the kitchen table, leaving an empty wine glass for Sozi. He knew that her parents' relationship had taught her a lesson: it is only through love that we get people to respond to our needs, not through force, anger, or temper. It was only because her father loved her mother that she couldn't throw him out and she put up with his addiction.

A few days after Khalid and Rozhin's wedding party, they went to the cinema together and then had dinner in a French restaurant.

'Lucy,' he called the waitress whose name was displayed on her waistcoat. 'What do you recommend? Steak or sole?'

Later, Sozi told him how she'd quietly observed him that night to see if he was a player. She'd decided, a long time ago, to rule out any man who gave off mixed messages and confused women. She'd promised herself that she wouldn't be in a situation where she felt insecure, attention-starved, and embarrassed. It had taken Hiwa years of practice to look at women's faces, not their bodies, to listen to them when they talked and not interrupt, to see them as people, not as objects of pleasure.

After dinner he wanted to invite her to his flat for a drink, but he didn't. He'd never been with a Kurdish woman before but knew that he had to take it slowly and be cautious. Hiwa had many short-term relationships when he was new in the country. He was still raw from his past when he started dating women.

He resented them for not being complicated, for having had sheltered lives. Once he got really drunk and ended up crying in the arms of a girl who he'd met her in a bar a few hours earlier. Another night he made love to a girl four times, each time he became more vigorous, each time he wanted to thrust himself into her as far as he could, empty himself inside her, and to love her and satisfy her.

Most of the time the women left him. His pains were too raw, his background was traumatic, his life was a mess. He spent many years starting courses and not finishing them, living on benefits, getting drunk, having one-night stands, hating his life. He was lucky to be handsome. There were always women who put up with him for a short while. He slept with older women, younger women, pretty women, unattractive women, kind women, cold women, but couldn't fall in love with any of them. Only when he met Sarah did he start trying.

The pain of breaking up with Sarah had made him reflect on his life and promise himself to do better if and when life gave him another chance at love. He was tired of short-term relationships, of being with women who didn't share his language and culture. This feeling became more pronounced when he finally summoned enough courage and went home in 1993. Suddenly he realised that there was a place where he belonged, a place with smells and tastes from his childhood, a place which wasn't as beautiful and tidy as Europe but was his home: all the shops where he'd bought candy as a child, all those neighbours, the safe neighbourhoods, and the graves of his loved ones. He was shocked to see how the house was in exactly the same situation as he'd left it twelve years ago. The same wall stood erect, amputating the

227

old bathroom from the rest of the house. He'd wanted to bring it down but worried that it may undermine the fragile balance his family had achieved.

After his visit home, he made more effort with the community, started listening to Kurdish music again, bought a satellite dish to receive Kurdish channels, started eating in Kurdish households, and felt ready to have a Kurdish family of his own. Eventually, after three months of dating, Sozi invited him for dinner at her place. It was a muted pastel pink studio decorated with golden candles, white flowers, and colourful curtains. She'd cooked him *tepsi bayinjan*- an aubergine stew he loved, with rice and chicken. They ate at her small dining table in the top left corner of the room which could be unfolded to accommodate four people. She was wearing a sheer blue and green dress with thin straps. Hiwa looked at her shoulders and realised that she wasn't wearing a bra. He wondered whether she was nervous, maybe that was why she was playing music.

She accidentally dropped a spoon full of rice and bent down to pick it up, her breasts were staring at him. He knelt on the floor to help her gather the spilt rice. She got up to get a towel, but he grabbed her wrist. She sat down again and looked at him, not smiling, nor annoyed. His hands started from her sandaled feet, tracing her slim toes. His fingers rose to touch her calves, then they went under her dress. When his hands reached the line of her underwear she sighed, moved forward, and kissed him.

That night he slept next to her on the sofa-bed, holding her each time he woke up. He stared at her with tenderness and wished he could have children with this woman—this woman who was soft but not weak, caring but not dependent, loving but not a pushover. He loved her because she could stand up for herself, because she would not put up with nonsense. He knew he needed that. He needed someone to bring him back.

Sozi was finally free of Shilana. She came and sat at the table, opposite him. He poured her some wine, but before he could say how beautiful she looked, and how he wanted to make love to her, the phone rang.

'Leave it,' he said, but Sozi picked up. It was Lana, calling to tell them that she was in hospital.

CHAPTER TWENTY-EIGHT

Gara

After hanging up with Lana, Gara found his way to his wife in the dark. The small lantern was burning low on the windowsill. His son was sound asleep on Aveen's left and he lay down on her right. He kissed her awake. 'How's Lana?' she mumbled. 'She'll be okay,' he whispered, putting his cold hand under her pyjama top. Aveen gasped and turned towards him, stretching her sleepy arm out. He rested his head in the crook of her arm and she gently kissed his cold forehead. His hand travelled up her warm body, resting between her breasts. Soon their body temperature was the same and Aveen was breathing slowly once again.

'You always sleep before me,' he once told her.

'Because I'm tired,' she said.

'You don't think I'm tired?'

'You go to work,' she told him. 'You socialise, hear jokes, exchange ideas, learn things… All I do is clean, cook, and look after Kawa every day. It's draining.'

'You give everything time but me,' he said, sulking.

'Maybe if you'd help around the house, I could finish faster and have energy left for you.'

Tonight, he wasn't going to demand attention. He thought about what his aunt had told him. Was he conjuring up his brother by continuously thinking of him? Did Kawa not walk around the house every day? Was he not living in this same room? Gara couldn't believe that it was all to do with him. He wasn't the only one who felt Kawa's presence. His son seemed to sense someone's presence in the house. His wife also felt it. Maybe it was her long conversations with him all those years that made him make a home in the house. Maybe she'd persuaded him to come back and stay. He wanted to wake her and ask her, 'Tell me, do you still speak with Kawa? Do you feel him close?'

He knew that his wife wouldn't answer him. She would feel hurt and withdraw from him. Once when they were in bed, and he was in one of his pushy moods he'd asked her whether she thought of Kawa when they made love. She'd burst into tears by his questioning and shouted at him to leave her alone.

'Did you marry me to get out of your depression? To have some fun?' he asked her.

'I could've gone with my brother,' she told him angrily. 'I would've had more fun in Sweden, don't you think? And no one would quiz me about my past.'

'If he was alive and you had to choose one of us,' he insisted, 'who would you choose?'

'If he was alive,' she screamed at him, 'we wouldn't be like this.'

'Like what?'

'Like this,' she said, throwing off the duvet and revealing their naked bodies next to each other.

She put her dress back on and tried to leave.

'I'm sorry,' he'd said. 'You're right. It's stupid.'

And together they had gently rocked in silence as his hands nestled her head.

231

'I chose life,' she told him in a calmer voice between her tears. 'I chose to be happy; I chose to be with you. Have I made the wrong choice?'

'No,' he answered. 'You did the right thing.'

Since then, they hadn't talked about Kawa, and it seemed to Aveen that they'd put those worries behind them. Gara never thought that he would be a jealous husband. He never worried about other men and knew that his fears were irrational. Was this because he was overshadowed by his brother? Was Kawa's presence a figment of his guilty imagination because he lived instead of his brother on that day and he took his place in the house, with his wife, with the child that should've been Kawa's?

He fell asleep on his wife's arm. In his dream he reimagined that day when he, unknowingly, replaced his brother in the course of living. Amongst the gunfire and smoke he told Kawa not to go forward. He told his brother that if he went forward, he would die and soon after that his child would be born in the rain, and it would die because he wasn't there to protect it.

'And before you know it, I'll be in love with your wife and marry her,' he told his brother. 'Before you know it, I'll sleep with your wife and have a son with her. We'll name him after you, but that isn't enough, is it?'

He grabbed his brother's arm and begged him, 'Don't go forward. Aveen will always remain in love with you, she'll never love me like she loves you, and if you die none of us will ever have a chance to be happy.'

Kawa listened calmly as Gara tried to explain the future to him.

'And what's the use if you die?' he asked Kawa. 'The Ba'athists will go, we'll have our own parliament and we won't be killed and silenced like in the past, the villages will be rebuilt and there will be no more mass graves.' He started crying. 'But you know what our own people will do? They'll steal money, marry many wives, and abandon the people who supported them and had faith in them. They won't fix the water and electricity shortages even though they have the money to do it, and in this oil-rich country we will forever struggle to get enough oil for winter fuel and gas for daily cooking. And you know what? We won't be killed for criticising and exposing them, but gradually our souls will decay, many of us will get exhausted, stop fighting, and give up. Many will put their heads down like cowards, join them, ignore them, or leave the country. We won't be able to provide a better alternative. We'll just suffer in a different way. What is the point, my beautiful brother? What is the point of you dying?'

Kawa shook his head at Gara's pessimism.

'It's true,' he told Kawa again. 'I know you don't believe me; I know you want to believe that things will turn out better than that, but they won't.' He grabbed his brother with both hands. 'Listen to me,' he said, 'I'll do some good things in my life and become known in this godforsaken community just for speaking up, for not running after money or advantage. I'll have a beautiful son with Aveen, I'll love her so much that jealousy will tear me apart. I'll wake up every day next to her and not believe my luck and I'll be jealous of you, my own brother. I won't be able to escape you, none of us will. Don't go forward!'

Kawa hugged him by the wall of the Red Security Headquarters and told him, 'It doesn't have to be the way you think. It can be much better. I know that you can be happy, this land can thrive,

233

people can change things, the leaders can turn things around.'

Gara shook his head and cried as Kawa looked him in the face.

'Now you listen to me, I'll go forward and if I die, I want Aveen to be happy. If you can make her happy, I would rather she marries you. But if you do marry her and feel unhappy it would have nothing to do with my dying today, it would be because of the two of you, so don't make an excuse of me.'

Gara wanted to interrupt him, but Kawa put his hand on Gara's mouth.

'Listen to me,' Kawa said, 'I'm telling you, things don't have to turn out so bad.' And with one last hug, with one last look from those deep blue eyes, he carried his Kalashnikov and stepped forward. And right there, in front of Gara's eyes, he exploded into a spray of blood.

'What was it?' Aveen said as she woke up from his screams. 'What did you dream of?'

'I can't remember,' he said.

She kissed his forehead, stroked his back. 'It's the war!' she said. 'It brings everything back.'

It was March 8, 1991, when Gara and Kawa put their winter coats on and picked up their Kalashnikovs to join the uprising. They said goodbye to their mother without hugging her. Kawa kissed Aveen and touched her pregnant belly. She whispered, 'Be careful!' She'd given up begging him not to go. Kawa laughed before they walked out. His eyes were full of blue flames. He was twenty-six years old.

Gara could still feel the excitement and anticipation they felt. The radio had been announcing revolution for days. After three years of silence, Ferhad Sengawi was back on top form, arousing passion for resistance. Since the chemical weapons turned the caves and hideouts into open graves and the revolutionaries fled to Iran in 1988, no one was listening to that radio station anymore. Its calls were the death throes of a dream that seemed impossible after that doomed year when dozens of locations were gassed, 2000 villages were bulldozed, the water springs were concreted over, and the villagers were made disappear.

Gara recalled the stillness and silence, and the crackdown on members of the underground movement in the two years that followed the Anfal genocide in 1988. One of his friends was captured, tortured, and later hanged in this period. Everyone thought it was over. The 'Kurdish problem' was finally solved and there was silence everywhere. Then, in August 1990 Saddam Hussein invaded Kuwait and Iraq was named a 'dangerous state' that needed to be stopped.

As the Ba'ath government was defeated, the Kurdish radio stations were promising freedom. Gara remembered the euphoria that spread as the old hymns were being replayed: 'No one should say the Kurds are dead, the Kurds are thriving. We're thriving and our flag will never be lowered'. There was a countdown to the 'wedding day' and people were urged to unite and fight. The days were charged with anticipation, fear, and hope.

The uprising started in Basra, in the south of the country, when demoralised soldiers joined the angry public against the state. It quickly spread to other cities where civilians attacked the government strongholds. The security and intelligence offices fought back and bloody battles broke out between the well-equipped but isolated Ba'athist fighters and the masses.

Those who fought against the public were killed, dragged on the streets, and mutilated.

In Slemani, a woman whose son was hanged by the government wanted revenge: 'He's mine,' she screamed as she pushed through the crowd to reach the wounded intelligence agent. 'Give him to me.'

The fiercest resistance was put up by the Security Headquarters, the large red building in Aqari. The building was surrounded by men who, like Gara and Kawa, were fighting their first battle. Those who were braver kept trying to go over the walls and the first few waves were shot down. Kawa exchanged a few looks with Gara and said, 'Cover us!' But before Gara had time to grab him, Kawa was gone. Four men went forward at the same time and Gara fired vigorously at the top of the building, terrified that his own bullets may kill his brother. The shooting intensified and he wasn't able to tell where the screams were coming from.

'Kawa,' he shouted as loud as he could, 'are you alright?'

A distant voice reassured him, a voice which he couldn't locate. He carried on firing at the right-hand corner of the building where shots were being fired from. A grenade fell on his left and for a moment he was blinded and confused. When he looked up the two men next to him were dead. More young men kept moving forward, the bodies were dragged away to make space for others. On the other side, the rebels managed to break through and got into the building.

'Kawa,' he shouted, 'Kawa!'

The shooting was dying down; more men were entering the building from all directions. Gara lowered his head and followed them. Leaning against a wall on the left, he soon felt safe and looked up. A man came out from the building, soaked in blood, and terrified.

'What is happening inside?' someone asked him.

'Dead... all dead... all dead,' he said in broken Kurdish.

Someone screamed: 'He is a...'

In one flash Gara recognised his brother's clothes on the man. He screamed and shot the agent until he had no bullets left. He found Kawa inside, stripped to his shirt, his chest an open wound. He screamed and cried, embracing his warm body. Kawa's blue eyes stayed open, but his lips were now sealed forever.

CHAPTER TWENTY-NINE

Hiwa

Sozi came to him as the prospect of orderliness was becoming possible and stood in the door frame waiting for him to notice. He looked at her for a second then carried on shifting things. He knew that this feeling of being at a loss was unfamiliar to her. She was usually clear and decisive, knowing what she wanted and how she could get it. He wasn't helping her either, he didn't want a confrontation. The day before, after visiting Lana, Sozi suggested that they go away for a long weekend, maybe to Devon or the Lake District. They could switch off their mobile phones, not check their emails, and spend some time walking, talking, and eating together. 'I can't switch off with all of this happening,' he said. 'I have to listen to the news every day.'

He knew that she was watching him with frustration, how slow he moved about, how slow he was in organising things. She stepped forward and stood close to him.

'Do you want to help me?'

'No,' she said, 'I want to talk.'

He put the box down and straightened up. 'Not now,' he told her in a calm voice.

'So when?' she asked.

'I don't know,' he said, 'but now isn't a good time.'

He felt the wave of anger and impatience that went through

Sozi's body before she left the room. He wasn't ready to talk about Sarah yet, not ready to clarify things. He himself wasn't sure what he was doing but he'd stopped questioning himself, given up reflecting or trying to understand things. He hoped that she would let him be until he was ready. Why couldn't she ignore the topic for a while?

It was nearly dinner time. He stopped working and went to the sitting room to join his family. Shilana was playing with her pots and pans. Her blunt plastic knife was struggling to cut a piece of cucumber. When she got frustrated, she screamed and Sozi helped her.

'Don't rush your fate *gullekem*,' Sozi told her. 'You'll do enough chopping and cooking when you grow up.'

He looked at his wife's back. He knew this was a complaint directed at him. When they were happy, she loved cooking and cleaning, but every time there was an argument, she resented the house chores. She felt used.

'Is there anything I can do?'

'No,' she said without turning towards him and went back to the kitchen.

On the news a woman and her five-year-old daughter had drowned off the coast of Cornwall as the waves came in and the rapid mist made it impossible for them to find their way back. He imagined the water rising to her waist, her calling for help on her mobile, trying to walk in the right direction. He imagined the woman carrying her daughter on her back for a while, trying to float, to remain calm. 'Everything will be okay, my love,' she was saying to her child. They tried to swim together in the mist, unable to see the coast from anywhere, without direction, without hope.

How long did they try to get somewhere? he wondered. How long did they maintain hope? When did they get too tired to try? Did a strong current drive them under? Did the child drown first? Did her mother hold on to her for long?

He closed his eyes. He imaged that death, that gulping for air, eyes wanting to pop out of the skull, the desperate attempt to get to the surface, lungs filling with water, veins bulging out of skin, skin going blue, going white, and then the muscles relaxing, taking you to the surface just when it was too late. But he knew that death by fire, by those beautiful, golden, and slippery flames, was a different story of pain. She had burnt slowly as layer by layer of her body was set alight. First a lively fire, her juicy cells burning vigorously. Then the fire penetrated her skin, into her flesh and bones. It had started with her head and face, going down to her shoulders, her breasts, her back and stomach, her arms. Her feet were normal when he saw her. The fire hadn't reached them. Her long toes, her toenails painted dark red, her orange soles—they were still beautiful. For years he was obsessed with the thought that if only she hadn't poured the petrol over her head, if only he was at home when it happened, if only he knew, if anyone had suspected it, maybe it could've been prevented. Now he thought it was inevitable, getting closer every day. It was her last desperate protest and he managed to miss all the signals.

He remembered that spring evening, a few months before their father died, when Tara announced her wish to join the Institute of Fine Arts the following year. 'Layla's father is going to be one of my teachers,' she said casually. 'I think it'll be much nicer than school.'

240

The family had gathered for dinner. The okra stew was soaking rice on the plates. Ahoo had also made some *treet*, torn pieces of bread covered in the okra stew and meat cubes. Each of them had taken some *treet* onto their plates. Akram's cheeks were full of food. He stopped chewing and looked at his daughter and then his wife. He then swallowed and calmly said, 'And what are you planning to study?'

'Drama,' she said, taking another spoonful of food while her brothers froze.

'No, you're not,' he said. 'You're going to university.'

'I don't like university,' Tara replied. 'I like to act.'

Her father threw his spoon in her direction. 'Who do you think you are? A male without a penis?'

She looked up at her father, as if she would shout back. Her mother's eyes told her to keep her mouth shut. Hiwa looked down on the *sifra* without a word, he didn't dare to interfere, or to look at her.

'Your daughter has no respect for anyone, what have you been doing all these years?'

'She's just young,' their mother said.

'Young? Women her age are married, with families.' He got up from the *sifra*, not finishing his food. 'How wonderful! My daughter wants to become an actor,' he muttered to himself. Then he stopped at the door, turned around, pointed at her, and said, 'Don't you dare bring this up again. We have no daughter who becomes an actor.'

For the next few days, Tara begged her mother to influence her father. She was convinced that Ahoo could make him change his mind. Their mother refused in as many ways as she knew but Tara kept trying until Ahoo became harsh like her father.

'Are you crazy?' she told her. 'Even without acting, people are about to eat you alive. What do you think will happen to you if you act?'

Tara refused to speak to any of them for days and their father wasn't speaking to their mother because he believed it was her fault that Tara had such ideas. One afternoon, when Hiwa went home from work, he went to talk to her but after what went on between them, she refused to confide in him. He knew that she didn't trust him anymore. He was a young man and he worked like his father, he'd become calmer and more observant than her. He knew that she saw him as part of the grown-up group in the family, the group that was making decisions about her life and holding her back. Only Kawa could speak with her.

'It doesn't matter if you can't study Drama,' Hiwa heard Kawa consoling her. 'You're a good actor anyway. You can always act for us, we love to watch you.'

Four months later, their father died without having time to say goodbye. Hiwa knew that his sister hadn't forgiven him yet, she was still angry with him when he died. His sudden death made her even more angry. It was typical of him, Hiwa thought, he did things like that. He rapidly made up his mind about things without giving them a second thought and surprised his family in his moments of love and anger. He suddenly left their lives, disappearing without making up, without a will, without a kind word.

Throughout his father's wake, Hiwa cried and cursed him in his heart. How could he be so cruel? he thought to himself, How could he just leave his family like that? How could he leave Ahoo with five children to support? He didn't even have a pension. Hiwa knew that he'd have to take on the burden and take responsibility for his siblings. He cried for his mother who was only forty-two years old, for the long widowhood she would live. Losing their father was also the end of protection from the world. It made them more vulnerable to everything and everyone, more exposed, more naked, more watched.

The desire to act was never again expressed by Tara. That year she gave up on her life changing and then a young man came into her life who promised freedom and happiness. He was her escape from it all. Why didn't Hiwa understand that? Why couldn't he at least help her be with him?

'Dinner is ready,' Sozi said in a calm voice, 'if you want to join us.'

He got up, turned the TV down, and went straight to his wife. He hugged her from behind while she was putting Shilana into her chair.

'I'm sorry,' he told her. 'I just need more time. Can you give me some time?'

She stood stiffly in his arms, not turning back and not saying anything.

'I'm just trying to sort things in my head, trying to keep it together. Please be patient with me.'

She touched the arm that was wrapped around her but didn't turn.

'Can you?' he said, holding her in his arms.

'I can,' she said, 'But not for long.'

CHAPTER THIRTY

Gara

The clouds had been lingering for days, as if waiting to catch people out, and then the thunderstorm started. Gara looked out the window as his colleagues talked. He remembered Aveen's prayers and smiled to himself, she'd been pleading for rain, not this violence. He knew she would be watching the rain and feeling guilty. Suddenly feeling the urge to be close to her, he ended the meeting and drove home.

He stood in the shelter of the front roof and watched the insistent drops fall on the pomegranate tree which strained to stay erect, its bare branches heavy and exhausted, its straight figure bent to the right. It seemed as if it would be ripped out of the earth at any moment, and it would lie down, roots exposed, rocking in the wind, a final sleep.

Is this what will happen to this country? he wondered. Will everything be ripped apart?

He thought about the families fleeing to the countryside and remembered the barefoot children crying in the mud, screaming in the face of rain, hunger, and exhaustion. It always rained at the wrong time, at times of crisis and disaster.

That late March in 1991 when his family joined the hundreds of thousands who were leaving the city, it was pouring down. As the Republican Guards were recapturing Kirkuk, the people of Slemani started heading towards Azmar mountain, their cars and backpacks filled with food and blankets. The city square was full of teenagers shouting, 'tanks, troops, aircrafts will not chase us from this city,' yet people were leaving in waves. There were talks of resistance, yet the *peshmarga* were joining their families and fleeing. It happened rapidly and Gara couldn't remember all the details, just masses of people walking in the rain, carrying their children on their backs.

It had rained for seven days, the raindrops turning into hailstone and snowflakes that the land kept absorbing. The thick mud sucked the crowd in and slowed down their desperate attempt to escape. Those who walked abandoned their drenched blankets and heavy coats, hoping to get lighter. The mountain routes were blocked as cars broke down in the mud. Gara regretted letting Aveen, a widow of three weeks, go with their neighbour. Everyone thought a seven months pregnant woman would be better off in a car as opposed to walking to Iran with the rest of her family.

'It's best for the baby,' Ahoo had told Aveen as the two of them hugged and cried. 'We'll see you in Iran.'

Gara remembered the soaking and muddy travellers whose backs were bent, their faces screwed up. Tears mixed with the rain, they were tears of grief, exhaustion, and hunger. As images of the exodus came back to him, water was building up in the garden, drowning the dead grass and struggling tree. Nobody kept the garden going anymore. Some days they barely had enough water to drink, so watering the garden wasn't a priority. The mulberry, vine, and fig trees had all died. He felt sad for the pomegranate tree, persevering through years of thirst only to be killed by too much water.

Life is full of getting it wrong, he thought.

Every thunderclap seemed like the world going into labour to produce more rain, every lightening flash looked like a shooting pain. He thought of Aveen going into labour on the third day of the mass exodus and his nephew being born two months too early. A few days later the premature baby was buried in a refugee camp alongside all the other babies, children, and elderly who'd made it to safety only to die there. By the time Gara found her, she was slim, empty, and looking like a ghost.

She's okay now, he thought, she's safe. And with these thoughts he entered the quiet house.

The raindrops were pelting down on the sitting room window. The constant drumming was a hum that didn't disrupt Sayran and Kawa's sleep. His aunt acted like a buffer zone, laying between the paraffin heater and his son. Gara looked at his son whose mouth moved as if he was suckling and thought of his wife.

Why isn't she in the warm sitting room? he wondered.

For a second, he worried that Aveen may have left them, having had enough of his insecurities and demands, of being a mother and a housewife, of the ghost-stricken house.

Where is she? he thought while searching for her. What is she up to?

He was about to enter the bedroom when he heard her speak. His hand on the door handle, he instinctively stopped.

'*Pura* Sayran asked me to say goodbye,' Aveen said. 'I thought I had! I've already let you go, haven't I? Are you still here?'

Gara's hand dropped to his side. So I'm right, he thought, Kawa is still hanging on.

'I want to explain a few things to you Kawa *gyan*,' she said in a calm voice. 'Maybe if I do that, you can forgive me, and we can all move on. Will you listen to me?' she stopped for a few seconds before resuming, 'All those years ago, when you died, I died with you. I was dead for many years, and it was horrible to be amongst the living who still hoped, enjoyed tastes and smells, and loved being hugged and kissed. I didn't. I couldn't feel anything anymore, do you remember? After a while, even grief became impossible, I had no sensation left in me, no feelings. This body was dry, it was like a land stricken by drought.'

He wanted to interrupt this monologue, as he had done years ago. He wanted to make his presence known. He was afraid of hearing what she wanted to say to his brother, but he was silent, motionless, listening.

'And then one day, when I was kissing your footsteps, I thought you'd come back for me. After many hopeless years, I felt hope, I felt happy for a few seconds, and I ran to you. But it was Gara who caught me before I fell. He was the one who held me as I cried, and he talked to me and kissed me. For the first time since your death, I re-experienced my body in his arms. I felt his hands on my back, his breath on my shoulder, and his lips, all warm and loving, on my neck. It was beautiful.

'In that moment I felt alive again. You know? And that smell, the smell of love was intoxicating. I realised that he loved me and not only that, I realised that I loved being loved by him, I loved embracing him, he who held me so kindly, who told me to stop grieving, who kissed me and made me feel precious. It was so simple, so touching.

'And you know, the first time when he undressed me, his

247

hands were shaking, that is how wonderful it was, I couldn't breathe. I couldn't believe that I could want so much again, that the trembling hands of a man could make me feel so beautiful and desired. And when I came, I was crying. He thought I was thinking about you, he always does, but I was crying because it was perfect. Gara is a good man, he doesn't know his own worth. I don't think he knows how much I love him. He still thinks that I'm in love with you.'

His hand reached his chest, shocked and heartbroken.

'Loving you didn't end with your death. You already know that. But it's not as he thinks. This is not either-or; I don't have to choose. I don't know how to explain it, but I love him. Do you understand me?' She stopped for a second, as if expecting an answer, and then started again, 'I knew you would. You were always good at understanding things, even if you didn't feel the same.'

Maybe this is one of my weaknesses, Gara thought, I sometimes don't understand her.

'And now we have little Kawa, who is beautiful... I'm so sorry about our baby my darling, my body pushed him out too early,' her voice broke down. 'He was a tiny, delicate thing with blue eyes, so beautiful, so perfect. I'll never understand what God's plan was when it came to him. Why couldn't I keep him, why did he have to die? I will never understand.

'Now we have Kawa, and he is such a wonderful little person, so clever, so unspoiled and caring. I want this little boy to have a good life. I want him to grow up with a sane mother, in a happy and healthy family. I don't want him to be moulded by the past, I don't want him to be haunted. Is it you? Are you the one who is coming to him? Is there anything that you need to tell us through him?' she stopped and then went on, 'I thought not. I know you are with us. I know it's probably our fault, we spend too much time talking about you, thinking about you, worrying about how you may be feeling.'

Gara nodded, they were guilty of not letting him go.

'If we carry on like this,' Aveen said, 'we'll all go crazy, we're all going to be hurt. I'm so sorry my darling, I just have to let you go for good. I have to live without worrying whether you are angry with us. We have to let you go.

'This is our last conversation then; it is time to say goodbye. I just don't want you to be angry with me. I know you understand how difficult it is for me. I know you do. I'll do my best. I'll be happy and I'll pass on happiness to Kawa. He'll know and love you, but I won't let him feel the burden of our tragedies. I hope you're safe where you are, beyond pain and grief. I hope you've found peace. Goodbye Kawa *gyan*, keep warm in this rain.'

When Gara looked up, he couldn't feel Kawa's presence anymore. Just like a blown-out candle, he was gone.

ONE WEEK BEFORE THE WAR

CHAPTER THIRTY-ONE

Lana

The clouds had parted. The weak sun made a stretched white rectangle on the floor. Lana was resting on her bed, watching the landing light and the folds in the curtains. Three days had passed since she'd left the hospital and she was feeling stronger. Her head was clear, and her mind was made up. The pregnancy had survived sepsis and she was going to keep the baby. This was doing her bit against the war. No more women ending their own lives or the lives of their babies for the sake of maintaining tradition or being in line with the nation's agendas, she thought. She was determined to give their baby the best chance of surviving.

Delighted by her decision, Amer cooked her food, accompanied her on short walks on Byron Road, read out poems to her, and hugged and kissed her. He played Arabic and Kurdish love songs. Songs that were sung passionately by men and women who seemed to have never been united with the objects of their desire, songs that bridged the gap between them and enhanced their love for each other. Lana thought about how easy it is to write about love when things were going wrong, when you can't be with the one you want, when you are hurt, heartbroken, or grieved, but it isn't easy to write about a peaceful togetherness, about happiness and satisfaction.

Hiwa had come to see her with his family, bringing her warm food. He tried to talk about happy things, but the conversation never took off. She quietly observed her brother and his wife.

'Is everything okay between you?' she asked her brother when her sister-in-law was in the kitchen.

'We're fine,' he told her. 'Just concentrate on getting better.'

'Why is she angry with you?'

'It'll be okay. I'll sort it out, don't worry.'

Lana looked deeply into his eyes. She wanted to tell him not to destroy what he has but she remained silent. She hoped that he could resolve it. She then told him what she'd been wanting to tell him all along.

'I saw Azad at the demonstration. Did you know that he lived here?'

Hiwa looked puzzled for a few seconds.

'Tara's Azad,' Lana clarified. 'Did you know that he lived in London?'

He closed his eyes for a second, as if from pain, then he shook his head.

'He has two daughters, and his wife is pregnant again.'

'You've probably met a different man,' he said. 'That was a long time ago.'

'Yes,' she said, 'he has to be a different man, otherwise, how could he live with himself?'

'It wasn't his fault,' he said and looked away.

'Wasn't it?' Lana asked. 'Didn't he raise her hopes and then desert her?'

'Yes, but he didn't have much choice, did he? He was young and couldn't stand up to his family. Plus, he wasn't Tara's only problem, he merely enhanced her loneliness. She was too lonely in this world.'

'How could anyone so beautiful and clever and talented feel lonely? Weren't those things a comfort?'

'It was exactly because of those things that she was lonely,' he said. 'Good things attract negative attention and envy; they don't do well in this world.'

Just like homeland, she thought, the natural resources and fertile land becoming a curse.

She looked at her brother who was lost in his own thoughts, looking hopeless. He didn't have the strength to be angry like her, or maybe he'd gone beyond that. Lana dropped the subject. She felt guilty for telling him about Azad when he was already struggling to keep things together. Before parting with her he gave her a hug and said, 'I only have one sister left, don't deprive me of that.'

Lana remembered her brother's compulsive visits to the graveyard after Tara's suicide. He'd withdrawn from his family, stopped shaving, and cried often. The war with Iran continued and her mother thought that Hiwa would either be conscripted and killed in the battlefield or kill himself while obsessing about his sister. It was the toughest decision she'd made in her life but one that she never regretted. One night, before making up her mind, she dreamt that the prophet put his hand on her shoulder and told her, 'Don't worry, Hiwa's your son.' She'd woken up at dawn trembling, prayed on her mat till the morning. She let him go so that he would survive. Lana wanted to do the same, to let him be and let him live.

The phone rang and she picked it up. It had been unplugged

since the demonstration and she'd only taken calls on her mobile from close friends and relatives.

'How are you *basaqa*?' *pura* Sayran shouted down the line, a habit from the past when the long-distance telephone calls sounded so far away.

'I'm well, thank you,' she replied, 'just tired.'

'Don't worry about us, Lana *gyan*. We'll survive this one too; you don't need to kill yourself. What will happen will happen.'

She was glad that there was an excuse for her exhaustion, that she didn't have to explain what was going on in her head.

'I know,' she told her aunt. 'I'm resting now.'

'I wish you were close to us; we would've looked after you.'

'*Qurbanit*, how is Kawa?'

'He's lovely, I hope you can see him soon.'

She'd only seen pictures of him and had promised herself that once the war was over, she'd go back to meet him. Two years earlier, when Gara phoned to tell her that they were going to name the baby Kawa, she wasn't sure whether she'd cried because one of her siblings was finally fulfilling her mother's wish for a grandchild or because Kawa was already present enough between the couple.

She lay back in her bed and wished that her mother could see her two grandchildren. The bad things happened too quickly for Ahoo and the simple things that she wanted so much never happened in her lifetime. In 1992 they were still grieving for Kawa and failed to notice her illness before it was too late. After a long history of stomach ulcer, bowel infections, and blood pressure, they assumed her symptoms had intensified because of Kawa's death. His death left destruction in their lives: his baby died, the house was looted when they fled to Iran, most of their books, clothes, and photos were stolen or destroyed. Yet people expected Ahoo to play the brave mother of a martyr who goes on TV and says that she's willing to sacrifice *all* her children for Kurdistan, that she feels lucky to be Kawa's mother.

'I don't want freedom if my son isn't here to enjoy it,' she said as she cried. 'I just want him back.'

In her mother's final weeks, Lana slept by her side every night, getting up when she coughed, moved, moaned. Sayran, Aveen, and Lana held Ahoo in their care, never telling her what was coming. She was too tied up in sorrow and prayers to realise how close her death was. She urged the younger women not to wear black. Years ago, she'd worn black for her husband and then Tara died. She was convinced that every time you think things are bad, they can get worse.

'Grief brings more grief,' she said.

But Lana saw how new grief awakened old hurt. Her mother often cried over Tara, felt that she should've been more careful, should've known better. She told them about a time when Tara got sick as a toddler.

'Whatever she ate, came back out,' she said, 'I tried to force-feed her, pushed spoons full of food into her mouth, held her nose until she couldn't breathe and had to swallow. She screamed, went blue, but refused to swallow. I knew then that she would not give in to pressures and restrictions, but when the crucial moment came, I forgot,' she said. 'I sided with the world against her.'

Lana got up, took out her mother's tapes for Hiwa, and put

one of them in the recorder. It was in the middle of side A. She sat down to listen to her voice, recorded eleven years ago, for her son in exile.

'... *dada* Halaw died a few years ago, do you remember? Her son Mahmood was two or three years older than you and he was a builder. Remember how he used to tease you that building houses is better than fixing cars? He's ill now. They cut his right leg off to stop the disease, but it's started again. He needs painkillers and medication. I was wondering if you could send him some strong painkillers from there. Even if you just send him money, it will help his family. Mahmood's son works with *wasta* Ali now, just like you *basaqa*. *Wasta* Ali always says you were his best assistant. He asks after you. Don't forget to bring him a present when you return. The neighbours remember how you bought them bread in the mornings, Hiwa *gyan*.'

Lana stopped the tape. Her mother's voice, so clear on the tape, brought tears to her eyes. Every time Ahoo wanted to send a letter to her son in exile, she'd plead with one of her children to write it for her. Eventually she turned to recording tapes for him, speaking in detail about the extended family, distant relatives, neighbours, passing acquaintances, those who were ill, poor, or in trouble, and she asked Hiwa for help. Ahoo prayed that the ill would get better, the prisoners would be released, the hungry would be fed, the lovers would unite, and the exiles would return.

Her illiteracy created large gaps between her and her children. She wasn't able to read the novels they talked about and the poems they loved. She wasn't able to read the bus destinations and only recognised the right bus because 'our neighbourhood has a long name and three dots,' she said. Even her faith was built on what the Imams told her; she couldn't accept that some of them made things up. From an early age she'd started reciting her Arabic prayers five times a day, facing Mecca, without questioning, and didn't realise that the prayers weren't in Kurdish. Once when they were young, her husband had teased her and said, 'Have you heard? The Imams are saying that from now on, if you don't pray in Arabic, your prayers won't be accepted.'

After a short reflection she would say, 'Let them say what they please, God understands my language.'

This was one of the family jokes. It was telling about her faith, her belief not just in God but also in whatever she knew about her faith through others. There was trust and forgiveness, but she couldn't forgive her own mistakes. In the last year of her life, before she was unable to walk, she spent her Fridays at the graveyard, sitting between Tara's and Kawa's graves. Lana cried because she had nowhere to visit, no tombstone to kiss and talk to, no grave to light an incense stick on, nothing she could hold onto. She carried her family in her dreams, saw them amongst the ruins and the rubble.

Maybe when all of this is over, I can go home, visit the graveyard, and tell them to rest, she thought. Maybe I can walk in the garden without shivering.

CHAPTER THIRTY-TWO

Hiwa

He lay facing down as Sarah traced his shoulder blades, held his tense muscles between her strong fingers until they relaxed, and drummed on his spine. Her fingers climbed the sides of his ribs, massaged the muscle that cupped his shoulder. He closed his eyes and surrendered to her touch. She slipped her hands under his shoulders. His armpits in her palms she lay down, resting her cheek on the back of his neck. He breathed in her breath. Her body was closely wrapped around him, and they didn't move for a while, closing their eyes. Behind the window the rain fell without a sound. The grey clouds made it seem later than it was. The winter day was shortened by togetherness.

Hiwa wanted to hold on to the moment and not think about his angry wife, his struggling sister, the approaching war. He turned away from the thought that he had to leave soon. He kept still and listened to her breathing. He didn't remember if during their shared life they did enough lying down together without talking or making love. There was always so much to say, so many things to disagree about, to misunderstand. If they weren't talking in bed, then their bodies were talking to each other. They were never still. Their love making was lengthy, full of winding around each other, full of force and passion. Hiwa wondered whether it was the process of growing old that had brought them to that peaceful moment. They understood each other without words now. He understood how Sarah's mother hadn't loved her father. After losing her loved ones she'd feared forming new attachments. She knew that Hiwa's family, like his nation, were not good at living, at best they just managed to survive.

Sarah kissed the corner of his eye and, while sitting up, told him, 'You must go soon.'

'Shhh,' he told her as if scared of breaking the spell.

'Come here,' he said, tapping the space next to him and she lay on her back. He raised himself onto his right side. Resting on his elbow, he looked into her grey-blue eyes and touched her face. She held his hand and kissed it.

'What will Lana do?' she asked him as she raised herself to face him.

'She'll get through it,' he told her. 'She's a survivor.'

'But falling so ill means that she's not coping,' Sarah said. 'Won't you at least speak with her?'

'The thing is,' he said while staring into her eyes again, 'coming to terms with the past, living with it, integrating it into one's life is a personal process which each of us has to do on our own. It's all come together for her in the last few weeks: the fatal combination of a complicated love, the stress of the war, and being confronted with someone from the past. It's a crisis, but I have faith that it'll pass.'

'Did she talk to the guy in the demonstration?' she asked.

'No!' he said. 'What is the use anyway? He probably doesn't even know what happened to Tara.'

'I think he probably does,' she said. 'He must've visited home, must've found out.'

Hiwa was quiet, looking across the room, where he felt Tara was looking at him disapprovingly.

'You know your sister better than I do,' Sarah said. 'I don't know her at all. But I think that speaking is better than not speaking. If she refuses to talk, then fine, but at least try to talk to her.'

He didn't respond. He worried that she may be right, and he may be wrong, just as he had been wrong about Tara who looked angry now. Was she angry for her own sake or for Lana? Or was she angry on behalf of Sozi? Hiwa felt that he'd wronged most of the women who mattered to him. Sarah kissed him gently, as if knowing that he was drifting away.

'Look at me,' she told him. 'You know what's best for you and your sister. Let's stay here, in this moment.'

She rested on her back again and put his hand on her chest. His fingers slowly travelled up her collar bone. Her small breasts nearly disappeared when she lay on her back. His thumb stroked her nipple and it rose for him. Her skin was covered with goose bumps.

'I can't...' she said but didn't finish her sentence.

His hand froze on her breast.

'You can't what?' he asked her. 'Tell me.' His thumb was stroking her pale forehead now.

'I shouldn't.'

'You can't see me anymore?'

'No,' she shook her head. 'I'm worried that I can't not see you again.' She looked at him expectantly. 'I feel selfish and awful, but I don't want you to disappear again, I don't want us to end

261

like we did. Can we stay friends?'

'I don't know,' he told her, 'I don't want you to disappear again either.'

She touched his face and kissed his lips and she got on top of him. For a few seconds he didn't think about anything else, he just kissed her back and his hands grabbed her hips.

'Don't disappear,' she whispered in between kissing him. 'Don't turn your back.'

Is this about continuity? he thought. Is it about consistency in loving? Do we want to believe that not all the good things in the world are beyond rescue?

He tried to hold her still, but she was rubbing onto him. He rolled over and was hanging over her. He held the corners of her mouth in one hand and kissed her.

Was all of that just foreplay? he asked himself. Is it about sex?

He kissed her nipple, and she wrapped her legs around him.

'There!' she said as he pushed his way inside her. 'There!'

CHAPTER THIRTY-THREE

Gara

It was not raining anymore but the clouds remained threatening. The *hamam* was lit, and its continuous hum took Gara back to the days when his mother washed the five of them and hand-washed all the clothes before washing herself. She used to take them inside the little steam room all at once so that they soaked, and their small bodies were cleaned properly. It was a once-a-week occasion, every Friday, and she would start with little Lana, washing her hair as Lana screamed and cried, her eyes stinging from the soap, and her lungs heavy from the steam. Each of them got two rounds of hair-washing before their bodies were tended to.

Gara could still feel his mother's firm hands as she forcefully rubbed soap on his skull, concentrating on the temples, where she believed dirt and grease accumulated. Then she rinsed his head with hot water, always too hot, and left him waiting until she had washed everyone else's hair before coming back to him for another round. When the two rounds were finished, she scrubbed their bodies with the coarse *lifka* until their skin was raw, until all 'the dirt came out of the pores,' their dead skin peeled off, and their blood threatened to circulate out of their bodies. Those steamy days were full of violence, full of muffled shouting, of slipping in the dimmed light, of eyes burning from the soap, of tender skin that wrinkled in the abundant dampness. It was full of being worn out by the force of it, and coming out completely exhausted, ready to have a long nap.

Gara had a clear image of the ceremony at the age of six when Kawa was eight, Tara and Hiwa were nine and eleven and Lana was a toddler. He remembered Hiwa and Tatty rubbing their own bodies energetically, competing on whose skin produced more peeling, who had greater and greyer shed skin. Kawa was shouting under their mother's hands, while Lana, sitting on a low wooden bench, tried to brush her hair with difficulty, too knocked out to do anything else.

Ahoo never stopped, her hands kept working fast to clean her children from the week's dust, mud, dirt, and sweat. She then dried them one by one in the changing room, traditionally called the cold room next to the *hamam,* and clothed them, the older ones first and Lana last. She released them into the quiet house where the laid-out beds were waiting for them. Water tasted the best after *hamam.* Gara still remembered the coolness going down his warm throat and into his hot stomach. Soon the chilled purity circulated in his body, calming him, and putting him to sleep.

Now little Kawa was being washed by his mother. No screaming or crying was coming from the bathroom. The place was not overcrowded with noisy children. It was much less fun and less painful. Unlike his father when he was young, little Kawa enjoyed being washed, his body was not scrubbed raw, his eyes were protected from the sharp foam, and he was allowed to help wash himself. He hoped that Kawa would have siblings to play with one day, siblings who would make childhood more fascinating and adventurous. He missed his brothers and sisters, all of whom he'd lost to death or exile. He missed eating around the big *sifre* with them. He missed their disagreements and fights, how they were all so different from each other.

Gara opened the photo album where the last few remaining family photos were gathered. It had often given him comfort. It started with early black and white childhood photos. On the top right corner of the first page there was a picture of Tara and Hiwa holding hands in the mud road. Their pyjamas were dirty and worn at the knees. Tara looked at the camera while Hiwa was looking away. They were nearly the same height. Tara was in the right-hand side of the picture but it was as if she was at the centre of it. He touched Tara's little figure with affection. He often wished that his sister had survived but understood how she couldn't wait for the world to catch up with her, didn't want to compromise. Throughout his schooling and working life, he met girls who were so used to their chains that they could no longer live without them, but Tara never got used to hers.

But why die so horribly? Why fire?

Aveen believed it must've had to do with how beautiful she was. Such exceptional beauty, she said, would've been the greatest nuisance in a community such as theirs. She imagined that Tara could never do anything or go anywhere without being noticed and without men falling in love with her. No one was able to see beyond what she looked like.

'She must've walked about guiltily,' Aveen said, 'knowing that she is reminding people of their deprivations, the things they could never have, the people they would never be.'

Pouring Kerosene on her head and upper body must've aimed

to destroy what the men desired, what the women despised her for, and what her mother was terrified of. It was an awful, calculated revenge, Aveen believed. They would never bury a beautiful body and cry and sing about it, she made sure none of that was left. It was a horrible way to die but it wasn't meaningless, it wasn't unintentional.

He remembered how Tara stirred up lust and envy. It was no wonder that her best friends betrayed her. How is Layla Ibrahim? he thought, does she ever feel guilty about passing the love letters to uncle Hassan? Does she regret letting her best friend down so badly? Gara looked at a portrait of Tara taken the year she killed herself, a colour photograph that could be used as a postcard or as an advert for perfection and symmetry.

Just where did she get this beauty from? he wondered.

He heard his wife's footsteps approaching as she talked to Kawa. Aveen was fully dressed with her hair wet, and Kawa was wrapped in a large towel, only his small pale face could be seen.

'Hello *gullebakh*,' he told his son. 'You're all clean and lovely again?'

She put him down by the heater and started towel-drying his hair. Kawa's fresh clothes were ready and warm, and his mother put his underwear and a little white vest on before letting him get out of his towel. Kawa ran to his father giggling. He leaned on his father's chest while his mother was putting his trousers on and then his jumper.

'We'll get warm now, my sweetheart,' his mother said. '*Pura* Sayran will wash and then daddy and then we'll all be clean.'

Kawa nodded as he caught a glimpse of the album and bent over to look. It was open on the same page. He reached out to the photo, nearly knocking the album over in excitement.

'*Jooja!*' he said as he pointed to Tara's picture. '*Baba, jooja!*'

Gara carried his son out of the room despite his wife's objection.

'He'll get sick,' she shouted behind them but that wouldn't stop him. He stood in the long corridor.

'Where is *jooja*?' he asked his son while kissing him. 'Where is she *gulle gyan*?'

Kawa pointed to the place his father suspected and they walked up to it together.

'Here?' Gara asked his son as he pointed to the new bathroom, carved out of the back garden.

'No,' Kawa said, 'here!'

The boy was pointing to the wall behind which her death place lay. The old bathroom had been a dead space for twenty-two years. It lay between the girls' room, where Sayran now slept, and the toilet on its left. It was a cavity produced by her death, a doomed space which his mother could not face entering. She demolished the changing room and sealed off the steam room by a thick wall. It was a black spot in their history but, she believed, the wall contained it and the rest of the family was protected. At first, they walked past it guiltily, putting their heads down and biting their lips, but as time went on it ceased to exist in their minds. It became an inert, meaningless space which had to be kept as their mother had wished.

He stood there watching the wall and soon his wife was standing behind him. She put one hand on his back and the other on Kawa's back. The three of them looked on without a word. He realised that it was the first time they stood together like that, holding each other, motionless and wordless, all of them looking at the same thing. Thoughts were rushing through his head.

Is Tara still trapped in this place, he thought as her smiling photo echoed in his head. Does she choose to stay here?

So the presence that his son felt was not Kawa's, but Tara's. Had he confused them out of guilt?

'*Awata*,' Kawa said. 'There she is,' he waved. '*Jooja* is pretty,' he said, 'very pretty.' He closed his eyes and giggled shyly, as if she was stroking him.

Gara could almost see her looking into his eyes. He froze in his place, his eyes wide open. Aveen must've felt her too as she squeezed her husband's shoulder.

'What calm!' she whispered.

Kawa was waving once again.

'Bye bye,' he said, 'bye bye.'

Aveen rubbed her husband's arm.

'Come back inside,' she said. 'We'll get sick, come by the heater.'

She held her arms out and grabbed Kawa who looked tired now. He squeezed his eyes and rested his head on his mother's shoulder. She walked away with their son and left Gara standing there on his own.

Tara! he called out to her in his heart. Tatty *gyan*, what do you want? Tell me.

CHAPTER THIRTY-FOUR

Gara

Gara put the little lantern by his bed and lit two candles in the windowsill overlooking the front garden. They were reflected in the window and doubled. The night was hushed and starless. His son was sound asleep. His wife sat up in bed, the duvet covering her up to her waist, she was waiting for him. The lines of her face were softened by the flames, making her look more beautiful. He smelt her perfumed hair and she leaned on his shoulder, locking her hands around his waist. His fingers started playing with her bundled hair.

'What does Tara want?' Aveen said, looking up at her husband.

He sealed her lips with a kiss, not a quick, friendly, or loving kiss, but a kiss full of greed. He held her face with both hands. She opened her eyes in surprise and looked into his. She closed her eyes again, her shoulders dropping, her neck relaxing and her head leaning backwards on the wall. He kissed her closed eyes, her nose, her cheekbones, her ears. He bit her lips.

'Take it off,' he said in a hushed voice as he grabbed her dress.

Aveen took her top off. She slipped under the duvet as he took his own clothes off. They always worried about being watched, so they hid under quilts and sheets.

'No,' he told her, and he pushed the duvet away, uncovering her naked body, all goose-pimpled and nervous. She pulled her knees together and covered her breasts with her arms.

'I'm cold,' she said, summoning his body close and embracing him.

He took off her hairband, and brushed his fingers through her hair, disentangling it. She touched his face as he played with her hair, tracing the curve of his forehead, cheeks, chin. His fingers moved down across her forehead and nose, down to her neck and chest. He pinched her nipple. His hand moved down her body. She held his hand, put his palm on her lips and kissed it. They stared into each other's eyes as they locked lips again. His hand tried to slip between her knees, but she didn't let him. She got up and sat on top of him. She held his wrists tightly, lifted his arms up until his hands lay by his head, as if he was surrendering. Then she kissed him and whispered, 'I'm not scared of you.'

Her body was cold and her back muscles were hard. His touch made her hair stand on end. He knew that if he looked at her from above, she'd be looking like a frog, her legs folded on either side of him, her back straight, her arms trying to hold his arms down. When she was tired, and she rested her head on his chest, he got up while holding her hips firmly. She was sitting on his lap, her legs enwrapping his hips. He grabbed the nape of her neck and kissed her throat and shoulders. Her loose hair fell back, covering her upper back. He held her there and looked at her in the light of the candles, she was nude and golden, scared and curious, full of greed.

He'd wanted to see his wife like this for a long time; he looked at her face, at her bare shoulders and breasts, her hardened nipples. He let go of her and she fell backwards. He balanced himself on his knees and hands over her. She stared up at him, looking slightly drunk. He then traced her left knee, her thigh and then rested his hand between her legs. She closed her eyes, but he pinched her and said, 'Look at me.'

She held his face in her hands and looked into his eyes.

'Here,' she told him. 'I'm here.'

There was a gap between their bodies which she wanted to close. She pulled him towards her, tried to lift herself up to him, but he resisted.

'Not yet,' he said.

He kissed her all the way down and she was motionless, all open and exposed in front of him. When she felt the pressure of his lips, she sighed. He kissed her and stroked her and pinched her until she was flowing. Then he climbed her body and suckled her nipple. She slipped her hand between them and squeezed him.

'Turn over,' he told her. She turned over and he massaged her again before going through her. She took a deep breath with his entry. Then he was leaning on the wall, and she sat up on him. He had her in his lap where he had access to her breasts and her vulva.

'Now tell me that you love me.'

'I love you,' she said as his arm pressed on her breasts. 'I love you,' she repeated.

And as they turned into one body, synchronised like the pieces of one clock, they were alone, no one was watching or touching them. This was their private moment, and they could do whatever they wished without worrying about being gazed at, without being shy or feeling guilty.

CHAPTER THIRTY-FIVE

Hiwa

His study looked large now, the rubbish thrown away, the bookshelves moved, the boxes gone, and the piles of books moved to the sitting room. The walls where the bookcases had been, were covered with cobweb, dirty fluff, and dust. He wore a mask and tackled the dusty space with the vacuum cleaner. The accumulated dirt and dust made him feel that he was entering an old cave, a cave that had not been visited for years, its mysteries undiscovered, its wisdom ignored.

The vacuum cleaner sucked the dust in. He could almost see the years that had been trapped there go up the tube and get compiled and compacted in the bag inside. He was the saddest about the cobwebs. It was painful to destroy these beautiful designs that had taken so much effort and brilliance to create. It was as if he was destroying someone else's impressive castle, someone else's life. He was careful, at least, not to get the spiders, murder would've been too much for him.

'Why?' he asked the two spiders hurrying away from him. 'Why have you built your lives around a flimsy, transient thing?' But maybe everything was flimsy and transient and there was no way to avoid it.

Sozi's footsteps approached, she watched from the door for a few seconds and walked away. He stopped vacuuming, took off his mask, sprayed a cloth with the all-purpose cleaner, and started wiping the wall and carpet. He tried hard to get the worst of it off but some of the dirt stuck to the wall. He knew that this would upset Sozi and she would make him repaint the room. The carpet was forever marked where the weight of the bookshelves had been. He rubbed it hard, hoping the marked rectangles would fade. It was as if the fabric's back was broken, and it would never look up again.

He felt tender towards every bit of that room that had carried his life on its back. He felt indebted to every corner, every inch of space for containing the strain of all the stories and images, ghosts, books. If he was a poet, he would've written a poem for his room, this quiet place that had taken in all his disasters, all his secrets. He was certain that no one could do this for him. No one could put up with all of him like this, no one who knew what he was really like, what he'd really done in his life.

He stood up and looked back at the cleaned space. The room would soon look like Shilana's room, filled with toys and happy images and sounds. He'd stopped his life in that room and soon it would all be hers to fill with her own pleasures, secrets, and worries. He hoped that Shilana's life would be free of guilt, of the heavy expectations of a community that made people do things they regretted. He hoped that she would fill her life with good things: books that would help her navigate the world, ambitions to change the things she didn't like, love in its different kinds and shapes, and a bit of luck. Maybe she would become an actor or an artist, a brilliant architect who would rebuild their homeland, a doctor who would cure pain, or a psychologist who would cure sorrow, maybe a teacher who would inspire young people to change the world, or a Human Rights lawyer campaigning for those who are silenced. Whatever she became, even if she went against her parents' ambitions for her, he hoped she would be happy and healthy. He wanted to never lose sight of that and to support her in whatever she chose to do, even if he believed it was below her capacities or not very interesting.

He unplugged his computer, the printer, scanner, and various hard drives. He put everything on the floor and started moving the desk. It was too heavy to move alone but he tried to move it corner by corner until his wife came through the door and scolded him, 'Why didn't you call me?'

He wasn't sure why he hadn't, but she was rightfully angry with him, and he felt ashamed to ask her for help.

Sozi picked up one side of the desk and together they tried to take the desk through the door. It was a little too wide.

'Can it be dismantled?'

'Let's see if we can find another way,' he said.

They then shoved the desk onto its side. It scratched the door frame and they struggled to hold it up. Half the desk went through the door until it got stuck in the corridor.

'Open the toilet door,' Hiwa said.

A quarter of the desk was already in the toilet opposite the room by the time Hiwa managed to get the rest of it out of the study. He then doubled back in the corridor until his wife was out of the toilet again. They put the desk down and looked at each other. Sozi placed a hand on her lower back.

'We're a good team,' he said.

'At least at moving desks, we are,' she said.

'No! We are a good team.'

They managed to get the desk into the bedroom, doubling back into the kitchen. They put it down by the window where the dressing table had been. They walked back to the door and looked at the room. The desk looked like an intrusion, but he knew that they would soon get used to it.

He followed his wife to the kitchen and sat opposite her. Dinner was ready and Shilana had already finished eating. Sozi tried to feed her more, but Shilana screamed and refused. She wiped her face and let her go and play. He looked at his wife, couldn't guess what she was thinking.

'If we're a good team,' she said, 'why do you go elsewhere?'

'She's not a replacement for you,' he replied.

'But she is,' Sozi said impatiently. 'You love her, don't you?'

'She is a good friend of mine.'

'Oh, come on! What friend? You hadn't seen her for eleven years.'

'It doesn't matter,' he said. 'Some people will remain our friends even if we never see them again. Even when they're dead, they're still our friends, and we talk to them inwardly.'

'So, all these years you've been inwardly talking to her?' she said mockingly but before he had a chance to say anything she continued, 'Are you trying to say that you haven't slept with her?'

He looked at her for a second and recognised the fire in her eyes.

She repeated, when he did not respond, 'Did you sleep with her?'

'Yes,' he told his wife and her face turned away from him.

Her face became hard like stone. She started eating without looking at him.

Shilana was playing in the sitting room. She pressed a button and 'Twinkle, Twinkle, Little Star' was played. Hiwa watched his wife eat calmly and wished she would look up. He wanted to apologise but he thought it was too early and she was probably not ready to listen to him. He wanted to touch her, to hug her, but he was frozen, unable to touch his food. Shilana pressed another button, and 'Humpty Dumpty' played.

Sozi drank water from her glass. They were one metre apart but to him it seemed that the space had stretched to miles. It was as if he was looking at his wife from a long way away, as if even if he shouted, he wouldn't catch her attention, she wouldn't hear him. The distance terrified him. He'd never felt so lonely with her before.

So this is it, he said to himself, these are the moments when you wreck your life.

He searched within himself and wondered what had led to this moment. Had he ruined his life by going back to the past? Was it his fault? He looked at his daughter who sat in the other room pressing buttons and listening to tunes. Everything seemed unreal, as if it was a bad dream. Now Shilana played 'This Old Man.'

Sozi got up, turned around and screamed at her daughter, 'Stop that, for God's sake, stop it.'

Shilana looked up in shock and started crying. Sozi headed to the bathroom, and he went to comfort his heartbroken daughter.

CHAPTER THIRTY-SIX

Gara

He walked into the office remembering to say good morning to the doorman, the cleaners, the receptionist and all his colleagues. He looked calm and happy.

'What's up?' Dara asked him before he entered his room. 'You know anything that we don't?'

Gara shook his head. 'Only that all the waiting and uncertainty is over,' he said.

Dara nodded in agreement. 'Yes, within the next few days.'

Gara smiled at the misunderstanding and walked into his room. He switched the computer on and entered his password. Ibrahim brought him a thick tea with a box of sweets. The tea pot was always on the heater, making the place smell like home.

'Many congratulations,' he said while choosing a sweet from the box. 'A girl or a boy?'

'A girl,' Ibrahim replied. 'We're arguing about what to name her. Her mother wants to call her Mizhda but I want to name her Lavah.'

'Why not both?' he said. 'An official name and one to call her by at home.'

'But won't that be confusing for the child?'

'It might be,' Gara answered as he chewed on the hard sweet.

'But it can also be a good thing for her, she can choose what she prefers later. You know, it can be an opportunity to be one way or another, a choice.'

Ibrahim nodded. He wiped the sticky tea rings on the glass table in the middle of the room. 'Do you need anything else?' he asked his boss while standing at the door.

'No, thanks!'

Gara skimmed the various websites for news. The paper was going out tomorrow, everything would go to the printers in the afternoon and the final changes had to be made before two o'clock. He monitored the news closely to make sure they were up to date. By next week when the new issue would come out the war would've begun.

Outside, Dara and Twana were arguing in the newsroom. Gara kept out of these disagreements as much as he could, unless they asked for help. The nation is full of egos that don't trust each other, the violent legacy of dictatorship and surveillance. He believed that decades of being betrayed by friends and neighbours left an aftermath of mistrust and selfishness. He often told his friends, oppressors turned people into what they wanted: broken spirits, competing individuals concerned with their own survival, unpredictable, irrational bombs that could go off at the slightest provocation. Yesterday's victims became victimisers, injustice and violence was normalised and reproduced. He was planning to put a stop to the vicious circles in his own life. He logged into his email and glanced through the urgent messages. He finished his tea, took a deep breath, and wrote:

My dear ones, Hiwa and Lana,

I've decided to demolish the back wall and free the long-imprisoned bathroom. I think it's time to move on from associating death and pain with the house we grew up in and some of us still live in. I think Tara would appreciate this; it's probably what she wants us to do. I know this may come as a surprise to you at this time and after all these years. We'd become so accustomed to it that we no longer noticed it. Somewhere in our minds it had become normal to have this wall amongst us, to live with this painful space. I've been living side by side with the past, in the same country, the same house. I've started a new family in this place, and despite having every reason to be happy, I haven't been.

It was little Kawa who drew my attention back to this place. He is the one who made me realise that some things remain unresolved, and this continues to shape our lives. It seems that putting things right is my duty as I'm the one who stayed behind. I think we have to let the past go, to free it, and ask it to free us.

Maybe it takes a child, an innocent being who doesn't share our history, and has not been shaped by habit, to sense how abnormal and wrong some things are. Maybe we need to start looking at things from a similarly open and fresh point of view. Maybe then we can understand what's happened to us, what's wrong with our lives, and how we can change all of that. I know that we can't change the past, it's beyond us, but we should try to understand the past and prevent it from sullying our lives and shaping it.

This nation is traumatised, and we are no exception. Even when things seem to be going right for us, we always find our way back to suffering and destruction. We're not free yet of what happened

279

in this place and the things that happened come into our most intimate moments with us. I want to try to put a stop to that. This isn't just about finding my way back to happiness, I think happiness is something that we build over time. I guess happiness means not being a mess, not being angry, and pessimistic, it's trying to do good, having faith, and making something good out of chaos. I guess happiness is having clarity of mind and a clear conscience that we're doing what we can to make our world a better place.

If, like me, you don't believe in God and you don't believe that the evil people will be punished and purified in another life, then you feel this responsibility, this urge to do all you can in this life, here, in this place. You feel that you must try to be aware of the bad things, support the good things, and do something about the injustices that surround you. And I don't think you can try to do this in the world without doing it first in your own life. So, I'm trying.

I'm still not sure what we'll do with the new space. Aveen says that it would be good to have a conservatory garden and maybe a little pond which would please Kawa. We're not sure but the past will have to leave this place, flap its wings and go, then we can decide about what to do with what it leaves behind. I hope that you're all well and that you'll always have peace of mind. Everyone sends their love to Shilana, she is beautiful.

I embrace you both,

Your brother,

Gara

CHAPTER THIRTY-SEVEN

Hiwa

After washing up, he sat down to have tea with his sister and wife at the dinner table. He'd invited Lana to dinner to alleviate the tension with his wife. She hadn't spoken to him since their last conversation, but she was polite enough to pretend to be on speaking terms in front of others. She co-existed with him, slept in the same bed, ate the same food but somehow her eyes never met his, her body didn't touch his, not even by accident. She turned away from him in bed and slept on the edge, making him feel cold and lonely. She did the cooking and left the dishes to him, washed Shilana and left him to dry and clothe her. He went to her twice, wanting to talk but he didn't have the courage to say anything. He'd ended up in the place he dreaded, a soundless place where love was dead, a place from which there seemed to be no return, where he destroyed the family he'd built, the family he loved. He lived in a daze. He'd received an email from Gara the day before, talking about the house and the wall, read the email a few times, realising that it was important, but wasn't able to understand what his brother was telling him. He gave up trying.

'You can't change the course of the war,' Hiwa said to Lana. 'So please look after yourself.'

'It's never one thing, is it?' she said. 'The rug rips from the thin end.'

'What's causing the ripping?' he asked. 'Love?'

'No, no,' Lana waved her hand. 'I'm being melodramatic. But tell me, why do the Kurds think it will be different this time?'

'It will be different,' Sozi said, 'because no two wars can be the same but that doesn't mean it will be better. My question is why do people want it? What is there to gain? We already have our regional government.'

'International recognition?' Hiwa said. 'With the sanctions removed and a new government in place, it's possible to negotiate a federal state, to demand a percentage of the oil revenues, to rebuild, to finally fix the shortage of water and electricity.'

'You think the new Iraqi government will accept federalism?' Lana asked.

'They'll negotiate because they will be a new, weak government.'

'Oh, come on!' Sozi said. 'We all know the Kurdish style! We pick up arms against the state, fight a bloody war, sacrifice our lives for freedom, but when it comes to the negotiations, we shake hands on very little. A bit like women who leave their homes, complain about their husbands, fight, and argue, and then go back to him without him making any meaningful change.'

'That's the style of those who have less power,' he said. 'But we're in a stronger position this time compared to the past.'

'So typical of us, isn't it?' Lana said. 'Either too optimistic or too pessimistic.'

'Either too proud with false confidence or too weak and insecure,' he said.

'The lion cubs,' Lana said, quoting a national hymn: 'Kurdistan is home to the lion cubs.'

'Or home to those who flee at the sight of attacks.' Sozi said.

The memory of the mass exodus made them all go quiet for a few seconds.

'That's unfair,' Hiwa said. 'It was fear of gas attacks then.'

'There's still the same fear,' Sozi said.

'Let's not talk about the war,' Lana said.

Hiwa realised that Lana was worried about them. Sozi was noticeably cold and dismissive of him. It wasn't what she said, they'd always disagreed politically, it was the way she disagreed with him. Lana stood up and looked at them for a second. 'Are you both alright? Is the war interfering too much? You should just ignore it.'

'We're fine,' he said.

Sozi looked at him for a second but didn't say anything. There was more than disagreement in her eyes, he saw anger and even hatred, it scared him. To avoid his sister's questioning eyes he got up and put Nasiri Razzazi on. Razzazi immediately started singing 'Why do you kill me with your alluring eyes?' Hiwa looked at the bookcase which was full of books now. He'd given some of his books away to the Kurdish Cultural Centre and only kept his most valued ones.

'Look,' he called his sister to the sitting room. 'My books are now in order. You can find things.'

Lana got up and joined her brother. 'Where were these books? I've never seen them before,' she asked him while pointing at Nawshirwan Mustafa's *The Fingers are Breaking Each Other* and Hawar's *The Immortal Sheikh Mahmud*.

'In my magical study,' he said. 'They were all waiting to come out.'

'A small magical place which had room for so many things,' she said.

'So many things,' he echoed. 'Too much, in fact, of some things.'

Sozi walked into the room, and he sang along with Razzazi as he looked at his wife. 'Why do you kill me with your alluring eyes?'

He refused to accept that all that love and togetherness was wishful thinking. He walked over and kissed her hand.

CHAPTER THIRTY-EIGHT

Gara

He watched Aveen as she prepared to go down to the basement, looking happy.

'Do you need anything from downstairs?' she asked, standing at the top of the stairs.

'No, but I'd like to help,' he said.

Looking at her all bright eyed and eager, he didn't need to ask her what she was doing. He followed her. Sayran entertained Kawa in the sitting room as the two of them moved and shuffled things in the small, damp place. It took some time to get used to the darkness. Aveen lit the Fanos-lantern which gave out the brightest white light. Still, it was difficult to see everything properly and they had to move the lantern with them to find what they were looking for. All the spare things, the things that had no space upstairs or were not needed anymore, were convened in the basement. It was also the place where the carpets rested in spring and summer, all rolled up and full of naphthalene to keep the moth and mice away.

Amongst the junk they found a large brass bowl which looked like it was rusting. His mother's grandmother had washed rice in this bowl, and it was the only piece Ahoo had taken into her uncle's house and later into her marriage. Aveen picked up the bowl and ran her hand over the eroding space inside.

'For more than a century the women of this family used this in their daily cooking,' Aveen said.

'And now it looks like a useless object that is good for nothing anymore,' he said.

He thought the life of the object resembled his mother's life: years of hard work and constant use and then old age and abandonment when she was reduced to enduring the hours to the end.

'I won't let it die,' Aveen said. 'I'll get it polished and find a use for it.' She put the bowl on the stairs.

They opened a few cardboard boxes, looking for what Aveen wanted. Most of the boxes were full of books, papers, and old clothes. Everything was penetrated by pure dark shadows that made them look sinister and even the soft clothes were not immune from this. He wondered for a second how at times, the most harmless things could look so dangerous and the most dangerous things so harmless. Not freeing the dead had seemed so harmless, just a non-risky exercise that helped them process grief, yet it had the potential to wreck all the things they'd managed to recover from the ruins. He finally understood how powerful the dead were, how present they could be in their absence, and how much this presence could suspend the lives of the living.

He closed the first three boxes and piled them on top of each other. The fourth box was filled with pots of acrylic paint. Aveen put the lantern down on a table nearby and took out each pot and brought it under the lantern to see what colour it was.

'Turquoise,' she said to him excitedly. 'This means skies, fish, horses, and people locked in lovemaking.'

The images raced through his mind. Some of them were too

fast to catch. He closed his eyes, endured the rush of ideas. The possibilities were endless. Aveen put the acrylic pots back in the box one by one. The two of them put the box on the stairs and returned to the top of the basement to find the rest of her things. In the top right-hand corner, where a vast space was cleared for the carpets, boards and canvases were leaning on the wall. She went through a few of them as he held the lantern for her. She separated the blank canvases from the paintings. Some of the paintings dated back to fifteen years ago when she was a student in the Institute of Fine Arts. Most of the work had been destroyed when the house was looted in 1991, those that had survived were marked with dirt, torn at the edges, and looked old and worn.

He particularly liked one of her paintings, that of a man and woman embracing each other, their faces joined in the middle such that they had one eye in common. Sharing one eye was the most perfect thing for him, to be able to see things with the same eye but also to have another eye, an independent one which saw things differently. A fish was swimming in the woman's hair while a bird was resting in the man's cheek. They were surrounded by large leaves, each standing there like an erect tree.

For the first time in many years Gara felt that creativity was possible for her, that she was flirting with art, standing right at the edge of it. He'd worried that art had deserted her, that she would never be able to get excited by a colour or a line again. Now, as she walked back and forth, touching the material, he felt that her sleeping senses were waking up once again. He imagined her artwork changing and growing with her, no longer focusing on love and nature. They'd all grown so much, and their world of concerns had grown with them. He thought about the war, the destruction, the trauma, but also about the new possibilities.

Together they carried the box of acrylics into the bedroom and went back to bring up the brass bowl and canvases. When they went to the sitting room Sayran looked up with a smile. She'd been cleaning the *aladdin* heater while Kawa played with his cars. Racing up and down the width of the room, his cars were crashing, turning over on their sides, but they were rescued by Kawa and recovered from their doomed fates.

Aveen lifted the bowl in the air to show Sayran. 'It's rusting,' she said.

'Yes,' Sayran replied. 'We shouldn't have left it in the basement.'

'I'll fix it,' Aveen said in an assured voice while inspecting it before taking it into the kitchen.

'She's determined to make it up to the object, make it up to *daya*, and to herself,' he said.

'Wonderful!' Sayran said. She was beaming, her cheeks lifted and her eyes twinkling. He understood what her smile meant. It meant that she was happy about their happiness, her years of endurance and hard work were made worthwhile, and her life wasn't wasted repairing the broken pieces of a vase after all. She'd felt the shift, as if a shadow was lifted, and everything was going to be okay. Aveen walked back into the sitting room and looked at her son, making all sorts of noises with the racing cars.

'Hello *gullekem*!' she told her son. 'From now on me and you will paint together. Wouldn't that be fun?'

The boy looked up at his mother, clapped his hands twice, and went back to his racing.

CHAPTER THIRTY-NINE

Lana

The night before the war she thought about the moment the pregnancy happened; how a drop of Amer travelled up her body, found its way to that impatient part of her which only waited around for a day or two before giving up and bringing the walls down upon itself; how an invisible part of her could unite with an invisible part of him and grow inside her, in that curved, dark place, padded for comfort, ready to nourish this little thing which would stay connected to her for nine months.

She knew that there was never a right time to carry life within, to put up with the demands it placed on her body, how it restricted her movements, changed her sleeping and eating habits, made her heavy, tired, swollen. She knew that however many classes she took, she would never be ready for the pain, the fragility of life that would pass through her body, spreading her open. She wondered what made women think that they would succeed, that they would gracefully accept this thing that latched onto them, ate from their bodies, and depended on them for its own survival. How many years would it take for this thing to become independent? How long before she could go for a walk without thinking about it?

She wondered if people had noticed her small bump. Sozi

and Hiwa seemed too caught up in themselves to notice and this was a relief to her. She'd put on a big jumper to see them and an old pair of trousers which were too big for her until recently. She now walked differently, it was as if everything was dictated by what she carried that gave her unhappy signals if she moved or turned rapidly. It wanted her to be gentle, not to carry heavy bags, not to run, not to get angry or sad. She worried that this little thing was making a slave out of her.

She imagined the little thing growing inside her.

'Today it's the size of a bean,' the book told her. It gained strength every day, it made her feel sick in the mornings, hyper-sensitive to the smells and tastes of the past. She felt terrified by this small being, so irrational, so rational. She considered disappearing for a few years, going somewhere where no one knew her, having the baby and maybe returning one day claiming to be a widow or a divorcee.

Why do people have children, she thought. When the world is full of conflict and is rapidly self-destroying, what is the point of bringing another person into it? The next generations would suffer more intensely, she thought, they would fight for water, for a cooler geography, for protection from the sun and moon.

But to have a baby with Amer was another dilemma. What kind of a being is a half Arab half Kurdish person? Isn't it a contradiction to unite two parts so utterly unprepared to acknowledge each other in reality? Two sides that coexist but the space between them is filled with blood, doubt, mistrust, and revenge. How could a history like that be wiped out by people of a mixed heritage? When this child grows up and reads her mother's and father's histories, what will she think? Will she be an angry person? Will she feel hopelessly depressed about her heritage? Will the wars of the past live inside her? What will she do at moments of crisis when she's asked to pick a side? Can she be happy? And keeping this baby, how could Lana face people like Khalid who could not forgive?

'You can't blame Arabs for what Saddam did to us,' Lana once told Khalid.

He looked at her in shock for a second and then shot back: 'Of course I can, I blame them for their support and cooperation, for the money they kept lending him while he was killing us... and as for the intellectuals! Where are they? I blame them for their non-existence. I blame them for their silence.'

Amer watched her as she walked about or stared at something absentmindedly, sometimes shivering, sometimes being absolutely still.

'This,' he said while touching Lana's stomach, 'is our baby. It is a blank sheet of paper that shouldn't be burdened with a past it wasn't involved in.'

For him the baby was theirs and theirs alone. It was the result of their love, and it would be raised with their love.

'Why should it matter what my ethnicity or yours is?' he asked her.

It was a cold night, too cold for late March. They went to bed knowing that the war would start at any moment. Lana's body was cold in Amer's arms, she couldn't sleep but it was as if there were no more words left, nothing more to say about it. She knew that Amer wanted to stay up to follow the news but stayed by her side as if he wanted to protect her from the imminent bombs.

It was as if the bombs that fell so many thousands of miles away were falling inside Lana's body. She felt nauseous in her sleep and her womb tensed up. She dreamt of babies struggling to be born, babies crawling down a canal that had no end, babies strangled by the umbilical cord, babies whose mothers' bodies rejected them, but they weren't ready to leave, babies spat out like garbage, all squashed and dead. Each dream made Lana sweat, each bomb became a flash of lightning that travelled through her body.

At dawn she woke up in pain. Deep inside her something seemed to be disconnecting. Lana got up and felt the wetness between her legs, she pulled the duvet away and saw the pink stain. She gasped and Amer jumped out of sleep, his head bent over hers. He looked at the stain, at Lana holding on to her stomach and looking at him, her face an expression of horror and pain. He put his arms around her as she started weeping.

Someone decides to enter our lives, she thought, another decides to leave it. A child refuses to be born, another refuses to die. Not everything happens for a reason, I can't believe that.

CHAPTER FORTY

Hiwa

On Thursday, 20 March 2003, at six am, they were woken by Khalid's phone call.

'Get up,' he said. 'The end's started.'

Now the two of them were in the sitting room, absorbed by images of Baghdad rocking under the bombardments. The targets were zoomed into, generals were giving their views about the progress, orders were being shouted, soldiers hunched over and moved forward, things were exploding. Hiwa's stomach was churning. Shilana had woken up crying as if she was in pain and he had to walk around, carrying her. Every now and then she screamed, demanding to be rocked. As he held her close, kissing her head and rubbing her back, he thought of the children dying in the war that had just started, those being mutilated and orphaned.

The map of Iraq showed the position and direction of the different troops. The American flag in the north was displayed alongside the Kurdish flag. It was the first time he'd seen the flag on a TV channel other than the Kurdish satellite channels. He remembered *mamosta* Ameen explaining the meaning of the flag to him when he was eleven or twelve: red at the top for revolution, sacrifice, and martyrdom, green at the bottom for Kurdistan's nature and the spring, and white in the centre, for peace. He was sitting beside Ahmed and Rabar when he learnt the meaning of the shining sun in the middle of the flag, spreading over the red above and the green below, the life force of the sun, its twenty-one rays of Newroz, the end of tyranny.

'It's the beginning of freedom,' he whispered to Shilana.

Sozi started to cry. Because of the war or because of him? Was she giving up on him, on their life together, on the possibility of still being happy despite everything? She wept quietly and kept brushing her tears away without a word. The period of calm between wars had ended, as had the calm in his own life. He looked at her, sitting on the burgundy sofa in her blue dress, her skin turning pale with fear, her hair covering her bare shoulders. He walked forward until he stood next to her, but she didn't look up.

Shilana seemed to have fallen asleep on his shoulder, he sat down beside his wife, still tapping his daughter's back. He wanted to reach out and hold her hand, the hand she'd worn the engagement ring on, the hand he'd kissed many times, the hand that cooked him so many meals, touched his body, gone through his hair, held his face. He wanted to hold his wife and tell her that he was sorry. He knew she wouldn't settle for 'the Kurdish style,' she wouldn't 'shake hands on' nice words and apologies. She wanted a commitment to change. Was he capable of that, he wondered.

'I can hear the children screaming,' she said. 'I can hear the mothers trying to comfort them. I hope everyone can see the violence and misery.' She wiped away her large tears and continued, 'There will be electricity shortages, the garbage will pile up without being collected, water won't run through the taps, shops will be closed, everything will become even more expensive, armed men will control the streets. More women will be controlled and oppressed. Did they even think about that?'

He touched Sozi's hand, he was unable to say anything back.

'I can't live like this,' she told him while turning back to look at him. 'You have nothing to say to me... nothing!' Her eyes were red and full of tears.

He broke out in a sweat. He didn't want to live without his wife and daughter, he'd promised Shilana to be there for her and help her realise her dreams. He put his daughter down between them and reached out to Sozi with a shaky hand. Everything felt unpredictable and terrible, anything could happen, everything could be lost.

'I'm sorry,' he finally told his wife. 'Can you forgive me and not worry?'

'Not worry?' she asked him as she cried. 'Wouldn't you worry if I was in love with someone else?'

'It's not that kind of love.'

'What kind of love is it then when you make love to someone?'

'I don't know,' he said, feeling confused. 'I know that I love you and don't want to live without you.'

'This can't continue,' she told him with fire in her eyes. 'It's either me or her, you have to make a choice'

'Please don't push me to choose,' he said. 'I can't do it right now.'

'You just did,' Sozi said, and she turned away.

'No,' he said, 'that's not what I meant.'

She detached herself from him. He knew he had to bring her back before it was too late.

'All I'm asking is that you don't give up on us so quickly,' he said.

He watched her profile, her determination and clarity. Sozi turned to look at Shilana but when she looked up at him, he walked away from her penetrating gaze. She wanted decisiveness and quick action, which he didn't think he was capable of. Everything was too much, too much war, too much confusion, too much love, too much guilt. He went to the kitchen and turned the cooker on, taking comfort in the circle of blue flames. He put his arms up to the fire. The dictator is falling, he thought, this is the eve of a new day. The Newroz song started playing in the back of his mind. He went over, brought Sozi to the cooker.

'It's Newroz eve,' he said. 'Let's celebrate his end and this new beginning. We should buy new Newroz clothes, like we used to. We should jump over the fire.'

'The past is like a fire,' she said as she stared at the flames. 'It'll burn you if you don't put up a firewall. I know you feel guilty about Kawa, about not seeing your mother before she died. I know you pretend to be okay when you're not. I also know that you loved Tara too much.'

She paused and looked up at him, as if she knew these last words had caused him to take a step back. Had she known all along? All this time, when he felt he'd hidden his dark side, had she seen through him?

'You can't change the past,' she said. 'You shouldn't destroy this family because of it. Shilana deserves happiness and I deserve you here with me. I don't want to share you, not with the past and not with anyone else.'

He wanted to run, to hide in his room.

His eyes started to burn, he felt the tears building up and started crying as she stepped forward and gently held him.

'No more guilt, no more shame,' he heard. 'You're free.' The voice was soft and gentle, it came from Sozi, it came from the walls, it came from his dead sister.

Also by Afsana Press:

Past Participle

A novel by Jane Labous

Dakar, Senegal, 1987: On a rainy night after a wild party, the British ambassador's wife, Vivienne Hughes, is involved in a car crash. Her vehicle hits the motorbike of a young Senegalese doctor, Aimé Tunkara, killing him. the story of two women bound together by the faultlines of the past, a study of love and guilt, power and desire, retribution and forgiveness.

Release date: May 2023 / 352 pages

Paperback: £ 10.99 / ISBN: 9781739982478

Inner Core

Short stories by Miki Lentin

Death, anxiety, masculinity, family and children, social good and rocks. All things that touch the life of a middle-aged man. Miki Lentin goes in search of a rock with his child in Ireland, travels to Istanbul with his wife while sleep-deprived, recounts memories of working and growing up in Dublin and explores what it means to do good in society today. Inner Core portrays, in a minimalist tone, Lentin's life on the edge.

Release date: April 2022 / 168 pages

Paperback: £ 6.99 / ISBN: 9781739982447 – e-Book: £ 5.99 / ISBN: 9781739982430

The Glass Wall

A novel by Goran Baba Ali

The story of a teenage refugee who must re-live the pain of his past to enter a land waiting behind a glass wall. Will his story be convincing enough to guarantee his safety? A story of struggle and persecution, yet abundant in hope, The Glass Wall is a clear-eyed, emotionally honest account of displaced people, illustrating the true hardship that refugees experience.

Release date: November 2021 / 352 pages

Hardback: £ 14.99 / ISBN: 9781739982409